Shape of the Sky

SHELAGH CONNOR SHAPIRO

More Praise for Shape of the Sky

At the center of *Shape of the Sky*, Shelagh Shapiro's brilliant novel about the effects of a Grateful Dead-like concert on a small Vermont community, is the murder of a young woman, but this is not just a murder mystery—if it's even a murder mystery at all. Shapiro's true subject is a much larger and deeper mystery, the mystery of human interrelatedness. Formally, the novel's chapters mimic the so-called "circle of fifths," the clock-shaped representation of the interconnections between music's twelve major and minor keys. Each chapter explores the effect of the concert and its surrounding events from a different character's perspective, and the result is a powerful, in-depth portrayal not only of the interrelatedness of everyone who comes together for one fateful weekend in Resolute, Vermont, but of the interrelatedness of all of us who share this planet under the blue and beautifully ragged circle of sky. And although the concert brings death to the community, it also brings love, hope, reconciliation, redemption, and, ultimately, peace. *Shape of the Sky* is that rarity, a work of literary fiction that is also a page-turner. Do your heart, mind, and soul a favor and read this wonderful book.

— David Jauss, author of *Black Maps, Crimes of Passion,* and *Glossolalia*

Shape of the Sky

SHELAGH CONNOR SHAPIRO

Published by

WIND RIDGE BOOKS of vermont

Shelburne, Vermont 05482

Cover artwork by Daryl Storrs
Cover and book design by Laurie Thomas

ISBN: 978-1-935922-55-1
Library of Congress: 2014947199

Publisher's Cataloging-in-Publication
(Provided by Quality Books, Inc.)
Shapiro, Shelagh Connor.
        Shape of the sky / Shelagh Connor Shapiro.
        pages cm
        LCCN 2014947199
        ISBN 978-1-935922-55-1

        1. Rock groups--Fiction. 2. Police, State--Fiction.
        3. Homicide investigation--Fiction. 4. Country life--
        Fiction. 5. Detective and mystery stories.
        6. Psychological fiction.   I. Title.

        PS3619.H3563105S53 2014   813'.6
                        QBI14-600151

Published by Wind Ridge Books of VT
PO Box 636
Shelburne, Vermont 05482
www.windridgebooksofvt.com

Dedication

*For Bennett, Connor, and Aaron, who make me proud
and happy every day.*

*And for Jerry, who pedals just behind—keeping watch
and keeping company.*

Contents

Acknowledgements

My parents, Mary Patricia Riley and John Houghton Connor, loved that I became a writer. I wish they could have seen this book come into the world.

Maura's love and support are unconditional: she reads it all. I count myself so fortunate that she is my sister, my cheerleader, my friend.

Debby Shapiro is a fantastic mother-in-law whose availability to baby-sit allowed me to go back to school and pursue this nutty occupation. I love her beyond description.

For the last eleven years, I've had the honor and pleasure of participating in a fantastic writing group. Thank you so much Susan Ritz, Coleen Kearon, Kathryn Guare, and Anne Trooper Holbrook. You are brilliant readers and listeners.

Another group of writing friends never saw a draft of this book, but our conversations were invaluable as I revised. Many thanks Angela Palm, Jessica Hendry Nelson, Kim MacQueen, Erika Nichols, Niels Rinehart, Patrick Dodge, Rachel Carter, and Kate Sykes (who, in fact, did read it – thanks, Kate!)

Maryellen Hebert, Mary Jane Shelley, Jennifer Vaughn, Taryn Austin, Jeanne Greenblatt, and Claire Butler are friends who are readers, whose wonderful feedback likewise changed the book.

Carol Mazuzan's honesty and insights were exceptionally helpful as I tried to find Becca. And Peter Biello made a comment in a Burlington Writers' Workshop meeting that changed Becca's life.

I am indebted to Lin Stone and the Wind Ridge Publishing team, whose hard work results in wonderful books. I'm honored that mine will now be one of them.

Many thanks to Daryl Storrs for her generous provision of art for the cover, and her interest in making it just right.

Each year, Carol Hewitt explains The Circle of Fifths in her fun and creative piano classes. I think I finally get it, Carol.

I found Bette Lambert's book, *A Farm Wife's Journal* (Stephen Publishing), and Kristin Kimball's *The Dirty Life* (Scribner) immensely helpful as I tried to build a farm for Bill and Georgia Farnham.

Thanks to David Dillon for advice. He and Sherry Mahady also shared valuable perspectives on the state of Vermont's raid on the Twelve Tribes community, once known as the Northeast Kingdom Community Church: June 22nd, 1984. I also found the church's website informative, as well as coverage in the *Burlington Free Press*.

The Vermont College of Fine Arts is a magical place. Francois Camoin, Abby Frucht, Chris Noël, and David Jauss each taught me something about writing, patience, humor, and humility. I am so grateful for their kindness and candor. I am likewise grateful to have interacted with so many inspiring VCFA students and faculty members in my time at the school and during the 2011 post-graduate conference.

Thanks to Hope Coppinger, Steve Lindstrom, Chris Zerby and Fred Ziemann for being smart and fun and hilarious, and for contributing to my understanding of what makes the best fiction work.

I'm delighted that writers in Burlington now have the support and community offered by such resources as The Writers' Barn, The Burlington Writers' Workshop, and the Renegade Reading Series. Through these groups, I've met writers whose work I admire and whose advice I appreciate.

For years of gentle support and encouragement, many thanks to Chris Bohjalian and Julia Alvarez.

Bennett, Connor, and Aaron trained me to write around cars, radios, guitars, saxophones, drums, video games, computers, and basketballs. The sounds that boys make have shaped my work and filled my life. Lucky me.

Last but always first, I thank Jerry. He makes quiet suggestions, he stands firm when I need to lean. He points out the little flowering plants that I am about to miss, or step on.

Introduction

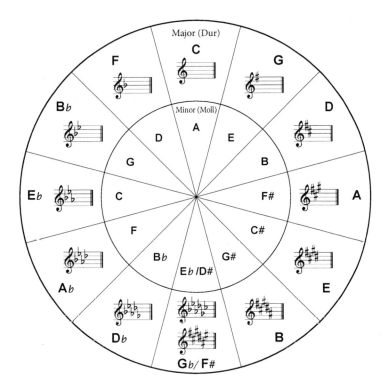

   The mountain watches. Large for the small state in which it resides, it stands protective, overlooking a valley dotted with small towns. Namito, the Abnaki say: Mount Witness.

   From the west, a flat sweep of snow-dusted fields can be seen leading into the foothills, where the beginnings of trailheads are just visible, but quickly disappear under ice-coated pines. At this time of year, the mountain's woods are a dark verdant cape sparkling with silver light. To the south, near the summit, a few ski trails remain, built long ago by a man who tried to make money off the mountain. In the right sunlight, Mardi Gras beads twinkle brightly and even a few faded pastel push-up bras can be seen, thrown—like the beads—into the tops of trees from a ski lift on New Year's Day 2005, the year that marked the failure of the ski area and the man who'd built it. The lift is gone, but a few trails remain visible, not yet erased by encroaching woods.

A bird soaring over the mountain would see the highest trees transform from conifers into gnarled old men, stunted by wind and cold and ice. The bald rock face just over the top was scaled last year by a twenty-two year old without a rope. *The first time*, said the experts, unaware of the Abnaki Indians who had achieved this time and again in the past century. Streams and waterfalls pour down the other side of the mountain and empty into crystalline Lake Pebon, the small body of water where people gather to swim all summer, or skate in the right weather, come winter.

In the valley to the east of Mount Witness lies a lonely ravine, the site where the body of a woman will be found. A young man will leave her in a stream; an old man will find her. Someday. Not yet.

And one day in the not-too-distant future, slightly farther to the east, fields that usually hold corn will be oddly trampled, filled instead with mysterious color and spark, gleaming as far as the eye can see. From a distance, it will look pretty, all this trash: glow sticks and lighters and plastic cups and cigarette butts, torn ticket stubs and broken CDs and abandoned ear buds. And thousands of purple bracelets required for entry into a concert: the kind of bracelets that are hard to remove from the wrist, but possible if yanked and twisted and torn. All of these things, thrown on the ground and left for the people of a small town to clean up, which they will gather to do. Triage on another kind of battlefield. Someday. Not yet.

Across the lake to the east is Resolute, Vermont, a town founded on surety, filled with proud, hardworking men and women. 613 of them, according to the last census. The original name has been forgotten, changed to Resolute in 1832 after a fire destroyed every building along Main Street. No lives were lost. Baldwin Thomas, the pastor of the church, declared the citizens "resolute in their determination to rebuild each structure." Because the church itself was a casualty of the fire, his next words became famous for a time, and remain so in Resolute. "A town is made of people, and not mere edifice."

That church was rebuilt, along with the general store and a restaurant. A tavern called Fassett Brothers was never rebuilt, but today two other bars exist along Resolute's thoroughfare, as a well as a diner, owned by Gil Fassett.

Just last night, in the church, the people of Resolute came together as they do each year for Town Meeting. The heavy, stained glass windows steamed up, thanks to certain tempers running high, and so the smallest window was opened, pushed by two men in unison: three, four, five inches wide, then propped with a stick of fatwood, borrowed from the corner stove. This year, Resolute is suffering, just as all farming communities are suffering. The cost of petroleum is affecting everything from fuel to fertilizer, machinery to livestock feed. Most of Resolute's farming families borrow money each spring to plant crops, hoping the fall harvest won't let them down and leave them unable to pay off loans. Fluctuating milk prices have them at a loss, unable to plan ahead. And so the town meeting began with a worried, contentious tone.

An institution, the Vermont Town Meeting. Each year different, and depending on whose eyes you watch it through, the event might be unrecognizable from one story to the next. The most comprehensive bird's-eye view of any town meeting would likely be that of the town manager. But Resolute's town manager is Stan Piper, an opinionated man. His version would be skewed and likely hard to follow. The better tack might be to see the meeting through the eyes of a considerate, empathic person. In Resolute, you can't get more empathic than Georgia Farnham. Wife of Bill, which is to say a farmer's wife. A woman who has no choice but to brace herself and look at the world straight on, with a wry smile and a balled fist. Surely there can be no truer start to a thing than looking at it through the eyes of a farmer's wife.

Georgia and Bill Farnham
March 2010

Georgia was having trouble paying attention. She and Bill and their son, Ray, had spent the day tapping maples along a steep area of the sugar bush, which wasn't terribly hard work, but crept up on you as the day ticked by. Between this and the early morning milking, her back was tight; it was hard to sit on these old wooden pews for over an hour under the best conditions. Church on Sunday was usually an hour, but it was full of singing and bible stories, and time went quickly. Trying to be inconspicuous, she sat up straight and stretched her neck, slowly moving her head toward one shoulder, then the other. At forty-nine, she was finding work on the farm harder year by year. Tonight she looked forward to sinking into bed and falling into oblivious sleep.

Happily, the town had almost finished with their business. They'd approved the school budget by a squeak, rejected the purchase of a new snowplow, elected town officials, agreed on salaries, and scheduled the annual Resolute Cemetery Beautification Day for the third Saturday in September.

A smattering of applause brought her back to the meeting. Stan Piper, the town manager, started hammering his gavel on the pulpit, as he was wont to do, and people settled back down.

"Congratulations," Stan said.

Georgia glanced over to where he was looking and saw that the handsome new state trooper, Chris Kozlowski, was smiling and looking down at his shoes. Apparently while she'd been daydreaming, he'd been voted in as town constable. She added a little clap to the dying applause; she liked Chris. He'd only lived in Resolute a few months, but people had taken to him quickly. There were, of course, the normal reservations; newcomers always raised suspicions, and he was no exception. He'd moved from a homicide department in Philadelphia to live in a tiny Vermont town and work as a state trooper—a perplexing trajectory. Still, he seemed fair-minded and friendly, and Georgia had a good feeling about him.

"Keep going, or break for grub?" asked Stan.

Everyone in the room shouted "Grub!" all at once, and people began to rise and stretch and make their way to the buffet tables that lined one wall. Looking at the copy of the warning she'd picked up at the door, Georgia realized there was only one agenda item left, mysteriously labeled: *Guy Masters' Band Concert.*

To her right, Bill stood and offered his hand. She smiled and said, "Thanks," letting him pull her to her feet.

"You all right there?" Bill asked.

"Fine. Hungry," she said. He gestured for her to lead the way to the buffet tables.

Georgia had always liked this part of Town Meeting, when her neighbors stopped for dinner, setting aside petty quarrels to break bread together. Tonight it meant a brown, molasses-infused bread, as well as beef stew; soldier beans cooked with bacon; barley and mushroom casserole; apple cabbage salad; and cider doughnuts.

She and Bill helped themselves to food and went to talk with Darren and Melanie Zucker.

"You see the latest projections out of Washington?" Darren asked Bill. He wasn't a farmer, and Georgia wished he wouldn't upset Bill all the time with woeful updates about dairy farming legislation. The news was always bad, and Bill was right on it without any help from Darren.

She turned instead to Mel, who sidled close and whispered, "That new cop is the cutest, isn't he?"

"Melanie Zucker," Georgia said, shaking her head and smiling. "You are a married woman nearly fifty years old, same as me. We could, either of us, be his mother."

Mel sighed sadly. "I don't even remember being single, do you?"

"I remember how cute you thought Darren was."

They looked at their husbands for a moment, taking in the thinning hair and lined faces, and jeans belted tight under round, firm bellies. Together they began laughing. The men looked up and blinked at them, perplexed, which just made them laugh harder.

Coffee was put out, and as people made their way back to their seats, they nibbled on doughnuts and drank from white paper cups. Guy Masters walked to the front of the room but didn't ascend the stairs to the pulpit, behind which Stan had resumed his position of authority. A handsome man, if balding and a bit heavier than he'd once been, Guy was in his mid-thirties. He wore a brown corduroy jacket over a white shirt and the triangle design tie he sometimes wore to church. He walked with his hands in his jacket pockets, slouching a little, ending up next to an easel on which stood a poster-sized pad of paper with a blank front page.

As per Town Meeting Rules, Stan redirected their attention to the warning, or "agenda of the business at hand," as he explained it. This was met with a few sighs and snorts around the room; they all knew what the warning was. Stan then formally introduced Guy to the room, which made Georgia smile. Of course, Guy knew everyone there, and everyone knew Guy. A life-long resident of the town and the music teacher at the high school, he had lived away from Resolute only once, for about seven months. Some people still smiled unkindly when they talked about this, and inevitably someone would say that Guy "had moved out to California to be a rock star, then moved back to Resolute to teach scales." But Georgia remembered the details of the thing; after graduating from high school in '92, he'd moved to New York, not California, and he'd only been gone a handful of months.

Guy cleared his throat and pulled his hands from his pockets. The jacket came with them, and he had to bat it down and then smooth it into place again. His mystery item on the warning probably had something to do with this year's increased attendance at Town Meeting. He cleared his throat again, reminding everyone in the room that he didn't like being the center of attention.

To her left, Darren Zucker crossed his arms and leaned close to her. "Can't for the life of me understand why he never became a big rock and roll star, can you?"

She gave him a cool look and he sat back, smiling ironically.

"I've been contacted by the manager of a band to make a proposal," Guy said.

"Speak up!" shouted Stan from the pulpit, clutching his gavel. People complained about Stan and his possessiveness of the Town Meeting, but they always voted him back.

"There's a band that started in Vermont. They were UVM students in the nineties," said Guy. "They're called Perilous Between."

"They're called what?" asked Stan with a single bang of the gavel. Someone behind Georgia tsked loudly and Stan looked out at the gathered crowd, making pointed eye contact with a few of his regular critics. "I asked what they're called again, because I didn't understand," he said.

"Perilous Between," called Becca Akyn's boy, Carter, from the side of the church. He stood behind Becca, holding the handles of her wheelchair. "They're a really famous band," Carter said. "And they're great. Lead singer is Kennedy Jackson—"

"That's fine, son," said Stan. "But I was asking Guy. He has the conch shell at this time."

The room got quiet for a few seconds, but for the yews scraping the side walls of the building in the wind.

Stan turned red. "The proverbial conch shell," he said.

To her right, Bill made a sound that might have been derisive. But when she looked at him, his face was placid.

Finally, when no one spoke but everyone continued to stare, Stan called irritably, "Go ahead, Guy. I just meant now's your time to speak. No one else's."

Guy watched Stan for a moment, then turned to face the group again, cutting his eyes to the floor. Georgia wanted to walk over and pat him on the shoulder. Guy was much too hard on himself. Always had been.

"This band, Perilous Between … Well, it's like Carter said. They're very big news. And they want to host a concert here."

"Here?" asked a number of people, Stan included, with another tap of his gavel.

Guy nodded. "Here in Resolute. They were all set to go ahead until I told them they'd need the town's permission."

Georgia smiled at this, and joined in a spontaneous round of applause, which made Guy blush happily. Nothing happened in Resolute without the local stamp of approval. It was in the town bylaws. Ever since the fire of 1832, which had been started by an itinerant junk salesman who fell asleep smoking in his guest room above the tavern, visitors could barely even park by the town green without a special permit. People were proud of it—the way they maintained control. No outsiders would ever change Resolute while her citizens slept.

Georgia wondered how it was that this band had chosen Resolute. She raised her hand. Guy pointed at her before Stan could object to an interruption.

"How is it they came to you?" she asked. Arms crossed, face serious, Bill nodded his approval of this question.

"Well," Guy said, smiling. "I called them."

"You did what?" asked Stan.

Guy looked back at him. "I read about the band, and how they might want to do a weekend concert somewhere in New England, and I called to suggest Resolute."

This extraordinary news, of Guy's proactive contribution, rendered most everyone speechless for a time. Georgia realized the pause was making him uncomfortable, which hadn't been her intention. And so she struggled to say something else.

"You called them?" she said finally. It was hard to believe; he was such a shy man.

"Yes."

"I have a question," shouted a woman from the back of the church. Georgia turned her head, but knew it had been Rita who'd spoken. Rita had a piercing, recognizable voice.

"Not now," said Stan, pounding the gavel twice on the pulpit. "This isn't a Q&A."

Rita Frederick got to her feet and stood scowling with her arms crossed. "Georgia asked a question, and Carter," she complained. Bill elbowed Georgia to let her know she'd started something.

"Troublemaker," he whispered.

"Hush," she said, smiling and elbowing him back.

Rita always made Georgia feel just a little bit sad. Not because she was a good woman who was largely misunderstood, but because she seemed to have no single redeeming quality, and Georgia could find no approach to helping her. Rita was a terrible gossip with a mean streak. She was obese, and her dark curly hair, shot through with silver, flew around her face no matter how much she combed it or tried to tie it back. Tonight she had on black sweat pants and a turquoise sweater. She'd knotted a sheer pink hair scarf too tightly to remove it once she got inside the church and out of the snow, and now it hung, lifeless, around her neck.

Stan's shoulders slumped a little. There always seemed to be a point in these meetings where he lost control, and that point usually involved Rita Frederick.

"I want to know if this means we'll be deluged in hippies and drug addicts," she said.

"We might be deluged *by* them," said Stan. "Or *with* them. But probably not *in* them." The room went silent again as people tried to work this out. Georgia smiled happily. Her back wasn't bothering her anymore. The evening had turned entertaining.

"Oh shut up, Stan," said Rita. She flapped her hands at him and took a deep breath.

"No, no, no," shouted Stan, banging his gavel. "It's Guy's time to speak, Rita, not yours!"

"These concerts bring in a bad element," Rita shouted back. "And we can't ignore that!"

"No one's ignoring anything," said Stan. "You'll get your turn, but Guy isn't finished with his proposal yet. You need to cede the floor!"

"Don't shush me, Stan," she said, putting her hands on her hips. "I know about these people. My cousin's son joined an honest-to-God cult out in Seattle and that's who'll show up in Resolute with their illegal drugs if we don't put a stop to it now."

People around the room exchanged glances. They were used to Rita's outbursts. Someone snorted, which seemed uncalled for.

"And you can't tell me it's not true, because I'm sure there are statistics to back up everything I'm saying!" Rita continued vaguely.

Henry Reese, owner of the Resolute General Store, stood and walked to the food table. He opened the spigot on the coffee urn and refilled his cup, then made his way back to his seat, rolling his eyes at Georgia as Rita warned them all about the crime that was sure would accompany a concert "of this sort of latitude." Georgia looked away to avoid giggling.

Guy had taken advantage of the bedlam to flip over the blank page on his pad and easel. Underneath, he had a poster, highlighting various points about the concert in red and black.

Rita's husband, Howard, tried to get her to sit down, but she pulled her sleeve out of his grasp, closed her eyes, and kept talking. Behind them, Rita's elderly father, Fisk Endicott, sat back in the scratched old pew and closed his eyes, as if to sleep.

Chris Kozlowski walked up the middle aisle. Watching him, Georgia grinned. It would take a little courage as a newcomer to get up and try to control this meeting, but here he was, hat in hand, and a considerate expression on his face, as if he could simultaneously agree with every person in the room. She'd heard so much talk about this man in recent weeks, she felt as if she knew him. The women speculated on whether or not he had a girlfriend back in Philadelphia. And the men wondered to one another what would make an able-bodied man move up to a town where he knew nobody and was sure to have taken a big pay cut. As their constable, he'd probably make a little extra here and there, breaking up fights and shooting not-quite-dead deer, but that wasn't like a big city salary, to be sure, even considering the state trooper job.

Rita was quieting down, her feathers still ruffled both from what she called Guy's *outrageous proposal* and from Stan's *browbeating*. She was breathing hard through her nose now and her eyes were wide and indignant.

"If I could cut in here," Chris was saying. Georgia liked his polite way of talking. It calmed the crowd. "Mr. Masters has put a lot of work into this presentation."

"And he's the speaker now," Stan shot. "He's got the proverbial conch shell at this very moment."

Chris smiled. "That's right," he said. "Mr. Masters should finish up before we weigh in with opinions. That all right?" He looked at Rita, who shrugged.

"Don't know why you're asking me," she said in a huffy tone.

"Stan?" Ken Comet had his hand in the air. Next to her, Darren groaned quietly. Ken always made these meetings drag on by asking questions that were beside the point. "What's the conch shell thing you're always talking about?"

"Read a book someday, Ken," Stan said.

"All right, now," Chris cut in. "It's Guy's meeting. Let's just give him some air time."

"Thank you, Officer Koz-loo-ski," Guy said. He stumbled over the man's last name, and a few people laughed.

Chris returned to the back of the room, seeming not to notice glances following him from many of the women.

Now that he had the floor again, Guy faltered. "Well," he hesitated. "I have some handouts on the table by the door.

"And this is a poster based on some of what the concert people told me. And I called the town managers in Highgate and Coventry, because they've hosted big concerts in the last several years," he said.

A door opened and closed from the kitchen down the hall, and the left-over smell of Marlene Reese's cooked cabbage drifted into the room. Already dinner seemed like a long time ago.

The church quieted as people studied Guy's poster. Local Revenue, Campground Rental and Parking Fees were in black. Band, Equipment and Damage were in red.

"Damage," Rita said in a significant Irish whisper. Outside the wind continued to howl, and a storm door toward the back of the church must have gotten unlatched, because it shrieked open, then slammed shut with a bang.

"What's the next step, Guy?" Stan said.

"We'd have to come up with a plan. These people want to move ahead. We need to decide if it would work for us. How much land could we set up as campground, how much sewage removal is available locally."

"Have to truck in Port-O-Lets from Canada, I'd think," Stan said, contemplatively tapping the gavel on the side of the pulpit to underscore his words.

Georgia raised her hand without expecting to. "Can you talk some about property rental, Guy?" she asked, tilting her head at the poster. "Is that for the campgrounds you mentioned?"

Bill turned to look at her, and she rested her hand on his leg.

"That's right." Guy was nodding. "These concerts attract too many people for the local hotels and motels to handle."

"Well, that's good, since we haven't got any," said Fisk Endicott, eyes still closed. Everyone laughed.

"Local farms can make a buck using their land for campground space," Guy said. "Or even just for parking."

"We're talking thousands of people, aren't we, Guy?" Stan Piper said.

Guy nodded. "Yes, I'm pretty sure."

"Hell," said Henry Reese, sounding worried. "Sounds like cluster flies."

Throughout the meeting, Henry had been sitting sideways to put some distance between himself and Zedekiah, the quiet and mysterious young man beside him. Zedekiah had arrived in Resolute some weeks before, seemingly out of nowhere. He had that strange first name, and no one seemed to know his surname. Niko Takis, his boss at the town garage, insisted that Zedekiah was a hard worker. But Niko Takis's ancestry was Greek and his family had only lived in Resolute for two generations; those points alone created drawbacks as far as having his opinion regarded.

"Well, see, that's the thing. This could be a huge opportunity for Resolute. It's a cash proposition, too," Guy said. "These concerts mean big revenue."

"We could use big revenue," said Henry Reese. Georgia could see his wheels turning. He'd be thinking about all those teenaged fans, coming into his store for flip-flops and sunscreen and Twizzlers and Kleenex tissues and cellphone car chargers. It would be all Henry could do not to take out a pad of paper and a pencil and start making lists of what to order.

Stan stood up. "Nothing needs to be decided right now. Guy just wanted to make his presentation. You got more, Guy?"

"No, sir. I think I covered it," Guy said, rubbing his hands down the sides of his jacket and surveying all the data on his posters.

"Next step is a public hearing, so people can voice their opinions." As the noise level started to rise, Stan added, "But that's not tonight! Tonight was Guy's presentation."

"I thought we could discuss some of this tonight," said Becca Akyn, raising her hand. Carter had walked around her wheelchair and was sitting a few rows ahead of her now, hunched forward, elbows on his knees.

"Constable Kozlowski said we'd get our chance to ask questions after Guy was finished," she said.

"You're right, Becca," Chris said from the door. "But I didn't mean tonight. I'm sorry if that was confusing."

"Oh, no. That's all right," she said quickly, blushing. She pushed her hands into her lap and folded them.

Mel leaned forward on Darren's other side to catch Georgia's eye. Becca was younger than they were: thirty-something probably. She hadn't had a boyfriend since the car accident that had put her in the wheelchair. Clearly, she liked Chris, though. *Join the club*, Georgia thought. She figured she was one of the only women in town who wasn't mooning over the new policeman.

"It's winter, Mom," Carter said to Becca.

"Right," she said brightly. "How could I forget? Nothing to do but count chickens and hold town meetings."

A chuckle went around the room, and Georgia smiled. She loved Becca. The idea that a woman could go through so much and still be so positive and funny all the time struck her as truly admirable.

"Next Wednesday, we'll have the public hearing," Stan said. "Tell your neighbors. Call your friends. Next Wednesday, you can all pass the conch shell."

"Oh for pity's sake!" Ken Comet said. But people were ready to head home, and his exclamation was followed only by the sounds of nylon coats being swept off wooden pews and voices rising in private conversations.

Bill picked up a set of Guy's fliers on his way past the table, then offered his arm to Georgia, who took it and pulled herself in close for the walk to the truck. Zedekiah arrived at the door just as they did, and he opened it for them, letting in a blast of wind that made Georgia gasp. He closed the door again quickly and they smiled at each other.

"Hard to believe spring is coming, with nights as cold as this," said Zedekiah.

"It hit thirty seven today," Bill pointed out.

Georgia thought of the sugar bush—all those maples still to be tapped. She nodded at Zedekiah, and he opened the door again.

"Thank you, son," she said to him, giving his arm an impetuous squeeze and smiling at him. He seemed like a lonely young man, in need of kindness.

"Yes, ma'am. You're welcome," he answered, and maybe he leaned into her touch just a little.

She wondered what his story was. Everyone had a story. And every story overlapped with countless others.

People were lining up behind them. Georgia gave Zedekiah one last nod, then she and Bill walked toward their truck under a fathomless Vermont sky, bursting with stars.

After the meeting, Georgia was quiet. Bill could tell her wheels were turning. The outside temperature had dropped while they'd been in the church hall, and they walked to the truck in that forced silence that weather sometimes imposes. *First get warm, then get busy,* Bill's father used to say on nights like this.

Bill waited until bedtime to ask what was on her mind, then decided not to come out with any direct questions. She usually got around to what was bothering her by and by. Now she stood across the room with her back to him, brushing her hair. From the bed, he could see her face in the mirror. She had once told him that her mother felt a woman should brush her hair a hundred strokes a day. Georgia had told him privately she thought that a waste of time. But tonight, as she stared at the brush moving through her thick, wavy hair, she seemed mesmerized, and he wondered if she might be counting to a hundred.

"You were chatty at the meeting," he goaded. She glanced at him and stilled her hand. "Big rock fan, are you?"

"I asked two questions," she said, putting down the brush. She rubbed lotion on her hands, then her face.

He wondered if this concert would be as big as Woodstock. Not likely. He remembered Woodstock, or the film clips, anyway. Hendrix playing "The Star-Spangled Banner" and thousands of people dressed in all colors, waving their hands in the air. Bill couldn't imagine that happening here in Resolute. There'd been a Woodstock II in the papers some years back. A girl got hurt. At that Rolling Stones concert out west, a biker had killed a man, Bill remembered. Some fool had hired Hell's Angels to do security, making law out of thugs. Coventry had hosted that last big Phish concert, Guy had said. And the Grateful Dead had played in Highgate, not long before Jerry Garcia died. Bill used to listen to The Dead some in his twenties, before he married Georgia and she found the Lord. Now they just had church music in the house, mostly, and some classical. It was calming.

"You're not thinking we should let a bunch of hippies camp on our land?" he said to Georgia now.

"You sound like Rita."

"Ouch," he said, and she giggled. "Hey, did you ever think how much she looks like a cow?"

"Bill!" Her smile gone at once, Georgia looked offended.

"Not in a mean way," he said.

"You know what I've said about that," Georgia answered.

He did indeed. She'd once said that, because of his livelihood, Bill tended to view the world through a "bovine filter," and that was right on target. She came up with these things sometimes. Georgia had a vocabulary that could trip a politician, but she never used it to embarrass or humiliate. She liked to look "beyond the obvious," as she put it, when it came to people. She watched for their hidden talents, disadvantages and secrets. It had something to do with her faith, and Bill thought she was the better person for it.

"Seriously, now," he said. "I didn't mean it in a bad way. When she got all prickly tonight, breathing hard like that, she looked just like Adelaide when she'd stepped on her own teat."

Georgia looked like she was fighting a smile.

"Foolish creature," Bill added with a laugh.

"Your observations are to stay in this room," she said, pointing with the lotion bottle.

"Yes, ma'am." He saluted.

"She has her burdens, just like we have ours."

"No doubt."

He decided not to tell her what else he'd noticed, in hopes of emulating her good nature. The truth was, he'd studied Rita closely tonight, looking for something beyond the obvious, like Georgia might have. And when Rita was standing up at the meeting, still panting with anger, and maybe a touch of a thrill at being in the spotlight, he'd seen that her lips were chapped and painful looking, from the way she constantly licked at them. There were purple circles under her eyes, as if she didn't sleep well. If he'd recounted this to Georgia now, he'd have felt like a little boy, trying to make a good impression on a favorite teacher, so he kept it to himself.

"I was thinking, though," she said, turning back to the mirror.

Here it comes, Bill thought.

"What if we did set aside some land for campers? *If* they even hold the concert here."

Bill lay back on his pillow and shut his eyes. He'd be lying if he said he hadn't done the math. He and Georgia owned close to forty acres, and their land abutted the proposed concert site. He could set up a lot of campsites and legally charge about the highest of anyone in town. But he didn't want strangers on his land, lighting bonfires, smoking who-knew-what near his cows. Still, he knew why she was asking. The nagging fear of getting enough rain, enough sun, not too much of either, kept farmers worrying their hats in their hands from March to September even in a good year. And this was not a good year. Just a week ago, they'd been going over the books, trying to work out how they'd make ends meet. Bill could almost envision taking a summer off. Not time off from work—a farmer never got that while he was still alive—but time off from the kind of tension that kept you awake when you needed sleep more than you needed air. If he didn't have to plant his corn and worry that it be "knee high by the fourth of July," he could focus on the dairy, build a new tool shed, put windows in the barn, maybe even learn that fancy computer program he'd bought three years ago: Cow Nutrition & Ration Planning.

But he didn't say this to Georgia. He said, "You want a bunch of derelicts on our land?"

"For I was hungry," she said, "and you gave me food, I was thirsty and you gave me drink, a stranger and you welcomed me—"

He didn't mind her quoting the bible, mostly, but sometimes thought she used it to unfair advantage.

"I don't think," he cut in, "that the Lord meant that we should shelter a bunch of wild drug addicts and keep them safe during their big party."

"… naked and you clothed me," she continued, "ill and you cared for me, in prison and you visited me."

"Well, there'll probably be naked people and prisoners, that's a good point."

Georgia shook her head and smiled. "I'm back and forth on it, to be sure." She slipped into bed beside him, propped up her pillow, then sat back and rubbed her hands together, working the last of the slick lotion into her skin. As they did every night, the smells of lavender and something else—rosemary, maybe—drifted in the air around him, making him drowsy.

He switched off his light and closed his eyes, but turned toward her, in case she wanted to keep talking. After a minute, her light switched off, too.

He had never learned to play an instrument, but his father had been a local favorite on the accordion. Bill remembered his father's band playing concerts on the green. And because of all the talk about Resolute hosting a rock concert, as he fell asleep, he drifted back in time and revisited those humid summer nights when the town would wander out to the green in search of a breeze and the relief that music brings. He and his friends would hop into the swings near the bandstand. Kicking out their feet, they would heave themselves higher and higher, surrounded by the sound of the music, carried on the wind into something like flight. Eventually, his mother would call him off the swings for their picnic supper: fried chicken and buttery oat muffins, grapefruit lemonade, corn on the cob. And the salt. Before handing 'round their corn, his mother would sprinkle each ear with Morton's finest mixed with dried herbs. She'd fold it up tight in tiny envelopes she made herself, out of spare scraps of paper, to keep it all from leaking in the basket. Up on stage, his father's accordion was more than music; it was comic relief. He'd sway and rock, getting into the beat, the rhythm, and Charlie Lavring would back him up on fiddle. The Resolute Band had four or five or six pieces, depending on who showed up, which depended on who had heifers calving, who had oats or hay to chop. They did popular songs mostly and an occasional religious piece, to keep the church folks happy. When he was a small boy, Bill used to fall asleep on the picnic blanket at these concerts. Tonight, for the first time in fifty years, he fell asleep to his father's music once again.

It took two more weeks for the populace of Resolute to decide it would host the Perilous Between concert, given the opportunity. An additional meeting in the church hall lasted over three hours. It was rowdy, even contentious. Bill tired of the subject of this concert days before the long-awaited ballot was held.

He and Georgia drove to town in silence that morning. They held hands on their way into the town hall and chatted amiably with their neighbors as they stood in line. The voting booths were cobbled together out of plywood and heavy dowels, separated by lengths of mismatched torn-up sheets that had been donated for the cause. Bill knew, watching Georgia's shadow through the pink sheet that separated them, that their votes would cancel each other out. He voted against the concert, if only to counter Georgia's now staunch position on hosting campers.

They stopped for a cup of coffee in the church kitchen before leaving. When Henry Reese asked Bill how he'd voted, Georgia drifted away to help a group of women who were putting brownies on squares of folded-up paper towels and selling them for a quarter. A few minutes later, Rita Frederick emerged from one of the voting booths and went to where the women worked. Rather than help, she began loudly expressing her opinion again.

"I can't believe it even has gotten this far," she said, looking around to gauge her friends' reactions. "I'll be glad when the town votes against this and it goes away."

Bill watched Georgia for her reaction. She'd stopped cutting brownies and stood with her arms crossed, legs planted firm, watching Rita. Nearing fifty years old, with new lines around her mouth and pale spots appearing on the backs of her hands, Georgia looked more dignified than the pretty young woman he'd married thirty years ago, but she was still attractive. Her wavy hair, once brown, had surrendered to the gray this year, making her look almost fearsome when she was provoked. As if sensing his gaze, she turned to look at him and raised her eyebrows. He saw a twitch in the corner of her mouth that might have been the beginning of a smile, but she turned away again to return her attention to Rita.

After a time, they left, walking back to their car, again holding hands, then driving home in silence.

In the end, sixty-five percent of voters wanted the income a concert would generate, and Perilous Between organizers wanted Resolute. Georgia left the paper open on the kitchen table the day the news was announced, and she kissed him and held tight around his waist as he read the article.

"Well, that's that," he said. "Rita will be disappointed in us all."

Georgia laughed and handed him a hot cup of coffee.

And although they pretended that everything was normal, by that night they still hadn't discussed what to do with their land in coming months. He knew the next day would demand the conversation. As stressful as farming life was, he and Georgia rarely experienced much tension in their marriage. He looked forward to the moment the decision would be made, and they could get on with their life. *First get warm, then get busy.*

He rose at 4:30. Having slept in long johns, he had nothing to do but pull on his jeans and thick wool shirt. Beside him, Georgia turned away and snuffled once quietly before her breathing returned to a steady rhythm. She'd be up soon, cooking breakfast. Yesterday they'd had home-baked bread with all sorts of special grains and seeds and who-knew-what else, turkey ham she'd bought in Johnson, an omelet that he knew had fewer yolks than whites. He wouldn't eat eggs without at least a little yellow mixed in, so she compromised, but she said her husband wasn't dying of a heart attack on any tractor if she could stop it. He let her cook her health food, so long as she didn't name the ingredients while he chewed. Privately, he felt fortunate that she looked after him so well.

Downstairs, he stepped into his boots and pulled on his coat and gloves, then wrenched open the door and walked out into the cold. Sometime in the night, the temperature had dipped again and now the trees were encased in glistening ice. On mornings like this, the cold had a smell of its own, a sharp, tinny odor that assaulted him and braced him for chores. His boots squeaked against the frozen ground. As he passed under the tall spruce between the house and the barn, a bird started, then flew loudly away into the dark morning. Maybe it was the red-tailed hawk he'd seen circling the farm all the day before, diving then rising, diving then rising, until finally flying off into the woods with some small critter—a field mouse, perhaps—in its talons.

Last year Bill and Georgia's son, Ray, had started the tradition of music in the barn to help with the milking. He didn't live on the farm anymore; he had an apartment over Sonny's Hardware. But he drove back and forth, and Bill paid him like a manager and gave him that title, in hopes that Ray might want to take over the family business some day. Tough as this life might be, it was what the name Farnham had always meant in these parts. Ray had installed a system in the milk house and they played CDs: Vivaldi, Mozart, Chopin. The cows seemed to like it. Bill liked it, too, though he didn't know a thing about classical music. All he knew was that it cheered him. There wasn't much that could cheer him at five o'clock in the morning in February as he saw to the milking of twenty-three cows. The stars sometimes, if the weather was right. But a single violin following a piano up and down a scale on the frigid night air? Even backed by streams of milk jettisoned into sterile tubes, that sound was enough to make him slow down and watch his breath fog inside the cold barn.

Milking was a pleasant chore, mostly because cows are pleasant creatures. Or, at least, Bill thought they were. Georgia said some days she wasn't so sure. Before he went to greet them, he turned on the music, something he didn't usually do when Ray wasn't around. But the hullabaloo about these Perilous Between fellows had him thinking about concerts and bands and his father's music, and he felt an urge to fill the barn with something other than cow breath. Reggae, as it turned out. He'd powered on the system and pressed play, letting whatever music was on the spindle go again, and perfect rings of sound pulsed through the building. Of course there was no spindle in these fancy new CD players, but he liked thinking of them the way he'd thought of phonographs as a boy. He remembered watching a stack of records on a spindle, dropping one by one. Remembered how that precision had once seemed so advanced.

"Stir it up," the man sang, but it sounded like *steer*. Bill smiled. There it was again, his bovine filter. He knew the song, and this surprised him. He even knew it was Bob Marley who'd sung it. Lifetimes ago, he'd known these things. And still, it seemed. The CD probably belonged to Vince, the man Ray had hired last month. If Georgia happened outside, Bill would have some explaining to do; the song sounded like it was about more than stew. But he remembered reading that reggae was religious music. Another man's religion, to be sure, but he let it play. Work to do.

He lit the kerosene heater, which droned loudly, almost drowning out the music, then led four cows into the milk house and lined them up, two on each side, "posteriors to the pit," as Ray liked to say. Bill washed two cows' udders, latched on milkers, then began preparing the cows on the other side of the pit for their turn. The milker added a rhythmic hum of its own to the music, which fanned out around Bill in hypnotic circles. He worked efficiently, methodically, sometimes murmuring to a favorite animal, sometimes patting a flank fondly. Before moving the heifers out of the milking parlor and leading in four more, he dipped their teats in germicide. If it got colder, he'd begin using the powder dip that guarded against frostbite.

When Adelaide moved into the milking parlor, he smiled and climbed out of the pit to look her in the eye.

"Hey there, Rita," he said. The cow gazed back at him mildly. She had deep brown oval eyes and her eyebrows were skeptical arches.

"Nah. You're nothing like Rita, are you? You're a proper lady." Bill patted her jaw gently. The cow remained still, watching him. "Well, sweetheart, what do you think? Farm the land? Or rent it to a bunch of excitable teenagers?"

Sighing, he walked around her, ducked under the bar and into the pit. He checked her injured teat before milking her. The music continued on, making his work pass quickly, so that when he finished with the herd just about two hours later, he was surprised.

In the kitchen, as Bill hung his coat on the hook, Georgia poured him a large mug of coffee.

"That wasn't Mozart I heard out in the milk house," she said as she handed it to him. He said nothing. "I started outside to help you, but changed my mind when I heard the music."

"You disapprove?"

"I didn't want to break up the party."

"The girls liked it," he said, nodding his thanks for the coffee and sitting heavily in a chair.

"Party animals, those heifers," Georgia said. And that was all.

Breakfast was blueberry pancakes—flawless circles she'd poured by hand—and syrup from the one-gallon can on the counter which bore their family label.

"Good," he said, after a bite.

"Skim milk, no cream," she said. He closed his eyes and let his head fall back. "Frozen berries, but oh, well," she said. He nodded.

They ate in silence for a few moments before she finally asked, "What are you thinking about the concert?"

He wiped his mouth with his napkin and squinted at her across the table.

Leaning forward on her elbows, she met his eyes. Bill looked away first. Then he took a forkful of pancake, chewed, swallowed, then took another bite, just so she would exhale in frustration. When she did, he smiled.

"What's the Old Farmer say?" she asked. They both knew the *Farmer's Almanac* was an unreliable source, but he had a fondness for it. His father and grandfather had depended on it. Even if he didn't fully trust it, Bill still found consolation in its pages. When it came to weather, every farmer was victim to his own helplessness and superstition. Bill tempered these burdens with the Old Farmer.

He was glad she'd suggested a solution. He was beginning to think they'd come to an impasse; they needed help, some resource, in coming to a decision. He half rose from his chair, but Georgia motioned him to sit down.

"It can wait. The pancakes are hot," she said.

After breakfast, he went to his office. The only room in the house that Georgia did not clean, his small office was crammed with furniture: two bookcases, three mismatched chairs, a desk, and a separate computer table. The computer table was clean; he hadn't used it much since Ray gave it to him for his last birthday. His desk was cluttered with notes, ledgers and receipts. From a middle shelf on the bookcase behind his desk, he pulled out this year's copy of the *Farmer's Almanac*, still clean and stiff. By year's end it would be soft, worn from use. He paged through for a moment, letting his eyes flit over ads and information: "Hydrogen Peroxide Can Heal What?";

"Two Seasons of Bulb Basics."

Weaving around obstacles, he left the office and wandered back to the kitchen, reading about how a bird's voice organ, or syrinx, allows it to produce more complex songs than humans can.

"Well?" Georgia asked.

Bill turned to the calendar pages, as if he didn't already know what they predicted. "May hath 31 days," he read out loud.

"And?"

"Says here the sunrise on May first will be at 5:40 a.m."

"William," she said softly, crossing her arms.

Rebuked, he raised his eyebrows. "All right. Hang on a minute." He flipped through. "What are we saying, here, anyway?"

"What do you want to say?"

"Good rain in April, good sun in June, we don't rent."

"Floods in April, frost in June, we do," she said.

"All right," he said, relieved the decision would be taken out of his hands. He sat in his chair, and Georgia slid his empty plate to the other side of the table before pulling up her own chair next to his.

"Region 1, Northeast," he announced, spreading the pages so that the spine of the book cracked, a habit of his that made Georgia grit her teeth and close her eyes.

"Sorry," he said, relaxing the open book an inch. He ran a finger down the column of text until he found April. "Wet," he said, then sighed. "Very wet."

Nodding, she crossed her legs and tucked her hands between her knees.

He moved on to June, then looked up at her. "Won't be needing the tractor this spring. Not for crops, anyway."

Georgia nodded. Her face, in victory, was drawn and worried. "We could use this money, Bill."

"I know."

"It'll be all right." She reached out and took his hand.

"'Course it will." He nodded and let her squeeze his fingers. "It's just one weekend."

"What's the weather for August fourteenth?" she asked, letting go. "That's the weekend the concert's scheduled."

He closed the book and placed it face up on the table. "Published Every Year Since 1792," read the yellow cover, which was familiar and comforting to him. But ultimately, that's all the almanac offered: a balm for his anxiety. He looked at Georgia and smiled.

"No way of knowing," he answered.

Carter Akyn
May ~ July 2010

Carter walked a few paces behind Mike, watching the way his own footsteps fell into roughly the same pattern as Mike's—left, right, left, right—but not exactly. Because Mike's steps were light and easy-going, ready to veer off at any new possibility, while Carter's were more dogged, determined. He'd noticed this before, but liked thinking about it in terms of temperament: his steps, his friend's. The way people's personalities might be represented by their gait. Also, there was the fact that Mike was hitting some of the sidewalk cracks, and Carter—despite being too old for it, at sixteen—still avoided them. His mother's back was long since broken, so he couldn't be sure why he did this, except the superstition had always felt aimed directly at him, like a gun. When he was little, he'd half believed that, by avoiding sidewalk cracks, he could fix her. Now it was just a habit.

They passed Duggan's Market, where almost no one shopped anymore because Mr. Duggan was old and pretty near blind and the store was full of dust and cobwebs, and the cement floor, caked with grease and dirt. They passed the G&B Diner, which gleamed in the late afternoon sunlight. Carter could smell bacon cheeseburgers in the warm air, although the griddle vent was around the back of the building. His mom was presently inside, working the dinner shift. He was tempted to go in for free food, but knew Mike wanted to find something better to do.

Mike crossed the street, and Carter followed. Thinking about footsteps and stride had him composing another new song in his head. *Retracing your footsteps,* he thought. Or maybe *rerouting. Rewriting?* He tried it. "Rewriting your footsteps," he sang in a whisper, the notes coming easily, since he already had some words twirling around his brain. That was how it was, when

Carter wrote songs. Usually it was the lyrics that came first, and the notes that popped neatly into place. It wasn't like that for other musicians he knew. A lot of people started with the notes, then filled in words. Just one more way his brain didn't work like everyone else's.

Mike was saying something.

"Sorry, what?"

"Grogan's," Mike said, indicating the hardware store with a little nod of his head. "Sonny's closed, but the door is open."

He was right. Sonny Grogan closed his hardware store at 5:00 on the nose every weekday. It was 5:30 now, but the front door was ajar.

"Weird," Carter said.

"Yeah."

The two of them stood and surveyed the dark storefront, hands in their pockets.

"We should call and tell him," Carter said.

"I have another thought."

"What?"

"Well, no one's painted the bridge yet this spring," Mike said, grinning.

Carter looked at him. "We're only juniors, and we don't play a sport," he said.

"You're not even a junior anymore," Mike snarled.

Carter had dropped out of school a month ago. At the time it had seemed like a good idea. School was really hard for him, and none of the testing had ever clarified why. So he'd dropped out. He wanted to devote his time to writing music. He was working construction, too, to feel useful, and to help his mother pay the rent. She was worried about him. Worried about his future, with no high school diploma. Lately, he was worried about his future, too.

"I mean, you," Carter said. "You're just a junior and you don't play a sport."

"So fuckin' what? Where's the rulebook that says only seniors and athletes can paint that bridge?"

"It's tradition."

"Huh," Mike said. "Not this year." He moved toward Grogan's, looking furtively over his shoulder.

"What are you doing?" Carter asked. "What does the bridge have to do with Grogan's, anyway?"

"You really are too stupid for school, you know that?" He'd been saying things like this, trying to get a rise out of him, since Carter had dropped out. Carter never said anything. Mike would get over it. They'd been friends since before he had memory.

"What are we doing?" Carter followed him again, and the notes to the new song leapt back into his head eerily, dogged as his own style of walking.

Rewriting your footsteps, taking back mistakes.

Mike walked inside the store, pulling Carter in his wake. He closed the door, pulling hard until the latch clicked. They stood in the quiet space, which under normal circumstances felt as familiar to each of them as a room in their own houses. With no people around, though, standing there was completely foreign. They'd never been in Grogan's with the lights out.

Rewriting your footsteps, taking back mistakes.

Question the familiar, when it's making foreign shapes.

"What do you need to paint a bridge?" Mike said.

"Paint."

"Let's find some."

"You want to steal from Sonny?"

"Steal," Mike scoffed. "It's a prank. Sonny would have done the same thing when he was a kid."

Carter wasn't sure. And he had enough concerns about the direction his life was taking without getting into trouble for stealing.

"What if the door was open because someone broke in?" he asked. "What if they're still here?"

Mike looked like this hadn't occurred to him. He glanced around, then put a finger to his lips and they stood for a long minute in the recycled light from the front window, just listening.

"I don't think anyone's in here but us," Mike said, but he was whispering now.

They stood for ten more seconds. Finally, Mike said, "I think I know where the paint is."

Carter followed him toward the aisle, but as soon as they walked between the towering shelves, tall shadows swallowed them and Carter couldn't see clearly.

"Need a light," Mike said, taking out his cellphone. He pressed a few buttons. A small, bright beam emitted from the phone and they continued down the aisle, between tubs of spackle, driveway patching, packages of sandpaper.

The paint stuff was at the other end, next to plumbing supplies. As Mike ran his cellphone light over cans of spray paint, Carter absentmindedly plucked various sizes and shapes of PVC piping, one at a time, from the next bin. He liked the smooth feel of them, the perfect curves.

"What are you gonna write?" Carter asked.

Mike glanced sideways at him, catching him sniffing a small white finger of PVC pipe, which smelled like vinyl and chlorine. Carter put it back, ignoring Mike's raised eyebrows.

"On the bridge. What are you gonna write?"

"Winooski Sucks," Mike answered. He set his phone on a shelf so that the beam shone out into the aisle, lighting a long, horizontal slash of paintbrushes, tarps, blue masking tape and orange plastic paint trays. One by one, Mike began picking up spray cans.

Carter studied a black PVC flange. *Winooski Sucks* was the expected and traditional message. The high school baseball team was due to play Winooski High School in a week.

"That's boring," he said, after a minute, putting the flange back.

"What?"

Carter shrugged. "It's boring. You said it didn't have to be traditional." He picked up a can of bright orange paint. "We're not seniors, we're not athletes, so why not paint something different?"

"Stop saying we," Mike said. "You don't get to say we anymore. You dropped out, remember?"

In reply, Carter just turned away. Mike had been upset about his decision to leave school, and raged about it just about every day. To some degree this had to do with Carter now working for Mike's dad, who owned Kaye Construction, but who also had a reputation as a mean drunk who'd been known to slap his wife around.

"Who the fuck am I gonna hang out with?" had been Mike's first response to Carter's dropping out.

"Why not paint something interesting," Carter said now, "instead of something stupid?"

"Like what?" a voice boomed from behind them. Mike jumped about a foot and dropped one of the spray cans he'd been holding. It rolled away, disappearing under a shelving unit and producing a round, repeating sound that appealed to Carter.

Carter turned to find Sonny Grogan standing in the dim aisle behind them. He was relieved it was just Sonny, and not a desperate thief looking to get out without being caught. "Hey, Sonny," he said. "You left the door open."

"That must be why you two are standing in the dark, helping yourselves to my paint."

Mike was on his knees, fishing the can out from under the shelf. When he stood up again, he handed it to Sonny.

"I don't need that," Sonny said. He pointed to the shelf. "Put it back."

"*Yes, sir,*" Mike said.

"Yes, sir?" Sonny asked. He was usually really nice, but now he sounded pissed. "Yes, sir?"

"Sorry, Sonny," Mike mumbled.

"When you're stealing from me, you can save your Yes, sir," Sonny growled. He turned and started toward the front of the store.

They glanced at each other, then Mike put the paint cans back and followed.

"We were gonna leave money on the counter," Mike lied breezily.

Sonny flipped a switch up by the register, making the overhead lights flicker, then bang full on, so that Carter squinted for a second.

"We didn't mean anything, Sonny," Mike said.

Carter wished he'd shut up and let Sonny do the talking. He thought that's all the man probably wanted. To be back in charge of his own store. To be the boss here on his own turf.

Sonny picked up the dirty white cordless phone and started punching numbers with a stubby finger.

"You're not calling the cops, are you?" Carter asked, knowing he sounded panicky.

"Hey, Sonny," Mike said. "You're not calling Kozlowski?"

Carter wanted to laugh at how Mike used the new cop's last name, like he knew him. The truth was, no one knew him.

"Kozlowski." Sonny shook his head and slammed the phone back into its base without waiting for the police to answer. Carter wondered if he'd just dialed his house or something, trying to scare them.

Sonny glared. "What kind of name is that, anyway? Kozlowski?"

"I think it's Polish," Mike said. "Cause my dad's been calling him 'that new Polack cop.'"

"Well, your dad's a racist," Sonny said.

"That's true," Mike said.

"It's no way to be."

"Yeah, Sonny, but you asked," Mike said.

"What did I ask?" Sonny roared.

"About the cop." Mike's voice was finally quiet, losing some of his normal bluster.

Sonny narrowed his eyes. "What kind of guy comes alone to a strange town in the middle of nowhere to take a nothing job after working homicide in a big city like Philadelphia?" He looked outraged, as if Officer Kozlowski's situation was the thing that was pissing him off. Carter had heard other people talking this way about the new cop. Resolute didn't get many strangers, let alone mysterious strangers. And between the cop and Zedekiah at the town garage, they'd gotten two in less than six months.

Mike opened his mouth to say more, but Carter poked him in the side with an elbow and he closed his mouth again.

"You know, I *should* call him. That Kozlowski guy," Sonny said, looking hard at each of them. "It's not right, you coming in here and taking advantage."

"The door was open," Mike said again quietly.

"That damn latch," Sonny said. "I need to fix it."

Carter grinned.

"What's so funny?" Sonny barked.

"It's just, you know, you own the hardware store. You should have what you need to fix the door."

A flicker of a smile might have passed over Sonny's face, but then Mike laughed and the moment was lost. The frown returned.

"What were you doing with all the paint, anyway?"

"We were gonna paint the bridge. No one's done it yet," said Mike.

"You're not baseball players."

"So?" Mike said.

Carter laid a hand flat on the old, worn wood of Sonny's counter. It was cool and smooth. He liked the feel of it against his palm. The grain was deep in some places, shallow in others. He moved his hand back and forth a few times, then stopped when he saw Sonny watching.

"What were you going to paint?" Sonny asked.

"Winooski Sucks," Mike said.

"That's original," Sonny said, tapping an irritated beat on the counter. He seemed not to know what to do with them, having caught them. He was too nice a man to do anything truly severe.

"How about you, Carter?" he asked. "What would you paint?"

"I'd paint, 'Reach up, that way, for the stars,'" Carter answered automatically. It's what he'd been hoping to talk Mike into writing.

"What the hell?" said Sonny.

"It's from a song," Mike said.

"A great song," Carter added. "By Perilous Between."

"Another ridiculous name," Sonny growled.

"It's a great name, and a great song," Carter said. He repeated the line to the beat of the song, but didn't sing it, for fear of embarrassing himself: *Reach up, that way … for the stars.*

"Yeah? Well, it should be 'Reach up, that way … for the bars,'" Sonny said, stressing the song's accents and intonation perfectly, making Carter smile.

In the end, he said he wouldn't call the new cop with the Polish name. He'd call Becca—Carter's mom—and Mike's parents, and then he would make the boys unload deliveries for a week after Mike finished school. It wouldn't be so bad, Carter thought. It would be something to do, which was what they'd been looking for in the first place. They wouldn't end up painting the bridge, but the baseball team would. Instead of "Winooski Sucks," they'd paint "Danville Sucks" because it would happen a week later, following their loss to Winooski.

After Sonny's phone call, Carter's mom was furious with him for about an hour. She'd been in a bad mood already, which was unusual for her; mostly his mom was a lot of fun. But she'd lost the necklace she always wore. It had been given to her by Carter's dad, on the day of their high school graduation. The necklace had a gold daisy on it, with a small ruby in the center, and she was forever touching it and playing with it, so Carter hadn't been surprised when she said it had fallen off. She almost never spoke about Carter's dad, but she must have loved him at least a little; her attachment to that necklace had always made Carter think so, in any case.

Then Sonny had called about the paint, making everything worse.

"You're better than this," she kept saying to Carter.

After she finally let him tell his side of the story, she could laugh about it.

"We're lucky Sonny's such a good guy," she said. And just like that, Carter's transgression had become hers as well. That's how things were between them. She was either his best friend or pissed as hell, and he never knew exactly which thing might come next. As long as she wasn't crying, though, he could handle just about anything she threw his way.

"Don't ever steal again," she said after dinner. "You can never steal enough to make up for what you don't have, and it can ruin your life in a second." She snapped her fingers.

"At least Sonny didn't call that new guy, Kozlowski," Carter said.

At the mention of the cop's name, Carter's mom had smiled for no reason.

"What?" he said, irritated.

She shook her head. "Nothing," she said. "Just that you're right. It's good Sonny didn't involve the police."

So it was a surprise, later that night, to see the cop on their front step. The bell rang, Carter opened the door, and there he stood: Chris Kozlowski, still in uniform and hat in hand. The state trooper car was parked in front of their house. Carter caught a flicker of movement behind the curtain at the front bay window of the Pattersons' house, across the street.

He opened his mouth in surprise, made a small sound of disbelief, a wet click in his throat, then closed his mouth again.

"Hi there," said the cop.

Carter put his hands in his pockets. They'd never met.

"How's it going?" Kozlowski said.

"I thought Sonny wasn't going to call you," Carter blurted, without meaning to.

Chris Kozlowski cocked his head. "Sonny Grogan?"

Carter shrugged in reply, and made himself be quiet. The cop was sweating—there were beads of it on the hair of his arms and damp patches across the chest of his uniform, which was probably made from some cheap material—and Carter was picking up a faint musky scent, too, which might be from the deodorant that was trying to keep up with the sweat.

"Carter?" said his mom from the door to the kitchen.

He backed up and opened the door wider, so she could see the cop.

"Hello," he called into the house, gesturing with the hat. "How's it going?"

Becca opened her eyes wider. "Hello."

"May I come in?"

While Becca started spluttering about "where were their manners?" and "so sorry," Carter backed up further to let the cop into the house.

"Thanks," he said, stepping around Carter.

"Officer Kozlowski," Becca started. But before she could say whatever it was she was going to say—and Carter was sure it had to do with his poor judgment at Grogan's and *please give a kid a chance*—the cop flinched as if she'd cursed him out.

"I'm off duty," he said, "uniform notwithstanding."

Becca smiled. She liked it when people spoke and behaved with a hint of formality. *Notwithstanding* had pleased her.

"Call me Chris," he continued.

"And Carter? What should he call you?" she asked. Carter noticed the slight tease in her voice and felt his stomach turn with discomfort and annoyance. Mothers weren't supposed to flirt. He walked into the living room and fell into the couch as if he hadn't noticed.

"He can call me Chris, too, when I'm off duty," the cop said.

"Hear that, Carter?" called Becca playfully. "You're on first-name basis with our new constable."

Carter shook his head, embarrassed about what a total mother she could be sometimes. He glanced at the cop. "Is this about me *at all*?"

"No," the guy said. "Not at all."

Carter nodded, trying to look nonchalant but feeling relieved. "I'm gonna go work on the song then," he said to his mother.

"Good luck," she said, grinning.

He made a face, to let her know she was acting phenomenally ridiculous, then went to his room. When he got there, he didn't take out his guitar. He pulled the door almost shut, then stood on the other side of it, listening for what the cop was going to say. He still felt like it was possible that he was here about Sonny and the paint.

"I hope I'm not interrupting your dinner," Kozlowski was saying.

"We finished," Becca said. "Not much of a dinner tonight. We just do sandwiches when I've worked the lunch shift."

"Makes sense."

"You want one?"

"No, thanks."

"You sure? I've got ham and salami and——"

"No, no, no," he protested.

What the hell was he doing here, if this wasn't about Carter?

Apparently his mom was wondering the same thing, because she went quiet then, like she'd run out of dumb jokes and casual things to say. Carter imagined she wouldn't be very good at flirting. He'd never known her to flirt, but then, who would she attempt it on, in this town?

"I'm just on my way home," the cop was saying.

"Where's that?" she asked. And then, when Kozlowski started to speak, she backed away from the question, apparently thinking it had been too personal. They talked at the same time for a couple seconds, and Carter could just hear Becca saying, "… none of my business!" Realizing she liked the cop, but was way out of practice, Carter felt humiliated for her.

"No, that's fine," Kozlowski said. "I live on South Maple, over near the bait shack."

"Oh, sure," Carter's mom said.

The living room got so quiet, Carter worried they'd hear him standing at his door. What the hell did this guy want?

"Anyway," Kozlowski said. "Zedekiah, that man who works at the town garage, brought this in to the station. When he dropped it off, Renee Sydall was standing at the counter. She said she thought it might be yours. She was in to pay her water bill." His voice died away at the end of the sentence.

"Oh my God!" Becca said loudly. And somehow, Carter knew right away it would be her daisy.

"I'm afraid Zedekiah said it wasn't on a chain," said the cop.

"I can't believe he found it!" she said.

"It was in the parking lot at the diner," Kozlowski filled in.

"I should have known," said Becca. "Probably it came off when Carter helped me out of the car."

Carter pulled his head back a bit at the mention of his name.

"… the beauty of a small town," his mom was saying.

"I thought that same thing, when Renee suggested it might be yours."

"To think that she knew that!"

Carter smiled, listening as his mom tried to come up with something nice to say about Renee Sydall, his school counselor. Her voice was guarded and polite. This voice liked everyone and would never find fault with a woman who helped to return a gold daisy.

"Thank you so much for bringing it by," Becca said. It was the first thing she'd said to him that sounded sincere, not put on or exaggerated.

"Sure thing," he said. "You're actually right on my way home."

This was followed by a silence that lasted so long, Carter realized with revulsion that the cop liked her, too. That's what had taken him so long to get to the point. Kozlowski had a crush on Carter's mom. Carter closed his door as quietly as he could and backed away. He knew they wouldn't be kissing. But it had almost sounded like that kind of silence, a loaded, heavy stillness, and he'd felt suddenly wrong about listening in. It had made him wonder—not for the first time, if he was to be honest with himself—if paralyzed women can have sex, a thought that sent him reeling and almost made him ill in the rush to think of something, anything else.

A week after the "Grogan's Hardware Incident," as he and Mike had come to call it, he'd nearly finished with the new song. Sitting on his bed on Saturday afternoon, he held his guitar across his lap and tried out the latest lyrics, which he was pretty sure worked as a chorus.

He strummed as he sang, his guitar pitch perfect, unlike his voice, which he kept low and raspy to hide the unpredictability of his tone. When he'd been twelve, his voice had lost all sense of sweetness. A couple years later, he'd picked up his dad's old guitar, which had sat in the basement for as long as he could remember. So Carter had asked his mother to buy new strings, and he'd taught himself how to string it even before learning how to play it. Since then, he'd been hoping a day would come when his voice would go back to sounding sweet or at least decent. He was sixteen, though, and it hadn't happened yet.

"And if you find you can't get free," Carter sang now, "Bring on the tears from long ago.

"You'll find a way through them, in the long, dark night. Bring on the joy, the fury, the fight."

He stopped playing to write in his black and red notebook, crossing out the words "long ago," and replacing them with "long dark night." The song wasn't right yet, but it was going to be. He could tell it would come through eventually.

The phone rang, and he fell over on his bed to grab it from the side table.

"You there?" It was Mike.

"Yeah." He pushed himself back up to sitting.

"We're going out in the truck. You wanna come?"

Carter checked his watch. "I've gotta drive my mom to work."

"Too bad. It snowed last night in Warren's Gore. Supposed to be very messy up there today."

"Can't do it. Sorry."

"Still working on the new song?"

"It's coming," Carter said

"All you need is a band," Mike said.

"Nobody else to play with around here," Carter said. "Nobody good enough."

"At least your ego's intact," Mike joked. "Hey, maybe Perilous Between could use another guitar."

"Hilarious," Carter said.

Since hearing that Perilous Between was coming to Resolute, Carter had been playing their music constantly. Their most recent album, Brilliant Deep, was awesome, but he'd pulled out their older stuff, too. There had been a time, a couple years back, when his love for the band's lead singer and lead guitar player, Kennedy Jackson, had verged on hero worship.

Before heading up Perilous Between, Jackson had been a nobody. Short as a kid, he'd shot up in his teens, just like Carter. He didn't have brothers or sisters and he'd grown up without a father, just like Carter. And they'd both come to music in middle school. Their first names were both presidents' names—though Kennedy was much cooler, and Carter had really been named for some uncle of his dead father. Finally, and Carter thought this was pretty amazing, the first Perilous Between album, *Rush Forward*, was released on October 7, 1994, the day Carter was born.

He used to talk about Perilous Between and Kennedy Jackson all the time. But one day last year, Mike had suggested in an uncomfortable tone that he "take it down a notch about that dude," and this had mortified Carter. He didn't want to seem ridiculous or obsessed, like some kind of stalker. Or a girl, with posters all over her bedroom walls. He'd stopped talking about the band. Now it was a relief to have an excuse to turn back to that music. What with them coming to town.

After he and Mike got off the phone, he went back to playing guitar, but was distracted, thinking about his friends taking Corey's new used monster truck up to Warren's Gore. He tried not to feel sorry for himself, but sometimes it was hard. Everyone else with a driver's license used it for having fun. Corey and Mike had been out tearing up the mud roads near Resolute every day after school. Yesterday they'd showed up in hysterics to let him see the truck, covered from top to bottom in soft mud.

"Next time," he'd said. "I'll come next time."

"Yeah, right," Corey had said before leaving.

His mother appeared in the doorway. She zipped her daisy up and back on the new necklace a couple times. It was a sturdier necklace, but not pure gold. "You almost ready?"

"Yup," he said, standing up. "You're gonna break it again."

She dropped the necklace.

"My dad gave you that, right?"

She glanced down, as if she'd forgotten what it looked like. "Right," she said.

"You never talk about him."

"Also right," she said.

He put his guitar away and placed the notebook on top before closing the case.

"I was listening," she said, probably just to change the subject, but also sounding proud. Becca always sounded proud of Carter, even—somehow—when she was chewing him out.

"Yeah?"

"The new song sounds good."

"Thanks." He didn't want to talk to her about it. She didn't really get his music. She liked folk and pop, he liked rock, blues, and jazz. Whenever she tried to talk about a song, he had the sense she was faking it a little bit.

"I've just got to grab my purse. I'll meet you at the front door," she said. Then she wheeled away, humming his song. And despite not wanting to discuss it with her, this made him feel good.

In the car, waiting for a light to change, Becca put the radio on, and Carter goofed around in the driver's seat. He pretended to like her music, shimmying his head from side to side, the way she danced in her chair when she listened to the radio and cooked dinner some nights. His imitation was a joke, exaggerated to insult her.

"Hey, mister," she said in her warning voice, but followed it with the pursed-lip smile that told him she wasn't really warning him. So he didn't stop. Instead, he turned up the stupid song and rolled down his window, then shouted silly lyrics to the song's tune. "Two farts that heat as one!"

His mother turned down the radio and stopped smiling, but he saw the corners of her mouth working against the frown, and knew she was just pretending to be annoyed. He closed his window, settled back into his seat and said, "Sorry," in a Homer Simpson voice, which broke her up, giggling, until she snorted.

"Nice," he said.

She laughed for the next mile.

"Mom, I'm not that funny," he said, happy that she thought he was.

"Oh, maybe not." She sighed, wiping her eyes with her fingers. "But you make me laugh."

When they arrived at the G&B, he transferred her from the front seat of the car to the "Super-Cook" Wheelchair that stayed at the diner. He noticed that she kept one hand over the daisy, to keep it from swinging.

"Short shift tonight," she said. "I'm done in three hours. I'll have dinner to bring home."

Carter nodded.

She reached up and touched his chin. "You okay?"

"I'm fine."

"Where are you going now? Mike's?"

"Nah. They're up at Warren's Gore, driving that truck around."

She tsked and shook her head but didn't start in again. She'd said enough the day before, going on about erosion and the environment.

"I'll see you at eight," he said, checking his watch.

"Thanks, hon." She leaned up as much as she could and he bent over her and accepted the kiss on his cheek. She ruffled his hair before he stood to go.

His dropping out had happened abruptly, after a couple of weird conversations with his mom. The first had happened on a Wednesday night. Carter's grandmother had been in the kitchen, making dinner. She came most Wednesday nights to cook them dinner and eat with them.

He called her Mad. Her real name was Marjorie, but his grandfather, who was dead now, had always called her Madge. Supposedly Carter had misunderstood this around the age of three, and had called her Mad, and all the grown-ups found that funny or cute, so the name had stuck.

His mom was in her bedroom, which tended to be what she did when Mad came for dinner, at least part of the time. His mom and Mad had a weird relationship. They were really close, but they drove each other crazy. He'd never really understood why. He loved them both, and thought Mad was the best. She was fun, and she brought him stuff just about every time she walked in the house. She was always happy to see him, and she said really funny things—goofy things that were mistakes, like mixing up Myspace and Facebook. *Are you on My Face?* And she called heavy metal music "heavy iron." Things like that.

"Hi! How was your day?" she asked, when he walked in the kitchen. She was chopping onions and had a pair of pink swim goggles on her face, to avoid the fumes. He'd seen this before, but never got used to it.

"It was all right," he said, staring.

His day had not been all right, in fact. He'd gone for math help after school, as he did most days, and had gotten just about everything wrong, and that idiot girl, Opal Payne, had noticed all the red marks on his paper when he walked out of the building an hour later. She'd asked if he'd spent the hour coloring. Mike had a thing for Opal, because she was blonde and skinny and wore low-cut tops and push-up bras. But she told jokes that weren't funny in her loud, donkey voice. Hee haw, hee haw. And she liked ridiculing Carter in order to make Mike laugh at him. She liked dividing people and picking between them.

Mad said, "Go ask your mom if she ever bought paper napkins, will you? I told her she needed some, but—"

"I got some." Carter's mom was coming into the kitchen. "They're in the pantry." She wheeled to a narrow door in the corner of the room and opened it with a jerk—ever since they'd painted the kitchen last summer, it always stuck—then reached up and took out a stack of peach-colored napkins.

"Hi, hon," she said, wheeling by him again. She stopped and he stooped automatically to give her a kiss on the cheek. "Can you set the table?"

He nodded, taking the napkins.

"So, how was your day?" Mad said to him again. She was finished with the onions and had taken off the goggles, but still had lines around her eyes where they'd pressed into her skin. She added some spicy liquid to the onions in the pan and the kitchen filled with a delicious smell that made his eyes burn. He walked into the dining room.

40

"Good," Carter said. "Well, except that I'm a moron."

"You're a Mormon?" asked Mad.

"No, Mom, that's not what he said."

"No, Mad," he echoed, placing forks on folded napkins, and knives and spoons to the side. "Not a Mormon. A moron."

In the kitchen, Mad started talking about how she'd misheard him, and that it would be funny—wouldn't it?—if he became a Mormon, since he'd probably be the only one in the town. And where would he go to church?

"What's this about?" asked his mother. She'd wheeled into the tiny dining room, and pulled up to her place at the table, since it was about the only spot where the wheelchair fit comfortably. "Why are you calling yourself a moron?"

He realized he'd done it again. As a kid, he'd gotten in the habit of exaggerating every insult in order to get his mom's attention. She'd cover him with kisses and hugs to make him feel better if some kid had said something mean, or if he didn't get invited to a party, or some other stupid shit. Now it was a habit, and a bad one. He needed to stop complaining to her. She could get truly crazy when people joked with Carter, or made harmless fun of him, the way friends do.

"Nothing," he said, knowing it wouldn't satisfy her.

She raised an eyebrow, then straightened her knife and spoon, which he'd laid crooked.

"Seriously," he said. "I just went to the math help session after school and it didn't help. So I felt like a moron."

"Did someone say something?"

"No, no one said something." He sat down in his seat. "But if they had, I'd be really dumb to whine about it to you, being sixteen years old and all."

She nodded.

"Look, it's just hard," he said. "If I get the numbers right, I forget the formulas. If I remember the formula, I flip the numbers. It's the same as it's always been."

As he straightened his own knife on the table, she reached and placed a hand over his. "Don't let it get to you."

"I don't," he said, shrugging.

"Did that mean girl say something again?" Mad was carrying the frying pan into the dining room with two purple oven mitts. She slipped one off to use as a hot pad, then put the pan on top of it on the table.

"What mean girl?" Becca asked.

"Nothing," said Carter, but at the same moment, Mad was saying, "The one who keeps calling him names. I think that's just terrible."

Becca looked at him and the eyebrow was raised again.

He remembered now that he'd told his grandmother about how Opal was stupid and mean. It had been funny at the time, because he'd been imitating her to get Mad to laugh, but now his mom would turn it into a federal crime.

"Nobody," he said heavily. "It's just that girl Mike's been hanging around with. She likes to put other people down; it makes her feel important."

"What's her name?" his mother asked.

"Nope," he said. "I'm not telling. You'll do something crazy."

"I think she should be suspended for that kind of unsportsmanlike behavior," said Mad, sitting down. "Who wants chicken?"

"For once, I don't disagree," Becca said.

Her mother rolled her eyes. "Bully for me," she said. "Who wants chicken?"

"Me," said Carter. She began to load him a plate. "Sometimes I think maybe I shouldn't be in school."

"What are you talking about?" said his mother.

"Getting a job, working on my music."

"Absolutely not!" Becca said, while Mad shouted, "No!"

"I'm sixteen and it takes me ten minutes to read a page. I'm failing math. I can't remember lists of chemicals. None of that's ever going to do me any good, anyway. If I can't make it as a musician, I'm screwed."

"Stop telling us how old you are," Mad said.

"Thank you," Carter's mom said to her mother. He hated when they worked together.

She turned back to him, looking hurt, as if he'd insulted her. "Why am I busting my ass working at the G&B if not to put you through college? I could have been on disability all this time!"

"You like your job," said Mad. Becca shushed her.

"Plus, your ass is already busted," Carter added. Usually this kind of wry comment at least made his mom smile, but not this time.

"Very damn funny," she said.

"Language," said Mad. "But your Mom's right, Carter. You need a high school diploma to get any kind of job in the world today."

"Not just high school. You need a college degree."

"Mom—college? Who are we kidding? I'd flunk out."

"No you wouldn't."

"I really want to drop out." He wasn't actually at all sure he wanted to drop out, but a kind of stubborn passion had overcome him and he wanted to argue.

Becca scooted her wheelchair up and back a couple inches, over and over, the way she did when she was upset and distracted.

"Becca?" said Mad. "Chicken?"

She looked at her mother, eyes full. "What?"

"Do you want any of the chicken," Mad said, maybe a little sarcastically. She'd only asked four times.

"Of course," Becca said. "It's all there is, isn't it?"

"Well." Mad shrugged. As she scooped the food onto Becca's plate, she added, "Not. Very. Nice," in a loud, hurt whisper.

Becca turned back to Carter.

"Don't cry," he said.

"Shut up," she answered, but smiled the pursed-lip smile.

"Well, just, please don't cry."

"I'm not."

"Come on. Everyone get along," said Mad. "This is family time."

For some reason, this was the comment that finally brought Becca out of her funk; she started chuckling, then laughing, and eventually put her head on the table. Her shoulders shook, and her mother said to stop acting like a monkey.

"Mom, it wasn't that funny," said Carter.

"And that is not appropriate table etiquette," Mad shouted, swinging the chicken spoon through the air like a truly crazy person. "Get your head off the table!" Becca laughed until she snorted.

Later that night, after his grandmother had gone home, Carter's mom said, "You're going to college."

"Why? So I can suck at that too?"

"You have a lot of talent," she said. "But I want you to have an education."

"I can get my GED if I decide to go to college."

"Carter."

"What?" he asked, frustrated. "Tell me what is so important about my staying in school when I'm terrible at it?"

She went all quiet again, playing with her necklace.

"Why do you like that, if you hated him so much?" Carter asked.

"What?"

He pointed at the necklace and she dropped it.

"You hated him," he said again, wanting her to disagree.

She swallowed and touched the daisy. Then she reached behind her head and undid the chain. She re-clasped it, off her neck, and held it out to him.

"He gave it to me when we graduated from high school."

"I know. You've told me. It's practically the only thing you've told me." He took it from her but didn't really study it. He'd seen it before.

"He's the only man who ever loved me. I think that's why I like the necklace. It reminds me that I was once someone lovable."

"I love you. Mad loves you. Lots of people love you."

She smiled, but it was a sad smile. "Thank you, but I think you know that's not what I meant."

"Did you love him?"

She touched her throat, where the necklace would be if she hadn't taken it off. "I did when he gave me that."

"Mike's mom says he was mean to you."

Becca narrowed her eyes, clearly working out what she thought of Mike's mother sharing this information. Then she said, "Lucas was mean to everyone."

"Why?"

"I don't know."

"Yes you do."

"He wasn't very ambitious; he loved to party." She sighed. "Well, we both did. But after high school, he started drinking too much and skipping work."

"Where did he work?" Carter already knew his father had driven a tow truck for Ingles Service Station, but he wanted her to keep talking.

"He did a few things," she said, surprising him. "He used to work the crew out at the car races in the summer. And he towed cars all year round. When he died, he was starting to work in Saint Johnsbury as a bartender. Which was a really bad idea."

"He had three jobs, but he wasn't ambitious?"

"The jobs came and went. They sort of overlapped. He had a hard time keeping them."

He became aware of a game of street hockey going on outside their house. Eight- and nine-year-old boys and girls, bashing into each other on roller blades, wielding sticks through the air in the fading light.

"Maybe," Carter said. "Maybe it was because he had a kid so young. Maybe I'm the reason he started to mess up."

Becca picked up her glass and took a long sip of water. Then she shrugged. "Maybe."

He sat back, stung.

"I won't lie to you," she said. "Raising a baby is hard, especially for teenagers who've barely had a chance to grow up their own selves."

Carter nodded, trying not to look hurt.

"What if right now, at sixteen, you had to feed a baby at midnight and again at three and then at five, and then get up at 6:30 and go to school or to a job? Can you imagine what that would be like?"

He shook his head, afraid to trust his voice.

"But I did it," she said. "I had a baby and raised that baby and I got a job and even managed life in this chair."

"You make it sound so awful. Raising me."

"No, no!" She widened her eyes and shook her head. "It was wonderful."

After a quiet moment, she said, "Look, Lucas was weak." She leaned forward, like she was confiding a secret and was worried someone might hear. "He was weak and lazy and he was born angry, and those things broke him."

She put her hand over his and he managed not to pull away, because she had that look where he knew it was so important to her that he feel better and that he be happy.

"He would have loved you if he'd been stronger," she said.

The next day, out of the blue, she'd changed her mind about his dropping out. He'd gotten home from school, having stayed late to retake a test he'd failed. No one had been in the house, even though he'd expected to find Mike and maybe also Opal, who tagged around with Mike now. They'd all been going to study together. But the house was empty. On his desk, a note from Mike: *Call you later. Your mom is up the street. She's batshit crazy, by the way.*

"What?" Carter said out loud, turning over the sheet in his hand.

But then the front door slammed, and Becca called out, "Carter?"

"In here," he'd said.

When she wheeled herself into the room, it looked like she'd been crying. "Are you all right?"

She nodded, waving her hand. "I've had a long day."

"Was Mike here?"

"I don't want to talk about Mike. I want to talk about school."

And then, instead of hammering her points home again, the way he'd have expected, she said, "You have to get a job. No way you're just sitting on the couch writing love songs all day."

"What?"

"You can leave school once you have a job lined up. Not until then."

"What happened?"

"You convinced me. Why? Are you changing your mind?"

"No!" She was actually going to let him drop out. He whooped. "Thank you!"

She shook her head, biting back what might have been a smile, or might have been a frown. He couldn't tell. "What?"

She shrugged. "I'll never get to see you wear a tux to senior prom. Or a cap and gown to graduation."

"None of that stuff matters," he'd said with confidence. "Plus, our caps and gowns are that bad green, remember? Really ugly."

Later, after dinner, he'd driven around for a while, trying to feel celebratory. His excitement was tinged by worry and a tapping finger of disappointment, which confused him. Mothers were supposed to convince their kids to stay in school.

So he'd gotten the job working construction. Mike's dad had hired him to help build the new houses going up on Pond Road, along the back route to town. He didn't have to work with Mike's dad. This had been something of a relief. The manager of the job was a guy named Harley, who everyone called Ride. It had taken Carter a day to figure that one out, and when he did, he was glad he hadn't asked. Ride had put Carter to work on the Payne house, which meant—incredibly—he was now sort of working for Opal Payne.

About a week after Carter joined the crew, the walls went up on the Payne house. Carter and Mike went there one night with their guitars and a thermos of coffee. Mike would have spiked it with whiskey, but Carter didn't drink, so they drank it straight—black. They hung out in the room that was going to be Opal's. Feeling like a pro at the construction game, Carter switched on the lights that were hooked over the naked ceiling beams. Sitting on half-full tubs of spackle, their breath appearing in ghostly bursts, Mike and Carter sipped at the coffee and plucked out tunes by Dylan and Clapton and Harrison. Carter played a few of the Kennedy Jackson songs he'd been working on, and Mike said he was impressed at how good they sounded.

Pleased but not wanting to look it, Carter shifted on the spackle tub and played around with chords on the guitar.

"You ready to come back to school yet?" Mike asked.

Carter stopped playing and laughed. "Where'd that come from?"

Mike shrugged. "It's just that I heard something you're not gonna like."

"What?"

"Mr. Masters made an announcement yesterday—they're holding tryouts for kids who want to audition for a band that's opening for Perilous Between."

Carter studied Mike for a second. He'd have thought he was joking, but he'd heard this sort of thing about Perilous Between. They'd done this before.

Before he could comment, Mike added, "You gotta be in school to try out. I asked."

"What?"

"It's true. I asked Mr. Masters about you in particular."

"What'd he say?"

"He said he was really sorry, but he'd already talked to them about you, and the answer was no."

"He talked to Kennedy Jackson?" Carter was aware of the whine in his voice, but couldn't control it right then.

Mike shook his head. "Don't know. But I guess he already wondered about you, and whoever's in charge said 'no.'"

Carter felt sick. He felt porous and insubstantial. "Are you sure?" he whispered.

Mike clapped a hand on his shoulder, then stood and walked around the room pretending to study light switches and particle board.

Carter took a sip of his coffee so he wouldn't have to say anything.

Mike looked around at him. "Don't you worry that you'll end up in this town forever, building houses?"

He shrugged. "That's not what I want."

Mike shook his head. "You're a dumb shit, divot-head. You should come back to school."

"I left because I am a dumb shit," Carter said.

Mike smiled a stingy little grin at that, but not like he meant it. "Maybe you could try out if you came back."

"But what kind of asshole would do that? If I made it, everyone would hate me for coming back just to try out. And I'd still have the whole stupidity problem."

"True."

Months later—after he'd gone to the prom as Suzanne Sprague's date, making his mom's day because she got a picture of him in a tux after all; after the Payne house was finished and they'd started on the Miller and Kimball houses; after Mike left to be a counselor for the month of July at Camp

Abnaki, where Carter had always wanted to go as a kid, but had never been able to because he was needed at home—Carter was walking by Grogan's Hardware and saw a HELP WANTED sign in the window. He recalled Mike's comment that maybe he'd end up stuck in this town, building houses. And he went inside to apply. He'd rather make less money in a temporary job for a good man like Sonny, than maybe end up permanently indentured to Mike's dad, who had turned out to be an asshole, after all.

Sonny hovered behind the counter, watching, as Carter filled out the application.

"Why the heck would I want you to work for me?" he finally said, when Carter slid the paper across the counter toward him.

"Why not?" Carter asked. He skimmed his palm over the smooth wood, enjoying once more the feel of the old counter, the polish of the grain.

"Because you stole from me, that's why not," Sonny said.

Carter remembered the way Mike had lied to Sonny, and he stayed silent, letting Sonny have the last word here in his own store. The bell over the door jingled, and they both looked over. The silhouettes of two people filled the doorway, backlit by the sun. They entered the store and clarified into two girls, maybe twenty years old. They were both pretty, but also odd-looking. One had dreadlocks. She wore red velvety pants and a camouflage jacket. The other was overweight and had a lot of earrings in one ear, but only one earring in the other.

"We're to needing a couple of deese keys made," said the girl with the earrings. Giggling, her friend in the red pants held up a house key.

"Granny Frank's new tenants," Sonny said. It took Carter a minute to realize Sonny was speaking to him, because he was still staring at the girls.

"You got dat right!" said earring girl brightly. Carter smiled. Granny Frank was a local character—a French Canadian grandmother who ran a daycare on the outskirts of Resolute. This girl had her accent just about down.

"Well," Sonny said, pushing off the counter. "I guess you may as well learn how to make a key." He crumpled up Carter's application and threw it in the trash.

"I got the job?"

"Trial basis only. Don't give up that job you've got working out on Pond

Road just yet."

"I'm gonna work both for a while, if that's okay." Carter followed Sonny's wide frame down the aisle toward the key machine, but nearly ran into him when Sonny stopped abruptly. "I promised Mike's dad I'd stay on for the summer, at least part-time."

Sonny nodded fiercely.

"Thanks, Sonny."

"You want to know why?" Sonny asked, turning around to look at him.

"Sorry?"

"You want to know why I'm hiring you after you tried to steal from me?"

Carter put his hands in his pockets.

"Because you were going to put something original on that bridge."

Carter smiled. He had not expected this. "Yeah?"

"Yeah." Sonny nodded.

"Three things impress me in people," he said. "Courage." He held up a finger.

"Honor." He held up another.

"And originality." He lowered his hand without raising a third finger. The unfinished gesture would bother Carter for an hour.

"I've been watching you," Sonny said. "You got all three."

"Honor?" Carter had to ask. "After I was here to rob you?"

"You didn't lie about it. And I'm guessing it wasn't your idea."

Carter shrugged.

"See there?" Sonny said, slapping him on the back. "You're protecting your friend. You have a little honor."

He and Becca had been having a terrible month. It turned out she'd known about the opening band auditions but hadn't told him, because of how upset she knew he'd be. He'd been miserable and angry, and he took it all out on her. When she suggested he could maybe go back to school, just to try out, he'd roared, "It's July! I can't go back to school in July!" He said even if they'd let him back in for the fall, that would look "stupid and obvious," and he didn't want to graduate a year behind his class.

So his news about Grogan's cheered her up. It cheered them both up, a little.

"It's a relief to be back in Sonny's good graces," she said. "He's a good guy."

"That's what I was thinking," Carter said. He didn't tell her that he also thought there was less likelihood of settling for a low-paying job at a hardware store, staying in this town forever, than settling for a higher-paying job in construction. Working for Sonny pretty much guaranteed that he'd leave this town one day and try to make it with his music. He smiled, thinking how he was tricking himself into working harder.

Becca watched him. "What?"

He shook his head. "Nothing."

He wanted to tell her that he was capable of more than she thought. That he knew she loved him, but that he had a gift she'd never fully understood. His refuge, his future, was music. He didn't really need a backup, wouldn't need the GED, because he was going to "reach up, that way … for the stars." But she wouldn't have understood. Her pride in him was misplaced, a fixed thing, anchored to love she'd felt even before he became who he was.

Back in his room a little while later, he went over the song, tweaked a couple lines one last time, and realized it was finished. He played it quietly, just for himself, enjoying how it felt to play it through fully, feeling grounded— secure in the knowledge that nothing needed fixing.

Rewriting your footsteps and taking back mistakes.
Question what's familiar, when it's making foreign shapes.
Spray painting answers, like a bridge from me to you.
Help yourself to reason, cause it'll get you through.

Jealousy and guilt are worthless, but they're hard to fight.
Joy shimmers out of reach. Bring on the night.
And if you find you can't get free, bring back the tears of old.
You'll find a way through them, beyond the dark and cold.

You're almost invisible, time ticks us apart.
I can't make out the borders around your beating heart.
They tell me you were dangerous, they say you made her weep.
Now you're just a ghost who wails while other men sleep

Chris Kozlowski
August 2010

Sometimes he still dreamed about her, but otherwise, Chris Kozlowski didn't think much about Andy. Why she'd left, where she'd gone: asking these questions had never gotten him far. She'd been there one night, doing geometry at the cheery red metal kitchen table, sipping tea from a large mug, giving him a warm, strawberry-lip-gloss kiss on the cheek when he went to bed. And she'd been gone the next morning: April 8th, 1985. As far as he could remember, there'd been no noises in the night, no cars tearing out of the driveway, no ladders against the side of the house. He'd been only eight, though, and a deep sleeper.

On the morning after his sister disappeared, his mother had circled the kitchen, worrying her hands in front of her waist and making a forlorn animal sound Chris was afraid to listen to. His father had placed several phone calls, retreated upstairs, then returned to sit at the kitchen table and sharpen every pencil in the house with a pocket knife. Chris could remember the way his father had slumped forward in the chair, an elbow on one knee. He could still hear the scraping of the knife shaving flakes of wood into an old bucket at his feet. He remembered the look of that bucket—the oxidized metal such a dark gray, it was almost black. He remembered, too, the arrival of the police, their guns and batons secured in holsters, their uniforms starched and blue. Wearing shiny badges and stiff caps, they'd taken notes on pads of paper. Later, people would assume he'd started wanting to join the force on the night of Andy's disappearance, but that had been another night and different police.

When she vanished from their tan brick row house in South Philadelphia, his sister had been fifteen. She was like a special, second mother to him—an outstanding mother who could pitch and catch: particularly cool, because she was a lefty—and rewarded hits with Tootsie Pops. Easily startled, she was easy to scare if he wanted to show off for his friends by jumping out at her—"BOO!"—from around a corner. His memories of her face were limited to the smiling pose she'd held in the picture that had hung in the front hall of their house. He felt like he remembered her, but could never call back more than that white sparkly blouse, the small, gold hoop earrings, the smooth, long sweep of hair across her forehead, and the way her eyes crinkled in the photo because she was laughing at something their mother had said.

What he had in great supply were *feelings* of memory. A sense that she had been kind and motherly, instructive, protective. He could almost recall the feel of her hand wrapping around his before crossing a street. He had, on rare occasions, snuck home movies into his bedroom and watched them on his parents' old projector. So he had false memories, as well. Of Andy doing cartwheels in their backyard at the age of about six, Andy in a Christmas pageant in second grade, playing a Wise Man, but mugging silly smiles and funny faces toward the movie camera the entire time. Then one when she was older—twelve? Thirteen? In this one, she wouldn't smile, wouldn't get silly, wouldn't respond to her father's urgings to, "Sing that song for the camera, Andrea. The one about the dog!" And although these movies felt like memories, they were not.

By the time he was in high school, the mystery of her disappearance had simmered from hysteria to concern to greedy gossip in his neighborhood. He could remember standing in line at Bruskin's Hardware, waiting with his father to buy enough Glidden "Colonial Feather" to repaint the house. Behind them, the school nurse and her fat husband had been whispering.

"Kozlowski," she'd said. "Andrea Kozlowski." And then, "Shh."

Despite, or maybe because of, the regularity with which this kind of thing happened—the sheer banality of the moment—Chris had been filled with a rage that sucked the wind out of him and made it hard to breathe.

Several times through the years, he'd tried to talk about Andy with his mother, but she'd always become quiet and weepy, retreating into whatever she was doing: needlework, maybe, or reading, ironing. So the mystery of his sister's disappearance disintegrated slowly inside him, buzzing with flies if he poked it. By the time he entered the police academy, he'd stopped poking it.

And until Fisk Endicott called about the girl in the woods, Andy had mostly retreated into his dreams.

As he pulled up to the little house, Chris groaned. Rita was looking out the old man's kitchen window. Nothing happened easily around Fisk's daughter, Rita Frederick, and if Fisk's story on the phone was true, a lot needed to be done quickly and efficiently right now.

The old man said he'd found a girl's body on one of his walks in the woods. Not a local, he'd said. An outsider. Chris had heard that Fisk Endicott used to go on long, vigorous hikes. When he was in his seventies, he was still climbing Mount Witness in ice-free conditions, bottom to top, once a week. Now he was nearly ninety, if you could believe local gossip, and apparently still walking the woods.

By the time Chris stepped out of the cruiser, Rita was on the porch, a threadbare yellow blanket wrapped around her shoulders. It was a chilly afternoon to be sure—sixty tops and breezy—but he was surprised by the blanket.

"I think it's time my father moved into assistive living," she announced.

Chris opened his back car door. From the seat, he took his hat and jacket and a backpack full of things he would need. He'd worked a lot of homicides before he left Philly, but this would be his first in Vermont. Resolute had only two murders on the books—both back in the nineteenth century. He'd checked that before taking the job. There'd been a suspicious drowning in the late 1960s, but foul play was never proven. Now he closed the car door, threaded the backpack over one shoulder and began walking toward the house in measured steps.

"My father shouldn't be out walking these woods," Rita said. "He needs to be in a safe place, but he won't listen. You're going to help me with an intercession." She crossed her fleshy arms, pulling the blanket tight around her elbows.

"Let's go inside, Mrs. Frederick," Chris said. "I need to talk to your father about this girl."

Rita shuddered and hugged herself tighter. "A dead body. In these woods." He heard fear in her voice, but could picture her gossiping in line at the hardware store, as well.

He climbed the steps and she blocked his entrance.

"Are you the only one coming?"

"It's my day off, so I was in town. The others are coming by way of the mountain road. Should be here soon."

She nodded, but didn't move out of his way. "Police protect and serve, isn't that right? Well, that stubborn old man needs protection from himself." A lock of pale silver hair blew across her forehead, softening her expression for just a instant.

"I understand your worry," he said. "We'll talk to him."

She shook her head and pushed back her hair with a yellow-blanketed hand. "I don't want you to talk to him," she said. "I want you to pick him up and put him in your car and drive him to Johnson."

"You mean the nursing home?"

"Assistive living," she said.

Chris walked forward so that, if Rita didn't want him on her toes, she'd have to move. She took two steps back, then turned and led the way into the house.

"I tried to keep her off you," Fisk called from the living room in his reedy old-man voice. Sitting in a brown Barcalounger, he, too, was covered in blankets. Next to him on a small table was a mug of something hot and steaming. "But she's like a bloodhound on the trail of a tired fox."

"You all right?" Chris asked.

Fisk nodded, throwing off the blankets.

"Dad!" Rita growled.

"Miss Nibs wants to keep me covered up like a child." He indicated Rita with a tilt of his head. "I can take you to the girl, though. Just give me a minute."

"No you don't," Rita said. "It's too much all in one day. You'll catch the grippe and die."

"What exactly are you saving me for?" Fisk asked, irritated, pushing on the arms of his chair so that he was boosted forward as the footrest retreated. His feet felt around on the floor for a pair of black leather slippers that were just out of reach.

"Don't do this, Dad," Rita said, and her concern sounded real. Chris felt momentarily sorry for her. Maybe Fisk did, too, because he relaxed back into the chair with a groan.

"Probably I can find this woman's body, if you tell me where to look," Chris said, and Fisk nodded.

"I'm sure you can. She's not far and it's a straight shot. I just wanted to help …" He sounded like he'd been going to say something else, but his words trailed off and he looked sadly out the window at the bright, low sun coming through the trees. "Anyone meeting you?"

"Medical examiner, forensics, more troopers." Chris nodded.

"Well then, we'll stay here and point them in the right direction," Fisk said. He rubbed his gnarled, blue-veined fingers for a moment, then pushed back in the chair to expel the footrest again. "I found her on foot, but you can get there in your car. Might be faster for you to go on foot, at this point. Whoever dumped her probably drove in by way of the old logging road around the other side of Mount Witness."

He picked up the mug. His hands shook, and it seemed to take him a moment to get a sip.

"I'll walk," Chris said. "Send the coroner by car."

Fisk nodded and put down his cup slowly.

"All right. You need to go out the back door. Rita can show you. There's a path to the left of the shed. Turns into a sort of trail. Not hard to follow if you use common sense. About half a mile out, you'll hear water. That road comes in there and stops altogether about twenty yards from your position. You'll see it. There's a big gravel turnaround. Look on your left and there are marks. She was carried from the car, I think, but he dragged her for a ways at the top of the ravine. Then he either chucked her down or dragged her all the way. I'm guessing he pulled her, because it would have been something for her not to get caught up in those trees."

"Sounds about right," Chris said.

"She's young." Fisk met his eye. "You brace yourself."

Rita was slow walking over the grass of the back yard toward the shed. She stumbled once, and Chris grabbed her wrist to steady her.

"Thanks," she muttered. "Dad says that girl was dressed strange."

"That so?"

"I'll bet she was here for Guy Masters' big hoop-de-doo concert."

"Could be," Chris said.

"We don't much get strangers here." Rita looked at him pointedly.

"I suppose I was the last one?" he asked. She shrugged, as if this were obvious.

"I tried to tell everyone," Rita said. "Having this concert in our town is a bad idea. If they'd just listened to me, this girl would still be alive."

He saw no reason to answer. Maybe it was true. Maybe not.

"There's the path," she indicated an obvious entrance, scored by several sets of what Chris assumed were Fisk's footprints.

As she started back toward the house, leaving him to the path, Chris said, "Rita?"

She turned and looked at him.

"Your father's sharp as a tack and fit."

"Runs in the family," she said proudly. "We don't get old timer's or d'mentia. Nothing like that."

"Well, I'll talk to him about his walks, if you like. But I won't help you take him to Johnson." She pulled her blanket tight around her shoulders and pursed her lips. He nodded to her, then started down the path.

In the woods, the air cooled and suddenly Chris felt chilled inside and out.

Before Andy had left, their mother had been a funny, easygoing woman. An old-fashioned mother who didn't work but stayed home, she took care of things Chris never really noticed until he was older: making sure there were towels for his showers, cleaning the front hall floor after his father forgot to take off his boots. Things like that. A lot of the mothers were strict and easily annoyed, quick to reprimand. But Chris's mother had always been fun. She and Chris used to make clay figures and cook them in the oven to dry them. The other kids in the neighborhood liked coming to his house because his mother cracked stupid jokes and didn't tell them not to laugh with their mouths full. She didn't call their houses to ask if they had permission to drink soda or watch TV. Before Andy vanished, he'd always been a little bit proud of his mother—how much of a goof she was, and how much everyone liked her. He'd been only eight, but Andy's disappearance had fixed that time in his mind. He would always remember at least his own sense of the before and the after. Of course, his mother changed after her daughter disappeared. Who wouldn't? She didn't become strict or mean, but she stopped joking and stopped playing and pretty much stopped smiling. She became very quiet.

His bedtime bible stories changed. Gone were Noah and his ark, the good Samaritan, the woman at Jacob's well. Chris's mother began reading darker stories about the wrath of God and the importance of faith. These used to frighten Chris, the same way certain movies frightened him, but he also loved the new, darker tales. He would ask for certain ones again and again, his favorite being the story of Abraham.

God tested Abraham's faith by asking him to take his son, Isaac, to Mount Moriah and sacrifice him. Abraham said he would. He took Isaac up the mountain and prepared to sacrifice him. Chris always wondered about that part; he'd ask his mother, what'd he do? How'd he prepare? She'd say he tied him down and sharpened his knife and started a fire. What was the fire for? His mother shook her head, saying it didn't matter, because, at the last moment, God told Abraham to stop. Just then, a ram came out of the bushes. Instead of his son, Abraham sacrificed the ram to God. Where'd it come from? Chris asked. How'd Abraham kill it? That didn't matter, his mother said. He just did.

Walking fast along the trail, still hoping to have his first good look at the crime scene before sunset, Chris had warmed up considerably. To distract himself from the unpleasant scene he was about to witness, he thought about Becca Akyn. He'd been thinking a lot about Becca Akyn. Certainly the most attractive woman in town, she was funny and kind, and she smiled almost all the time, as far as he could tell from the handful of dates they'd been on. Which was interesting, since being paralyzed would have justified a much less sunny outlook. Living in a wheelchair was not easy. Chris used to work with disabled vets in Philadelphia. He knew that life couldn't be sugarcoated.

But Becca was beyond positive or brave. She was funny; she made him laugh every time they got together. On their first date, he'd taken her out to dinner and a movie. When he asked what she'd like to see, she'd answered without missing a beat: "Something without aliens or decapitations."

As often happened when he thought about Becca, he wondered what kind of sex life they might be able to have, if they were to keep seeing each other. And these thoughts made him feel vaguely guilty, like this wasn't something to work out in his own head, but something they'd work out together, if it came to that. So he walked on, looking for the girl, not thinking about much beyond the darkening sky and his grim task.

It was just like the old man had said. The trail got thin, but never disappeared. After he heard the stream and saw where the road died into a parking lot, Chris began looking down the slope. Soon he saw her at the bottom—a colorful figure splayed by the water's edge. Before he climbed down to where she lay, he walked the perimeter of the graveled lot, pulled a roll of crimescene tape from his pack, then tied it between two trees to block access. The coroner, Doc Hunter, seemed like a competent, careful man, but Chris didn't know him well and he wanted to be sure no one inadvertently wiped out evidence driving in. A single set of tire tracks was visible in the small, snowdusted lot, and a pair of footprints—just one pair—leading to the ravine.

Normally he'd have treated Fisk as a suspect, given that the old man had found the body and called her in. But Fisk's hands shook just in drinking a cup of tea. And when he walked in town, he had to stop frequently to catch his breath. Maybe he still went for hikes in the woods, but those were sure to be very slow, shuffling hikes. It would take a miracle for the old man to shoot someone without being knocked back by the recoil, let alone pull her down a ravine.

Chris avoided the drag marks Fisk had told him about. He climbed down the slope a good ten paces south of where the girl had been either pushed or pulled to the stream. What the old man had said was true: she was young. He'd have guessed eighteen at most, but it was hard to tell. Her face was white as an eggshell, her lips, pinkish blue. Chris shook his head, imagining the phone calls. There would be parents to notify. Siblings. He set his pack on a large rock and took out a camera.

The first body he'd ever seen had been his father's. Chris was fifteen, the same age Andy had been when she was taken. Back then, at least, he used to think she'd been taken. He walked home from school and found a note from his father on the red kitchen table.

Your mother is at the church. She won't be home until six. I'm in the basement. You need to take care of everything before she gets back. Don't let her see.

That was it. No words of love or apology. No signature. No goodbye. There had never been notes. If his father needed help with anything, he just shouted. Already understanding something terrible he could not have expressed, Chris walked down the basement steps. He did not call out for his father, and later he would wonder why.

Chris hadn't seen him at first. He walked into the cluttered basement and looked around, filtering out green plastic bags of sidewalk salt, shelves of varnish and paint, and boxes marked "Andrea's Records," "Andrea's School Books," "Andrea's Artwork." He was quite close to his father when he finally made out his shape, hanging from a beam in the dark corner by the boiler, above a toppled stack of snow tires. Still and heavy, he was foreign in his lifelessness, like another kind of object: a bag of sand, an old metal bucket lowered down a well. Chris saw him and stopped, unable to move. Matthias Kozlowski's face was bloated and alien. Watching his son take in the scene, his eyes were swollen, glassy slits.

Chris felt acid rise in his throat, but he breathed in and out fast, swallowing, and didn't throw up. Then all at once, he felt uncomfortable, embarrassed to see his father this way. He looked down, shoved his hands into his pockets and turned to walk back up to the kitchen. When he was little, he used to tear up these same stairs, worried something might follow him out of the darkness. But today he felt no such fear, no rush. Nothing in this basement could hurt anyone.

Chris called the police and told the woman who answered what he'd found. When she asked if he was sure his father was dead, he said yes, completely sure. So she said, in a soft, sorry-for-you voice, not to touch his father, and he wondered why anyone would want to touch something so terrible. Then he sat in the kitchen, folding and unfolding the note, waiting for them to come.

Out of the blue, he was reminded of the story of Abraham. In the past, he'd always identified with Isaac. Poor Isaac, whose father would have sacrificed him to prove his faith. Now, though, it seemed clear for the first time that Abraham's sacrifice only meant something because of how much he loved his son. And in this moment, Chris no longer felt like Isaac at all, but much more like the unfortunate ram caught in the thorny bushes. A creature that accidentally stumbled upon the scene. A last-minute, unarranged sacrifice.

He wondered why his father had killed himself, but almost immediately closed his mind to the question. Instead, he thought about why his father had chosen hanging. In a way, this was easier: a question with an answer. For one thing, the basement ceiling was high. Also, his father wouldn't have known where to get pills or what kind to get, how many. He didn't own a gun. Jumping off a roof was too public. The rope, though, that was simple. He'd have gone back to Bruskin's Hardware, waited in that same slow line at the register.

By the time the coroner arrived in the woods, it was almost fully dark. Chris had shot a first set of photographs. He'd taken notes, measured and drawn the tire track and the pattern of footprints. Far from the body, he'd tied a rope to a tree at the top of the ravine, looped it around several trunks on the way down, and knotted it tightly around another at the bottom. Then he'd settled on the large rock and waited. The coroner had lights and equipment for the rest of the forensic work. He didn't want to touch anything before they'd done their part.

Back in Philly, he'd had a partner, Walt. Those homicides felt much different than this one. Whenever they waited for the coroner in Philadelphia, they were busy the whole time, keeping people out of the crime scene, interviewing people, asking if they'd noticed anything unusual. *Did you hear a shot? Did you hear a scream? Did you notice anyone acting strange?* Out here, the only witnesses were animals, birds, Mount Witness itself. The old man might recall something more, but Chris suspected he'd already heard most of what Fisk had observed.

"Officer Kozlowski, that you?" The voice was immense, and Chris jumped, surprised he hadn't heard a car, but then remembering it would have parked outside the lot, beyond his yellow tape.

"Doc Hunter, hello." He walked back to the rope—his makeshift railing—and held onto it as he scrambled up the hill to the top. Three people were walking around with flashlights, carefully skirting the parking lot, just as Chris had. A fourth stood at the top of the slope, peering down toward the general area where the girl lay, concealed by darkness.

Dr. Earl Hunter was a big guy, burly like a wrestler, and tall. Except for a ring of bristled gray hair, he was bald on top.

"We'd better get set up," Doc Hunter said. "Hell of a time of day for this report to come in. Too bad Mr. Endicott doesn't take his walks in the morning."

"I'll ask him to consider that next time."

"Is it murder?"

"I'd say so. Looks like maybe she was shot. Somewhere else, though. Not here, I don't think."

"Anyone moved her or messed with the scene?"

"I had the impression Fisk left her alone. Pretty sure no one else has been out here."

"And you? Touched anything I should know about?"

"Me?" Chris wasn't sure whether or not to be offended, so he laughed dismissively as if the man had been joking. "I know how this works."

A switch was thrown, a generator buzzed, and the woods sharpened in bright, counterfeit light, throwing shadows that made Chris look twelve feet tall.

"Good man." Doc Hunter clapped his hand against Chris's shoulder in a conciliatory way. After all, Chris reminded himself, they didn't know one another well. He wouldn't have touched the body, Doc Hunter wouldn't have driven over the tire tracks in that graveled lot, and neither of them would question the other again, if the opportunity arose. It probably wouldn't.

"Looks like you've rigged some kind of staircase for us there," Doc Hunter said.

"I had some time on my hands."

"Well, now we're all going to get busy." He turned around. "Helen? You here somewhere? We need a camera down there."

Before untying the rope and releasing his father's body, the Philadelphia police had taken pictures. From the kitchen, Chris had heard the noise of the camera down in the basement and had asked what it was.

"They're just taking some photos," the cop said. He'd introduced himself, but Chris wouldn't remember his name. He was a small guy—Chris was taller—with long sideburns, and Chris had the impression he'd been assigned to sit with him. He was there to make him feel better if his father really had committed suicide. But he was asking a lot of questions, too, which made Chris think that he might also be there to find out if this was murder. Maybe they thought he'd done it. Though it seemed pretty obvious that he couldn't have lifted his father's weight to the high beam, alive or dead.

It was weird, sitting there, not knowing what to feel. He'd always been comfortable with, even occasionally glad for, his father's strength and the silent force of will that seemed to surge through him. But despite Chris's best efforts, they had not been close. His father had never been warm or loving, even before Andy's disappearance. He'd been strong and had seemed, for a time, important. But after Andy was gone, his silence turned sour and anguished; he'd become prone to furious outbursts and persistent pacing, like a man in a cage.

Without immediate access to grief over his father's death, Chris had unexpectedly and intensely re-experienced his grief for Andy. He missed her all over again, in a new and terrible way. His throat tightened, breathing was hard. He laid his forehead on the cold, metal tabletop for a minute or more, then finally made himself sit back up.

The cop made Chris tea before sitting down with him and asking to see the note. He'd put honey in the tea, expecting maybe that this was what a boy would want to drink—tea with honey—upon finding his father hanging by a rope. The tea had sat on the red table between them, steaming at first, then not. Eventually, a fly landed on the rim of the cup where the policeman had dripped some of the honey. The fly got stuck and struggled there, then died, while they talked.

It was late afternoon. Outside the window, it was cloudy. The low light made the kitchen feel gray and cold.

"Has anyone called my mother?" Chris asked.

"She's at your church. They sent an officer over, a woman. She's very nice. She'll stay with your mother until we're finished here."

Chris nodded.

"Are you all right?"

He shrugged.

"This must have been a hell of a shock, huh?"

He nodded again.

"Was your father upset about anything? Do you know if he was particularly sad lately?" The word *sad* seemed wrong coming out of the man's mouth. It sounded like a word he didn't use much.

"Do you know about my sister?" Chris asked, surprising himself. He hadn't expected to say this.

The man—what had his name been?—shook his head.

"Andrea," Chris said. Then he corrected himself, "Andy."

"What happened to Andy?"

"She disappeared a long time ago. So my parents were both pretty sad after that."

"How long ago?"

"Seven years," Chris said. "I was eight. I hardly remember her." White sparkly blouse, gold hoop earrings, smooth, long hair, laughing eyes. Strawberry lip-gloss. Baseball. Tootsie Pops.

"Did they ever find her?"

He shook his head.

"Well that explains a lot."

"Maybe."

The cop nodded and leaned forward, elbows on his knees, reminding Chris of the way his father had leaned down to sharpen pencils the day Andy disappeared. Why had he done that?

"It's very possible that she's out there somewhere, you know. She might have run away to be with somebody. Happens a lot."

"Really?"

"Oh, yeah." He nodded. "This is gonna be hard on your mom. You'll need to be strong for her, probably, don't you think?"

"Probably."

"She'll be upset."

He could see the man was saying things but he was also asking questions. He was very smooth, and Chris liked the way he'd set up the conversation to be both sympathetic and questioning.

"Your parents—they're close?"

"Sure," Chris said, but it wasn't really true. His parents didn't talk much, that he'd noticed. His father worked at a carpet company. His mother did a lot at the church.

The cop nodded and sighed. "Maybe your father just missed your sister, maybe that's what this is about."

"I don't know," Chris said, shaking his head. He'd been embarrassed, seeing his father's body hanging in the basement. Embarrassed, to see his father as a weak man. "I really don't know."

"And you don't remember her?"

"I was little."

"But what are your larger impressions?" The man's voice was louder now, a little.

Chris looked up at him. Larger impressions? He shrugged. He'd been just eight. At eight, you're still afraid of the dark. You sleep with the door open. You hear people creeping down hallways sometimes.

Chris wiped his eyes because he seemed to be crying now. "I really don't know."

"Of course not," the cop said. He reached out and put a hand on Chris's shoulder. It seemed like a fatherly gesture. It was the message of strength that had not been in the note. The signature, the apology, the reassurance that everything would be all right.

While Chris wiped his face on his shirt sleeve, the cop walked over to the kitchen window and looked outside. Then he turned back and asked, "You want more tea?"

"No, thanks." The fly was curled in on itself now—a minute black orb stuck inside the cup.

Doc Hunter gave him a ride back to Fisk's house to get his car. He'd have been fine to walk—the moon was up and the path would have been visible—

but Doc Hunter insisted. They talked about the girl. No I.D. So he wouldn't be making those phone calls tonight after all. Not that this was any comfort to him. In one of the deep pockets of her crude, quilted skirt they'd found a letter. "Dear You," it had started. "Love, Me," it was signed. Had another person written it? Or had this girl written it, but never signed or mailed it?

She'd been wearing a leather fanny pack with eighty-four dollars in it. Also in the bag was a blue ticket etched with wavy lines, like water, and the words "Perilous Between: Shape of the Sky, August 13 & 14, 2010."

After the body had been loaded into the coroner's hearse, Chris followed Doc Hunter to a blue Grand Am parked just a ways down the road. They drove out of the woods behind the hearse. At the main road, the hearse turned right to start back to Burlington. Doc Hunter turned left.

"Thanks for the ride," Chris said.

Doc Hunter nodded. After a second, he said, "Well, she wasn't robbed."

"Doesn't look like it."

"This band—this Perilous Between. Some of the fans spend their lives following them around. I read that in the paper."

Chris wasn't sure why, but he didn't think this girl seemed to be one of those fans. Unable to articulate why he felt this way, he just said, "I think a lot of these kids just work between tours, make enough to be able to afford to follow the band around on its next tour."

Doc Hunter shook his head. "I think that's nuts, don't you?"

"I couldn't live that way." He cringed inside, hearing himself, then waited for the inevitable comment about how this girl wouldn't be living that way anymore, but Doc Hunter didn't say anything, and Chris liked him better for it.

Now he sat in his living room, going over his notes. She'd been petite and probably not very strong, but there'd been no signs of a struggle. Maybe her killer hadn't gotten close before killing her. Chris hoped not. He hoped it had been quick and unexpected. Though, as Fisk had warned, she looked like she'd known what was coming. Hard to tell; she'd been dead for hours, certainly. But something about her eyes held the look of fear.

Suddenly, without expecting to, he remembered the last homicide he'd worked in Philly. A chubby-cheeked little boy whose father had been aiming for the mother. She had wailed and clawed at her own face when they'd zipped his body in the bag before driving him away. But the father had shown little emotion about his son's death. After the cops cuffed him and led him out to the car, he'd shouted, "I'm comin' back, Simona! And I'll kill you next time, bitch!" That was the one that had driven Chris into the woods. He'd read an article about Vermont, and had pictured himself fishing and taking long hikes. He'd decided country work might be more his thing: drag races and cow-tippings and the occasional general store robbery. But for whatever reason, in Philly he'd never worked the homicide of a teenage girl. The fates had spared him that, somehow. Yet now here he was, living in the woods and haunted by Andy in a way that she'd never troubled him in the city.

He wondered if the girl in the woods had run away from home, or if someone was waiting for a phone call: *Just checking in, Mom. I'm fine.* Andy had never called. Since his father's death and the conversation with that cop, he'd accepted that Andy had probably run away. She'd never called their parents; perhaps because she'd been too angry, the way teenagers are always angry at the restrictions imposed by their parents. But now, reading his notes about the body in the ravine, he was forced to ask himself the question he'd always avoided. Why had Andy never called him?

If he closed his eyes against the present, he could still remember the feel of her lips on his cheek—his sister's last goodnight kiss. Also, he could feel the cold metal of the red kitchen table biting into his lowered forehead on the day his father died. And his mother's worried, vise-grip hug when he'd left home to attend the academy. Each moment in his life, layered in unshakeable sense memories.

He closed his notebook and set it on the coffee table. He wasn't tired, but it was late. For dinner, he'd heated up a frozen mac and cheese and fried a steak. In the sink, the orange cheese and red juice pooled together, looking grisly on the white plate. He'd clean up, read the paper, go to bed. Maybe by then, he'd be tired.

He soaped the sponge and immersed his large, callused hands in warm water. An animal moved through his yard—fox or coyote or cat—a tall, stray shadow momentarily sharpened in the floodlight thrown off the back of his house. The animal tensed in the light, rigid, then darted toward the juniper bushes in the side yard and was gone.

Becca Akyn

June 2010

Becca could sit upright on her own, which was a blessing. She could push herself to a sitting position and stay there, and pull her legs one at a time from their tangle within the sheets. She could hover on the edge of the bed, almost falling, never quite falling except that once but never again, and angle the wheelchair just so to move herself from the bed—built to particular specifications so that the transfer would be easier—into leather that was both firm and soft, like Carter's old catcher's mitt. Her arms were muscular, almost burly-looking compared to the thin strain of her neck, the protruding bones of once-graceful clavicles. Her arms had been delicate when she'd been a young woman—a whole woman who walked and danced and occasionally kicked out in joy or anger. The woman who had walked down the moonlit driveway against her better judgment, tiny baby asleep in the seat hanging from her then-thin branch of a forearm, who had leaned into the back of the car to push the seat into place and buckle him in with shaking hands. Small sleeping boy, completely dependent on her.

That was what most haunted Becca, now. The way she had buckled him in, slammed that door. Sliding into the front seat had meant turning her back on him in more ways than one.

Back when he'd still been in school, her routine would have meant waking Carter next. Not such a tiny boy anymore, but nearly full-grown and thankfully whole and healthy. Whenever she felt cheated by her fate and the way she'd lost the use of her legs, she quickly reminded herself that Carter had been fine, despite her mistake. Lucas had died, she'd been paralyzed. But Carter had suffered only a jolt to the head. At her best, she was able to believe the doctors who said it most likely hadn't harmed him.

Carter was asleep in his room and would get up in half an hour and head over to the construction site where he'd found work after dropping out in April. His idea: dropping out. And, for a complicated set of reasons that she listed over and over to herself these days, she had let him. Mainly, though, the decision had been made in a hot spike of emotion, as was so often the case when it came to her feelings for Carter. She worried endlessly that this had been a mistake, brought on by the less obvious disability the accident had left her with: a blind spot for Carter and a wild, fierce need to protect him.

She'd never told him he'd been in that car. The crash had been up north, near the border, and the EMTs were from Newport. No one in Resolute knew. Only Becca's mother, who'd taken care of him when Becca was in the hospital, and she'd never tell. She'd said it was Becca's secret to share or not share, though it was clear from the way she'd said it that she thought Carter deserved to know.

The woman on the radio announced that it was 6:15, and the radio's volume, designed to wake the sleeper at any cost, began to rise in pitch. Soon it would be deafening. 6:15 was about as far as she could stretch it and still be ready when her mother arrived. She turned off the alarm, then pushed herself up from the mound of pillows and dragged her legs out with her hands: one … and then two. She inched the wheelchair closer, closer, and then ejected her body out of the bed, propelling herself with a bounce of those strong arms into what she thought of as a leap of faith, landing safely in that leather seat. Ready to start again.

Becca's mother, Marjorie, came to help out on Tuesday and Thursday mornings and Wednesday and Sunday evenings. She'd offered to come more often, every day even. What she really wanted was for them to move in with her. Becca always said, "No, thanks," trying not to let a look of horror cross her face. The idea of moving back into her childhood room, of watching TV in that same brown living room, eating dinner off those same metal folding tables from her childhood, filled her with angst. She and Carter were just fine, she always told her mother; they could manage on their own.

Marjorie usually arrived carrying one or two Tupperware containers of food—casseroles and occasional chops or soups—her brown string bag swinging over her forearm, her smile broad and determined. On Wednesdays, she cooked at Becca and Carter's house, then joined them for dinner.

This morning Marjorie would help Becca clean out her closet, then drive her to work before going to Thrifty Madge's, her thrift shop. Marjorie regularly brought clothes from the shop for Becca and Carter, and once or twice a year she helped clean out their closets: throw away whatever they didn't use. Marjorie had a real knack for her work. When Becca was little, she and her mother used to have such fun, trying on clothes at the shop, picking things out for one another. Marjorie would always dress Becca for Halloween and make her up. And later, when Becca was a teenager, her mother would find her the best dresses to wear to the formals, the prom.

Becca wheeled into the bathroom. She brushed her teeth, then got herself onto the toilet and managed to go without much trouble. Successfully going to the bathroom could mean the difference between a terrible day and a good one. Not wanting anyone else's help with this part of her life, she'd developed a routine that involved a special diet, laxatives, and a lot of patience. Some days it wasn't pretty. But she knew there were people who needed a lot more help than she did, and she was grateful to manage it on her own.

She washed up, then wheeled out to the kitchen to make coffee. She made it strong, the way her mother liked, then sat by the front window to wait with a steaming cup. This lasted only a few minutes. Carter had mowed the lawn the day before, and clippings were scattered all over the front walk. It looked sloppy. She shrugged on her jean jacket and went outside, stopping in the garage to grab the push broom. Grasping it halfway down, she started pushing the grass clippings off the front walk.

She managed to clear about a third of it before any cars came. She was feeling good—strong and capable—when the first of her neighbors passed by on his way to work. George Hilary's car made a short screeching sound, he applied the brakes so abruptly. He opened his door and started to get out, actually looking irritated, as if she was trying to make him late.

"What are you doing, Becca?" he asked.

"I'm cleaning my oven," she said, but he didn't laugh.

"Let me get that." He started to cross the street.

"Get back in your car, George," she said, trying to remain friendly. "I need the exercise. I want to do this."

"Don't be ridiculous."

He was walking up her front lawn now, putting his big dumb footprints into the pretty dew on her grass.

"George," she said sternly.

He stopped in front of her, hand out.

"Thank you, but I don't want help."

He looked like he couldn't leave, like his mother was watching from heaven and this was some sort of test about whether he'd turned out to be a gentleman or not.

"You sure?" he asked.

She nodded. "Thank you, though."

As George walked back to his car, Stan Piper drove slowly up in his shiny blue Chevrolet. He put his window down. "Need a hand, Becca?"

"Yes, please, Stan," she called, just to see George whip his head around, looking scandalized. She laughed, then said, "No, Stan, thanks. I'm good."

"All right," he said, continuing down the road and making George wait to cross until he'd gone by.

Chris Kozlowski was the next to pass. He slowed, watching, and she smiled and waved. He waved back, then tipped his head in a meaningful way before driving on without offering to do the work for her. She liked this, his acknowledgment that she was capable of physical labor, his respect for her as a person. A whole, unbroken person.

Marjorie arrived five minutes later, a garment bag over her arm. Becca was in the garage, now, putting the broom away.

"What are you doing?" Becca's mom asked.

"Perming my hair."

"Ha ha. Did you just sweep that walk?"

"Doesn't it look nice now?"

"Where is that son of yours?" Her mother put her hands on her hips.

"Still asleep, big lump."

"Carter!" Marjorie yelled. She went into the house ahead of Becca, hung her jacket on a hook in the closet and draped the garment bag over the back of the couch. She charged down the hall to her grandson's bedroom. "Do you know what your mother is doing while you lie here in your bed?"

"What?" came Carter's sleepy voice.

"Mom, it's fine!" Becca said. "I wanted to."

Marjorie came back from Carter's room, glowering. Behind her, Carter was briefly visible, making his way to the bathroom in his boxers.

"There's coffee," Becca said to her mother.

Marjorie harrumphed once more, then went into the kitchen, and Becca picked up the garment bag, inched the plastic up from the bottom to look inside.

"What's this? I thought today was for getting rid of stuff," she called into the kitchen.

"Just a top I couldn't not bring," Marjorie said. "It's got buttons up the front."

"I like the pattern."

"Isn't it pretty? I thought it would be good." Her mother walked back into the living room holding a shiny blue mug.

Mostly it felt like they were still close. But always, between them, was Becca's wheelchair, and how she'd come to be sitting in it.

Her mother had never liked Lucas. *I'm worried he's going to hurt you.* How many times had she said it? Back then, Marjorie hadn't known how much he'd hurt her already. That twice, Lucas had cheated on her with Renee Sydall, that superficial bitch who'd pretended to be Becca's friend. Before he'd dropped out, Renee had been Carter's guidance counselor, something that irritated Becca no end, and one small silver lining to his no longer being in school. Renee always started any family meetings with a handshake for the student and parents. Whenever she shook Becca's hand, she'd always give it an extra little squeeze.

There was much more Marjorie had never known. Like how Lucas had bullied and yelled and pushed, and had twice hit Becca, bruising her shoulder once, her neck another time. That's why she'd gotten in that car when he yelled at her to. She'd gotten in and she'd brought the baby as well, because he'd yelled. She'd put them both into that car even though Lucas was on his fifth beer and angry. She couldn't even remember why now. Why had they argued? She didn't know. He'd raced the old Saab along that winding farm road, trying to scare her.

"Stop it, Luke, slow down!"

Maybe it was hearing the anxiety in her voice that had started the baby crying. Maybe it was just the way Lucas was driving, whipping the car along like a ride at the fair, so that they were all slammed from one side of their seats to the other. Eventually Carter had started screaming.

"Can't you shut him up?" These, the last words Lucas ever said before taking the turn too fast.

The car had rolled twice, eventually hitting a parked tractor in a field. She had memories of this: the rolling, the abrupt, horrible stop. The devastating silence and hollow numb nothingness that had followed.

Marjorie and Becca spent forty-five minutes going through the closets.

Carter checked in with a quick, "See you later," before stumbling out to work.

As Becca wheeled into her room, the arm of her chair snagged in the doorway and Marjorie almost walked into her from behind.

"Ooph," she said, and then, "Sorry."

Becca backed up and Marjorie took little mincing steps behind her, trying to stay out of the way, but mostly still being in the way. Finally Becca just let her arms fall and dropped her head back. She looked up at her mother.

"Wheel me in?" she said.

"Well, sure, honey, just say so." Marjorie took hold of the handles and pulled Becca back awkwardly, then pushed her forward into the room with a loud sigh that made Becca grit her teeth.

At first, as they went through Becca's clothes, they were quiet. Then Becca felt bad, because Marjorie was here to help, and Becca was in a bad mood for no reason. So she asked if Marjorie had heard about the fight Mel and Darren Zucker had had in the diner on Thursday, and Marjorie had asked if it didn't have to do with his watching porn, which made Becca laugh, and she said, no, it was that he'd been gambling online and had lost eighty dollars. Marjorie laughed then, because it wasn't Darren's style, to look at porn, but eighty dollars wasn't anything they could afford, and he should cut it out. Soon they were chatting like always, catching each other up on gossip. Marjorie pulled down the hangers three or four at a time, put them in piles that she must have understood, and then went back for a few more.

Marjorie helped Becca undress then, though Becca could have done it herself. Faster, though, with help. From above, Becca pulled off her own cotton top, and from below, Marjorie slipped off her pajama pants and underwear. Becca did her best to manipulate her body, using her arms. Then they reversed the process and gradually dressed her again. She wore a pair of "stylish pull-on pants," rescued by Marjorie from one of the piles, and the new button-front top, to make her mother happy.

When she dropped Becca at work, Marjorie took her time pulling the wheelchair from the rear of her van, then unfolding it to put it together.

"Any problems?" Becca called out the front window, but her mother didn't answer.

As she wheeled the chair around the car a minute later, she was wiping her eyes.

"What is it? What happened?"

Marjorie shook her head vigorously and waved a hand. "Nothing. Never mind."

"No, honestly. What's got you crying?"

"You know, sometimes I take out this chair and it puts me back to a time when I'd open your stroller for you." Her mother's voice cracked.

Becca almost said this was insulting and ridiculous, but then remembered how it used to feel, opening Carter's stroller for him. Unfolding the legs, locking the wheels, then slipping him onto the soft, fabric seat. She remembered walking behind him, pushing the stroller, how his happy round face would sometimes slide back to look up at her, and his wide, giddy smile let her know he loved her more than anyone else.

"I worry about you," Marjorie whispered.

Becca sighed and stared at her.

"What'll happen when Carter leaves?"

"At his present rate, I'm not sure when that'll happen." Becca tried for a smile.

"Not funny."

"Mom, I'll be fine."

"Will you move back home?"

"No! God!" She shook her head. Seeing her mother flinch, she said it again more calmly. "No, Mom. Really, I'll be fine."

"There'll be no one to take care of you, no one to get things off a high shelf or carry a package or help if you get hurt …"

"If what?" Becca laughed and took her mother's hand in her own. She squeezed it. "Can you stop being so crazy, please?"

Her mother wiped her eyes and nodded unhappily.

"I gotta get in to work."

Marjorie nodded again. When she helped Becca transfer into the wheelchair, Becca noticed she seemed to take a few seconds longer than usual. Her arms felt so thin—when had that happened? Her mother was getting older.

She gave Marjorie a peck on the cheek. "Bye." She turned the chair and started toward the diner's front door.

"See you Sunday." Marjorie's voice was almost normal again.

"Right." Becca met her mother's eye. "You okay?"

Marjorie rolled her eyes. "Of course; don't be silly."

Three hours later, working the lunch shift at the G&B, Becca was feeling the strain of her day in her upper back, which had full sensation down to T11, below which she felt nothing. Or actually, below T11, she occasionally felt the twinge of something mysterious and painful and futile. Something that only ever reminded her of what she'd never again be able to feel or put to use. A week after high school graduation, she'd gotten a tiny blue and gold hummingbird tattoo on her lower back. Sometimes she thought about that, and was sad she never saw it anymore. No one ever saw it.

She lined up buns on the griddle, nudged them into a neat row with her spatula, threw on the burgers, one by one. Frozen discs, they skittered out of line at first, but she slid them into place an inch below the buns. Caitlin clipped another slip to the length of wire stretched above the griddle, and Becca moved all five slips to the left to read the new one. G CHS TOM—

another grilled cheese with tomato, special of the day. She wheeled her chair back and forth to move sideways, opened the fridge, peeled two slices of orange cheese off the open, unwrapped stack on the plate. Normally she'd cover them with plastic, but today she was pulling cheese out of the fridge faster than it could go dry.

Behind her, Nowell Heath was talking. "I don't give a care about any band. It's the money interests me. Like in that movie: Show me the money." He laughed, then coughed. Low and raspy, his voice was always thick with smoke and phlegm. Becca didn't much like him coughing at the counter, up by all her food.

"Show me the money!" Nowell said again, laughing and slapping his palm on the counter.

"Well, I hope so." That'd be Guy, the music teacher, the one who'd brought the promoters' idea about the concert to the town in the first place. Guy seemed now to be living out his fifteen minutes of glory, as everyone who came into contact with him wanted to talk to him about the band, and which famous people he'd met or talked to so far.

"None," he kept saying, in his quiet, unassuming voice. "Nobody."

The whole town was buzzing now that it was official, Carter most of all. Becca liked seeing him so excited about something. Ever since he'd dropped out of school, he'd seemed itchy for something to happen. That's why he'd gotten in trouble at Grogan's, Becca felt sure.

Wheeling back to the griddle, she paused to close the refrigerator door with an elbow. At the counter, she stopped to pull four slices of white bread out of the bag, then batted it shut again. Behind the counter, Gil's radio shot out a thin version of The Allman Brothers' "Jessica." The radio lived inside a Ziploc bag to keep splattered grease off the leather. It had half an antenna. The top had broken off last spring, when Gil threw a potato at Baby for moving too slow with the lunch orders. Gil and Baby were the G&B of the G&B Diner: prime example of a married couple who should not work together, let alone drive off to the same yellow ranch house every night. Gil wore his hair in a duck's ass, slicked back with a weird fussy curl at the back, though he was mostly gray and it made him look old. He was always grumpy, impossible to please, while Baby was slow and pale and long-lashed: pretty as a piglet. Baby wasn't allowed at the griddle anymore.

Nowell's "breakfast-for-lunch" was ready. She peeled his sunny-side-ups off the griddle, slid them onto a plate and added bacon. Wheeled back and over, got the toast. Buttered it with one hand.

"Order up!" she shouted, wheeling again to put it under the warmer. Something on the griddle hissed and popped, and Becca felt a sting of grease spatter her wrist. She sucked in her breath and quickly put her mouth to the burn and tongued it.

"You all right there, Becca?" asked Guy.

She glanced over her shoulder and nodded her head and her hand up and down together once.

Guy was half-standing, his brow furrowed in concern.

She took her hand away from her mouth. "I'm fine, Guy."

He sat down.

"You shouldn't put your mouth on that, you know," Nowell said. "Loads of germs in the mouth."

"Yeah?"

"Loads of germs," he repeated.

She lowered her hand, remembering her mother's words that morning. *No one to take care of you. No one to get things off a high shelf or carry a package or help if you get hurt.*

Out the front window of the diner, Mount Witness drew her attention. The texture of all the different trees—brights and darks, swirling striations—reminded Becca of pictures of earth, taken from space. She stared, wondering at the way the mountain had always made her feel watched over. From the time she'd been a tiny girl, Mount Witness had seemed like a protective presence. After the accident, when she'd suddenly found herself alone and paralyzed, with a little boy to look after, this sense of shelter had wrapped itself around her like a cloak, infusing every neighbor's offer of a ride, a meal, every friend's stopping by to hold her hand or sing the baby to sleep, with a larger sense of well-being and love. People liked to tell Becca how much she impressed them. They marveled at her inner strength and humor in the face of so much struggle. But it was this place; something about Resolute, and the mountain. She'd be all right. This place would keep her safe.

The bell over the door jingled as someone came inside, jolting Becca out of her reverie.

It was Rita Frederick. The sight of her made Becca forget all about the mountain and what it looked like or felt like, and even about the burn on her wrist. Rita could do that to people. Becca thought she was a gossip and a liar and a phony, always trying to get attention, even by acting like a fool. She used to try to cut her some slack, because she'd had a difficult childhood in some ways, but no more. Thanks to Rita, everyone in town had known right away when Carter and his knuckle-headed friend broke into Sonny Grogan's store. Sonny hadn't called the cops. But he'd told a few folks, including Rita's husband, Howard, who was his friend. And Rita had told the town.

"Hi there, Becca!" Rita said, smiling a pretend smile. She waved and walked up to the counter.

"Rita," Becca said. Nowell and Guy exchanged a look.

"Gil's not here, is he?" Rita asked with a furtive glance around the room. Everyone knew she and Gil didn't get along.

"No," said Nowell and Guy at the same time.

"That man is not nice to me," Rita said.

"Gil hates everyone without prejudice," Becca said. People laughed.

Rita took a seat next to Nowell. "Can I get a Reuben with two pickles?"

The griddle hissed with melting provolone. Becca shouted, "Order up!" and left two plated burgers under the warmer.

"Damn, girl, but you're fast," said Millie Sullivan, passing by on her way from a table to the ladies room.

"Faster than me," Caitlin said, picking up the burgers. "I want a Super-Cook Chair, Becca."

Becca glanced down at her wheelchair. "It's pretty nice, isn't it?"

Gil and Baby had bought the chair last year at Christmas and surprised her with it, calling it her Super-Cook Chair. Really a fancy sports wheelchair, it was extra tall and light and fast, and Gil had fitted it with an oilcloth apron to protect her legs from grease spatters. When she thanked him, Gil had gotten all gruff. He said she wasn't to take it home, because it was diner equipment, just like the new freezer, and he had written it off. Then he'd stomped back into the office to pay bills.

Nowell had gotten his coughing under control and was working on his eggs. Wedged in next to him, Rita leaned low to one side, probably depositing her purse at her feet because there was no room under her lap at the counter. Becca let herself direct all the mixed-up feelings she had about Marjorie's visit into a renewed wave of dislike for Rita. She used to be one of the people in Resolute who'd tried to explain away Rita's behavior by saying that her mother had been a difficult, disapproving woman, either ignoring Rita, or bullying her to lose weight, to stop talking so much. But Becca didn't care anymore if there were reasons for how Rita acted. She'd crossed a line when she gossiped about Carter.

"Order up!"

"Shit, Becca, slow down." Caitlin's face was red. She clipped a new slip to the wire, took away the grilled cheeses.

"There's no call for swearing," Becca said. "Be a lady." It was a joke, an imitation of Rita, who was a prude and proud of it. Caitlin snickered and Becca brandished the spatula at her.

She slid her orders over. The new slip said CROAK MESS. She smiled. Stanley Piper had come in once and ordered some French thing with a ridiculous name that turned out to be ham and cheese. Baby had tried to write it the way he'd said it, and it came out CROAK MESS. Gil had been working the griddle that day and had shouted, "What the hell is a croak mess?" They'd written ham and cheese that way ever since, and it had become one of the stories everyone in town knew.

Rita said, "That band—the one that's coming here—"

"Perilous Between," Guy said.

Nowell broke out laughing at the mention of the band's name. He spat an untold quantity of toast back onto his plate. A communal groan rose up from the counter and everyone looked away while he cleaned it up.

Rita raised her voice. "Perilous Between—right. I hear they're letting some of our kids perform at the concert. There's gonna be try-outs."

Becca dunked a new basket of fries in oil and wheeled around. "What?"

"Oh, now, wait," Guy said, holding up a hand.

"It's true," Rita interrupted him, nodding. "They're having auditions. All the kids in the school band can try out. He wants a small group of them to perform during the concert breaks."

"Now that hasn't been officially announced …" Guy seemed anxious to dispel the rumor.

"Well it's only a matter of time," Rita said.

"No way," Nowell said. "That's crazy."

"Why?" Becca asked. "Why is that crazy? I think it's fantastic."

Guy looked happy when she said this, but he kept his hand raised in the air, saying, "Listen, we should wait until it's been made official."

"You spearheading this, Guy?" Becca asked.

He lowered his hand and smiled, blushing a little. "I'll be involved if it happens."

"Well, this could be an incredible opportunity for Carter," she said.

Guy's smile faded.

Rita cleared her throat. "It's just for the kids in the band," she said. "The school band."

Becca was about to say that Carter did play in the band—she was that close to it—when she remembered he'd dropped out.

After the accident, after she'd woken up, a doctor had told her about Carter's head. There was bruising above one ear that had healed over time, leaving only a tiny depression, hardly noticeable. In the crash, his head had been hit by the middle seat belt, which had whipped around somehow, hurting him, despite the car seat. All that rolling and then the impact. They'd warned her there might be consequences. But there'd been no problems with his early development. He'd been right on time learning to walk, to speak, to play with toys and interact with other children. Then, in fourth grade, he'd started having trouble in school. Reading was hard, and math. She never mentioned it to anyone—had never seen the point—but deep down, she knew his problems in school were from the accident, which meant they were her fault.

Rita was watching her, and Becca turned her attention back to the griddle. Over her shoulder, trying to sound offhand, she said, "Is that so, Guy? Only for the school kids?"

"This hasn't even been made official yet," he said. His voice registered a misery equal to her own.

"But," said Rita happily, "it'll be just for the kids at the school."

Becca put a chicken salad sandwich on the counter and shouted, "Order up!"

She didn't look at Rita, who would be still watching for a reaction. Instead, she let her gaze fall on the bulletin board across the room, cluttered with photographs and ads. There were pictures of the diner staff and customers hamming it up—the whole town displayed on the wall like a big photo album. A few were from vacation spots: Florida and Virginia Beach and Lake Dunmore. And in these, people from Resolute held signs that said things like, "Hey there, Becca!" and "I miss Gil's California burgers." She could see the picture of herself and Carter, arms around each other's shoulders, mugging silly smiles. They'd been doing a transfer from one chair to the other, and someone had shouted for them to look up and smile. It was one of the only pictures in recent memory where she didn't look tense and unhappy and old.

Becca had been pretty once. Slim and fit, even without trying, she looked like a movie star, people used to say.

"It's your eyes," Lucas had insisted. "You've got movie star eyes."

Now, though, the bones in her face looked sharp. And her eyes, though still large and brown, were underscored with dark circles. There was never time to put her head back in the sunshine and get a little tan. Never time for makeup, and why bother, when you lived your life tethered to a chair? In that picture, though, Becca hadn't been thinking about her looks. She'd been thinking about Carter, the one person who made her happy. So it was ironic that she looked pretty there, at her most super-gimp, being transferred between wheelchairs.

"You all right, Becca?" Rita asked, her voice full of mock concern.

"I'm fine, thanks." She dumped Rita's corned beef onto the griddle. She pretended to throw up in it. Caitlin noticed and snickered.

"Your fries are smokin'," Nowell said.

"Oh, shoot." Becca moved over and pulled up the basket.

"How'd you hear about it, anyway, Rita?" Guy asked.

"I heard it from Alice Sisley this morning," she said, her tone all uppity. Alice was the school secretary.

"She probably shouldn't have—"

"She got a call this morning from the concert pro-mo-ter." Rita said this like she'd been practicing, trying to get the words right and sound offhand at the same time. "Calling to organize the try-outs. Seems that famous band is coming ahead of time just for these try-outs!"

"None of that is for public consumption, though, Rita," Guy mumbled.

As they talked, Becca glanced out over the tables, as she sometimes did, just to make sure she hadn't forgotten anyone. Her gaze faltered when it fell on the state trooper, Chris Kozlowski, sitting at the tight table by the bathroom door, his uniform neat and pressed, his hat placed with care on the tabletop across from him. He must have come in when her back was turned. She'd have noticed.

He'd been watching her first, and she nearly jumped when their eyes met. He nodded and smiled, and Becca looked away, wondering if he'd seen her pretending to throw up on the griddle. Then she wished she'd smiled back.

Nowell was again doubting that Rita's information was any good.

"Just wait, Nowell, you'll see when they announce it," Rita said. "Won't he, Guy?"

Guy made an impartial noise in his throat.

"Too bad about Carter, though," Rita said, and Becca turned her chair to look at her. She was struck hard by how sad Rita was—always trying to get a rise out of people, even if it meant hurting them, sacrificing their friendship.

"Carter's a talented musician with his whole life ahead of him," Becca said. "He'll be just fine." She smiled to reassure Guy, who was sitting small on his stool, watching her mournfully, as if he'd be more sorry than she would be if these auditions happened and Carter was barred from trying out. She found herself wanting to make him feel better, and turned back to her griddle.

"CROAK MESS!" she shouted, adding a little gravel to her voice as she put up the order. Everyone laughed, even out at the tables.

On the day she'd changed her mind about letting Carter drop out, Gil had given her a ride home from work, grumbling all the way about how much paperwork he had to do, and how worthless Baby was about helping with any of it, and Becca had been relieved to get out of the car and leave behind all of his problems, kind as he'd been to drive her. It was early April, and she'd wheeled herself into the house through the garage, because it had snowed, and this was easier than negotiating the front walk. Inside the house, she'd heard kids in Carter's room.

"Hello?"

"Oh, hey, Becca," came Mike's voice.

"You call her Becca?" said a girl in a grinning whisper.

"Who's there?"

"Mike," said Mike.

"And Opal!" called the girl. She giggled.

Opal would be the one who'd just moved here last year. Or moved back. Her family had lived in Resolute all their lives until 2002, when Opal's father got a job in Albany. That hadn't worked out, though, and they were back. Carter had told Becca that Opal was "cute, but kind of annoying." Becca wheeled down the hall. Carter's door was open just an inch. She pushed on it. Mike was on the floor and Opal was on the bed. Books and papers were spread everywhere, and she could tell they'd been studying. Or preparing to study, anyway. Just to be sure, she opened the door wider until it made contact with the wall. Clunk. Mike looked at her and she saw that he knew what she was thinking: *No funny business.* He smiled and looked away.

"Hi," she said.

"We're here to study with Carter," Mike explained without being asked. "He said we could wait for him here."

"That's fine," Becca said. "But where is he?"

"At school," Mike said.

"Still," said the girl with another stupid burp of laughter. Becca had the sense this was the continuation of a conversation they'd been having already. A conversation about Carter.

"Oh?"

"He'll be home soon," Mike said. "He's got some work to make up." He'd adjusted his tone into something mild and harmless, the way he could when he wanted to make a good impression. Mike could be very smooth, Becca knew. She narrowed her eyes at him.

The girl was still laughing.

"Did I miss something?" Becca said.

"No," Mike said. His voice, so earnest and sincere, made the girl lose it entirely.

Becca decided they were just flirting. She didn't want any part of it. She wheeled herself backwards out of the room and spun around to leave.

"Well, tell him to come see me when he gets home," she said, just for something to say; the house was so little, she'd know when he got home.

"All right," Mike said.

She started down the hall toward her room.

"But it might be awhile," the girl said with a little snort. "Because he's failing, like, everything!" She'd said it quietly, almost quietly enough.

Becca could hear Mike, then, shushing her, trying not to be amused. She knew she should continue on to her room. It would be better for Carter if she didn't make a scene; he accused her of always making a scene. But she couldn't help it. The anger she felt, the burning fury, as this stupid nobody girl criticized Carter in his own bedroom, felt like it might melt the house. She wheeled back to Carter's room and parked herself in the doorway, watching them. The girl hadn't seen her return, because she was flopped forward on the bed in hopeless giggles. Mike saw Becca though, and his grin flickered away immediately.

"What was that?" she said.

"What?" The girl sat upright, whipping her long hair up and over her head. She put her hands to her mouth.

"Nothing," Mike said.

Opal wore a pair of trendy mittens—blue and white striped, with tops that folded back to let her fingers wriggle free if they were hot. Somehow, the cute mittens and the cute girl and the lazy way she made herself comfortable on Carter's bed while she mocked him all merged together, making Becca see red.

"Go home," Becca managed to say.

She looked at Mike. "Get her out of here," she hissed.

He nodded without questioning her, and began collecting papers and shutting books.

"Oh my God!" the girl said, scandalized. "I was just kidding."

"Shh," Mike said.

Becca had left the house. With no plan, she turned and began wheeling herself toward the end of the road.

"Um, Becca?" Mike had followed her outside. He walked slowly after her without a coat, arms crossed.

"Leave me alone, Mike."

"Are you all right?"

"I will be." As she wheeled away, she heard him go back inside to get the girl.

The road wasn't fully cleared of snow, and it was hard to push herself forward. She knew she was acting crazy. Knew this was what Carter hated most—the way she tried to protect him like he was a little child.

He'd tried to explain about school. Why hadn't she listened? Why had it taken this snotty little bitch to convince her that Carter was right about school?

Nearing the dead end, her road went up a mild incline, and she really had to work to push herself all the way. It was how she'd first trained herself in the chair, this trek: up and down her road, strengthening her arms and learning to handle gentle hills. But that hadn't been through snow. The turnaround at the end wasn't plowed, but she pushed herself hard, ignoring the angry thumping of her heartbeat, the tears on her cheeks.

People were so fucking mean.

She'd always been glad for the view of the mountain at the end of the street. It had been her reward, in the years when she'd had to master the wheelchair and face her future: Mount Witness, rising up to meet her. She sat and faced it now, watching her breath shoot out in frosty blasts, wiping angry tears from her cheeks, and swallowing, trying to get her temper under control. Strong and permanent and the same as it had been when she'd been little, Mount Witness felt like proof that things had not changed as much as she might think. That her world was still in place.

Her shift ended at two, after the lunch rush slowed. She transferred back to her own chair, asked Caitlin to put her Super-Cook Chair in the office, then wheeled out from the diner to wait for Carter to pick her up. He had permission from his boss to leave the construction site every day for an hour to grab a bite of lunch and bring Becca home. Although, twice in the last few weeks, he'd called at the last minute to say they couldn't let him out that day, and she'd had to trouble Gil for a ride, enduring the humiliation of his having to lift her into his car. She couldn't transfer into cars on her own, had never quite mastered it. The one time she'd fallen while trying to transfer had been between a wheelchair and a car. She'd scraped up her face and her wrists and had been left with a dread of car transfers.

Before Carter had been big enough to help her, and old enough to drive, she'd had to rely on other people a lot. It was a relief not to have to do that anymore. She felt grateful for his size and strength. And grateful, too, that he'd never once balked at having to pick up his mother and move her around. He'd been doing it since the seventh grade and driving her places for almost a year.

Before that, different people—men and women—had helped her by coming to take her to work, or to bring her home. After the accident, she'd needed so much help. And the town had healed around her like the edges of a wound.

Chris Kozlowski came out of the diner, hat in his hands and Rita Frederick at his heels. She was battering him over some concern or other, and he looked like she was getting on his very last nerve.

"I'm just saying, the element that's going to come with this concert will mean problems with a capital P," she said.

"And that rhymes with T?" he asked playfully.

Rita looked stumped.

"And that stands for Tool!" Becca finished from a short distance across the lot. It was from a rap song by some band Carter sometimes listened to—a spoof on *The Music Man* number. Apparently Chris liked rap, too. Or knew the song, anyway. She exchanged a smile with him, but Rita's face darkened.

"I wish I could find some member of this community to take me seriously. This concert is going to hurt our town."

"Mrs. Frederick," he said. "The troopers are going to do everything possible to keep that from happening. I'll be working here in both that capacity, and in my role as constable."

She made a noise that might have been her way of disrespecting the troopers, or disrespecting his role as constable.

Chris ignored it and kept speaking. "I've gotta say, I'm not quite sure what else it is you'd like me to do."

"Cancel this concert before it's too late!"

"Well you know I don't have that authority."

"Obviously!"

"Rita," Becca interjected. "The town voted. No one can cancel it. We agreed to have it here."

"Well," she huffed. "It's a big mistake." And she ground her heel into the gravel as she turned, then stomped away to her car, parked across the lot.

"Thanks," Chris said to Becca.

Her cellphone rang from inside the backpack on her lap, and she cursed it silently. She'd have loved the chance to talk to Chris Kozlowski all alone for once. He was kind and smart and handsome, and she knew from the way they'd caught each other's gaze on more than one occasion that he had noticed her as well. She pulled the phone from her bag and held it up.

"Sorry," she said. "It's my son calling."

"No problem." He took a few steps back to the front door of the diner, and made a show of reading the fliers that were posted there, but did not walk to his car.

"Hello?" Becca said. "Carter?"

"You gonna hate me if I can't come today?"

"What?" she crossed her free arm over the backpack and squeezed it into her ribcage. "Gil's not here today."

"I'm sorry, Mom, but Mr. Kaye says—"

"I'm going to call that man and —"

"No, Mom! You can't. He's been doing us a favor. No one else leaves for lunch. They all take fifteen minutes, sitting in their trucks."

She was tempted to tell him that before Harvey Kaye had ever been called "Mister," he'd been just Harvey. A loser in her high school class who'd partied too much, failed algebra and English, and tried every Friday without fail to get Becca to agree to go out with him. Or just sleep with him.

"Can you find someone else to help you?"

"Who am I going to ask to transfer me?"

"There's no one at the counter? Come on, you know they'd all be happy to help you."

Chris was studying her, and she turned her head and spoke into her lap.

"I'm just not sure who's still here." She thought about telling him what Rita had said, and how the band might audition school kids to play during breaks. Maybe he'd quit the job, come get her, go back to school. But that was bribery. Not fair.

"I'll figure something out," she said.

"Thanks."

"You'll be home for dinner?"

He paused long enough that she knew he wouldn't.

"Where are you going?"

"Mike and I were gonna go hang out at Seth's house."

"Well, that sounds like fun."

"So is it okay?" Carter asked. "You don't need me tonight?"

"I'll be fine."

"You sure?"

"Have a good time."

"Thanks."

"Drive safe tonight, okay?"

"I always do."

This was her way of asking him not to drink and drive, not to be like Lucas. And his way of saying that he never had and never would.

Becca shut the phone and put it back into her purse.

"You need a lift?" Chris started to walk back.

She looked up at him, so handsome and strong, smiling over her.

"That would be very nice of you."

"I'll bring the car around."

She wondered if she'd have to tell him how she needed help, but when he parked the car, he hopped out quickly and came around, opened the passenger door.

She wheeled forward, heart pounding either from humiliation or excitement, she wasn't sure.

"You need a hand, right?"

"I do like help at the car."

He nodded, bent down and picked her up, as if he knew what he was doing. She found herself grasping his sleeve as he slipped her into the passenger's seat, and she ran her fingers across the fabric as he let go of her, trying to smooth a wrinkled patch that had been left where she'd been holding on. She wondered what his arm felt like, under that sleeve. Muscular, probably. He'd picked her up like it was nothing.

"Well," she said. "You did that like a pro."

He smiled. "I used to help out some with a rec program for disabled adults in Philadelphia."

She thought, *Because you weren't perfect enough already?* She looked away, knowing she'd be blushing.

He started to close the door, then stopped himself. "All in?" he asked.

She glanced back up at him, then checked her legs, and pulled her right leg farther in with her hands and nodded. He shut the door. She thought about asking if he needed her to explain what to do with the wheelchair, but he'd already folded it up and was putting it in the backseat before she could open her mouth. She hoped he hadn't noticed the ratty blue duct tape she'd used last week to keep one of the armrests on.

In the car, they made small talk. Then she thanked him for not stopping to help her sweep her walk that morning. He said, "Okay," but in a way that made her wonder if it had been a stupid thing to thank him for.

After a quiet moment, he asked about Carter. She explained about his music and his decision to leave school.

"He was never much of a student," she said.

"Neither was I," Chris said.

"I think it might have had to do with the accident," she said, wildly aware that she had never shared this thought with anyone and confused about why she was telling him. "He hit his head."

He paused a beat, looking as if he was trying to decide whether or not to ask something. Finally he said, "What happened?"

She looked at him, not sure what he meant.

"I know it was a car accident." He gestured at the wheelchair in the backseat with a hand. "But what happened?"

She was surprised he didn't know already. Of course, being a cop, if he'd asked, someone probably would have told him. She felt a new respect for him, because it seemed that he hadn't asked.

"Drunk driver," she said, knowing it was misleading.

He nodded.

"My boyfriend, actually," she added with a shrug, acknowledging the small lie. "Carter's father. I was a passenger, and Carter, too."

"What happened to your ... to Carter's—"

"Lucas ... Luke. He died."

"I'm sorry."

She looked down at her hands in her lap. "At least Carter was all right."

"That's the truth."

"He was buckled into a car seat, of course," she said. "Should have buckled my own belt, but Luke and I were arguing. I was upset; I just forgot."

Watching her, his gaze looked open and sympathetic, not judgmental like some people might have been in his line of work.

"My mother had warned me. She'd said it again and again. 'Lucas Axedale is trouble. Get away from him.'" Becca forced herself to smile, suddenly worried that she might cry. "She was right, of course."

Chris nodded. "Mothers are right more often than is good for anyone."

"That's the absolute truth." She laughed. "Now you have to tell me something about yourself."

"I do?" he glanced at her, his expression serious and very policeman-like, and she wondered if she'd overstepped. But then he smiled and she felt a swoop of relief.

"Why did you move here?" she asked, feeling impetuous. It was the question everyone wanted to ask him, and here she was, doing it.

"Oh, that," he said. His smile faded, and she felt again that she might have overstepped.

"Unless you don't want to say."

They drove for a few seconds before he spoke again. She thought about directing him to her house, but he turned left and she realized that, of course, he'd been there once, to return the gold daisy from her necklace.

"It was a homicide case," he said finally. "There were a lot of homicide cases, mostly drug-related or domestic. This one was domestic."

"It must have been terrible."

"It was." He looked at her. "A kid."

"Oh, God."

"A boy. Seven years old. He got in the way when his father tried to shoot his mother."

Becca put a hand to her mouth. At seven, Carter had loved Legos and Batman and spaghetti with meat sauce. At seven, he had still called it "pisketti."

"I saw an ad the next week," Chris said. "State trooper job, up here. Seemed like a good change. I know people wonder why I did this, but the truth is, it was the right thing. I took a pay cut. But it's cheaper to live up here, and I've never needed much money." He shrugged.

They pulled up in front of her house.

"So now we know each other's sad stories," she said, hopeful to salvage some sense of optimism out of this car ride.

He nodded, but didn't say if she was right about that.

At the curb, he easily set up the wheelchair again, then helped her out of the car and placed her into the chair with no more trouble than if she were a doll. If they'd been on a date, this is when he'd kiss her, she thought. Then felt stupid, because she could imagine it perfectly well. She felt wonderfully weightless, a heroine in a romantic movie.

"Thanks," she said. "This was really nice of you."

He stood at his open car door, not getting in, playing with the set of keys that he'd pulled from his pocket. She didn't want to turn the chair, turn her back on him, but wasn't sure if they were still talking.

"Well …" she said.

"Well," he answered. "Do you ever go out?"

She was taken aback by the question. "Ever?"

"Other than work, I mean. Would you ever want to catch a movie or go to dinner or anything?"

She had the mad impulse to say, *No, I'd never want to*. It made her smile, thinking of saying that. The absurdity. *I'm sorry, but I don't go out with perfect men. Only disasters.*

"Yes," she said instead.

"Yeah?"

And now it sounded like it had maybe been a joke, something hypothetical he was asking her opinion on. She raised her eyebrows and watched him. Her heart raced predictably.

"When are you free?"

She smiled. *Pretty much always.*

"How about Saturday night?"

"Saturday night." It was like she was reading a script. She wasn't even sure she'd said the two words "Saturday night" all in a row like that in fifteen years. She swallowed and it hurt.

"Yeah. We'll get some dinner."

"I'd like that." She found herself again picturing the kiss, only this time, it seemed like a real possibility. She looked into her lap for a second, in case her thoughts might be visible on her face.

"Great," he said. She looked up. His smile of relief was flattering. He liked her. "How about I pick you up at six?"

"Six. Sure." She could not stop smiling. But it was all right, because he was still smiling, too.

Then he was gone. Driving away in his silly cop car with its Vermont state seal and overly serious lines. The car of someone's father.

She wheeled herself to the house, barely even noticing how she had to work harder against the ramp's pitch, or the way the screen door banged up against her feet, conspiring to keep her out.

She was going to have to tell Carter he'd been in the car. She'd have to tell him. Tonight.

She kept the truth of her upcoming Saturday night to herself all that afternoon. As she slipped a Stouffer's Lasagna in the oven for later, as she wiped down the counter from that morning's coffee, as she folded shirts and boxers and socks at the couch. The truth of it—the rare joy of something special to look forward to—followed her through her day, keeping a persistent smile on her lips, a reassuring warmth around her face, her arms, her unnecessary legs. But the shadow of what she had to tell Carter also followed her around the house, and loomed larger as the day wore on.

At 5:30, the front door slammed and she flinched. Carter dashed past her. "Where are you off to?"

"A bunch of us are going to Seth's," he called from his room. "The XGames are on TV tonight."

He appeared in the hallway, looking worried. "Why? Do you need me?"

She shook her head, and he went into the bathroom. "I got paint on my good jeans. Can you get that out?"

"Probably not."

He hopped into the hallway, pulling on clean brown corduroys, a sour expression on his face.

"Leave them in the sink," she said. "I'll have a look."

"Thanks!" He ran into the living room barefoot.

"You in a big hurry?"

"I told Suzanne I'd pick her up and drive her there."

Becca smiled. He'd had such a crush on Suzanne Sprague for months. According to many people, including Caitlin, who actually knew her well, it was mutual. "Actually, I was hoping we could talk. Do you have time?"

He looked at his watch. "What? Now?"

"No, I guess not."

"What is it?"

She thought about her conversation with Chris, thought about the wrongness of his knowing something she should have told Carter first.

"Actually," she said. "If it could be now, that would be good."

He took out his phone and started typing on it. "Let me just text her. How long will it take?"

Becca wasn't sure. She again wondered if that wasn't the right time? Would he even be able to hear her, in his excitement about his date? She looked at the pair of socks in her hands. "Um."

"Fifteen minutes?"

"Sure."

He put the phone back in his pocket, grabbed the socks out of her hands, and sat on the couch with a bounce that spilled over one of her laundry piles.

"Sorry!" He fixed it before she could complain. "Okay, what is it? Am I in trouble?"

She shook her head. This wasn't how she should have done it. She should have had a plan. There had been so many moments like this through the years, where she almost told him, but stopped herself. This time, though, this time she'd announced it. No going back.

"Mom. Seriously. What's wrong?" His look of frustration reminded her of the way she sometimes felt with her mother. Such exasperation, trying to love parents!

The thought made her smile. She reached up and he flinched away, not sure what she was doing. "Sit still," she said. She touched his jaw, then slid her hand around to the side of his head, behind his ear. It had been years, but she found it quickly—a small indentation. Barely there, but there. Small, but important.

He reached up and displaced her hand. "That's my divot."

"Your what?"

He flashed a goofy grin. "My divot. A hole in my head. I showed Mike when we were kids. He calls it my divot. Sometimes he calls me divot-head."

"Charming."

"Yeah, he's a tool."

She laughed.

"I didn't know you knew about it."

"Of course I did. You were my baby."

"Sure, well, I guess it was always there, so you'd have noticed. Like, before I grew hair."

"Not before you had hair, no. Not always."

Maybe he picked up on something in her voice. "That sounds ominous," he said.

"Ooh, ominous! Good word." She was trying for a light tone, but didn't know if her voice could pull it off.

"So what's the story? How'd I get it?"

"You got it the day I got this." She pounded the arm of the wheelchair softly. His eyes followed her hand up and down.

"I thought I was at Mad's house when that happened."

She shook her head. "You were with me. With Lucas and me."

"I was in the car when he died?"

It was not what she'd expected him to focus on, Luke's death. She put her hands on her knees and glanced over his shoulder, out the window, where the late sunshine was making the tops of the trees shimmer.

Carter said, "So why didn't I know that?"

"Because I never told you."

"Why not?"

She shrugged, almost saying I don't know. "It was my fault." She licked her lips.

"The accident?" He slipped his phone out of his pocket and glanced at the face of it, checking a text, she realized.

"Carter, this is important."

"Yeah, sorry, okay." He shoved the phone back in his pocket.

"I knew Lucas was drunk. I shouldn't have gotten in the car. I shouldn't have put you in the car."

He stared at her for a few seconds. "Yeah, I guess so. You knew he was drunk, and you took me with you?"

She braced herself for his anger, felt a flare of the familiar guilt. Then, speaking all in a rush, to be sure she'd said everything she'd intended, she said, "Maybe you wouldn't have had trouble in school."

His hand floated back up to his head and he touched the spot again. "You think?"

"I don't know. The doctors didn't know. But maybe."

He put his hand back in his lap. "Well, that's good!"

She couldn't be sure she'd heard it right. He was smiling; why was he smiling? "What?"

"Yeah. Mom! That's great!"

"What are you talking about?"

"If it happened in a car accident, then I'm not just a stupid, lazy sack of shit!"

"Carter." Even now, she couldn't let him criticize himself like that. Outside, a warm breeze was blowing, and the screen shook in its frame.

"Mom, don't you get it? If it's from a head injury, then it's not my fault."

"I've told you all along it wasn't your fault. I've told you all along that I saw how you were working, how you were trying."

"Nah." He leaned down and put a sock on one foot. "I could have tried more."

"Harder," she said automatically.

"Harder," he laughed at her. "Okay. Harder—I could have tried harder."

He put on the other sock, then touched his head again. "It's a lucky divot!"

"I don't think that's exactly true."

His eyes glanced down at her chair and a look of regret flashed over his face. "That's not what I meant," he said.

"Of course it's not."

They sat looking at each other.

"So, can I go now?"

She couldn't believe he'd taken it so lightly, didn't know what to feel without the fury she'd anticipated. "Don't you have any questions for me?"

He looked at his phone again. "Not really."

"But–"

"Maybe later, okay? I gotta go." He pecked her cheek, hopped up and slipped on his shoes at the door. "I'll be home around eleven. Gotta work in the morning."

He was gone. She wasn't sure what to do with herself. She slipped the folded laundry into the basket, wheeled through the house, leaving piles of soft, clean clothing on Carter's bed and in her dresser drawer. Without warning, the insistent patter of an unexpected rain shower drummed the outside wall of the house, and she quickly moved around, closing windows.

Before letting herself think any more about the conversation, what she perhaps should have said differently, how she should have worded it, she decided to focus instead on her upcoming evening with Chris Kozlowski, and that warmth from before. The joy of something to look forward to. And as soon as she let herself feel this happiness again, she pulled her cellphone from the pocket in the side of her wheelchair.

It was strange, she thought, that her first instinct was still to make this particular call. But then, this had been a very strange day.

It rang twice before Marjorie picked up.

"Thrifty Madge's," she said. Her voice was a song, a tribute to happiness. To living a carefree life. It made Becca grin, hearing her mother's joy.

"It's me," Becca said.

"Becca?" Her tone changed to worry. "Everything all right?"

"It is. Yes." Stupidly, she was crying. "Everything's great."

Her mother waited.

Wiping her tears with a hand, first one cheek, then the other, Becca took a moment to speak. She picked at the blue duct tape, already starting to peel away from the arm of the wheelchair. Then she took a deep breath and said, "I have a date."

Jeannie Lynam

July 2010

Even before she saw the girl in the ridiculous dress, standing at the side of the road, shaking her thumb frantically, Jeannie had been grinning to herself all alone in the car. Not just because she was on her way to find Russell again. Though thoughts of his smile, the way it took his whole face along for the ride, had been stirring in her for weeks. And not necessarily even because she was on her way to Resolute, the pretty little town where Perilous Between was scheduled to play in two weeks. True enough, there was a certain delight in preceding the band to its next town, making that place her own even before they arrived and set up their drum kits and their amps. Apart from these happy thoughts, Jeannie had just been in a hell of a fine mood, big stupid smile on her face, Rusted Root on her radio. But then she rounded a bend in the road and saw her, a girl of about twenty years and considerable size wearing the shiniest raspberry-colored bridesmaid dress you ever did see, and Jeannie near to drowned in a kind of "joie de vivre" thing she'd have had to dance to express. Of course, she pulled over. She had to. It was the only thing to do.

"Fantastic dress!" she shouted, reaching across the seats to open the door, and then the girl kind of pulled back and looked at her for a second, like she was trying to decide if Jeannie was nuts or something. But she got in the car, which probably took a little courage, Jeannie looking as she did in her dreadlocks, her homemade red pants, her U.S. Army camo jacket with PFC Alder's name still on the breast pocket.

"Thanks," the girl said. She settled in and pulled the seatbelt around herself with a swishy noise of satin and tulle, then disentangled a tiny gray-and-pink beaded purse from her wrist and threw it on the floor. She smelled like stale cigarettes.

"Are you going anywhere near Connecticut?" the girl asked.

"Connecticut? Honey, that's south. You're standing on the wrong side of the road!"

At this, the girl looked over her shoulder and all around, but it was pretty clear she had no idea about directions or anything.

"You had a few drinks at the wedding, huh?" Jeannie said. The girl looked so confused, Jeannie couldn't help laughing. "You were in a wedding, right?" She indicated the dress.

"My cousin Cyndi's wedding." She was a pretty girl, with wavy brown hair and neatly plucked eyebrows that brought out her very large, blue eyes. She had a long, straight nose and carried herself with a kind of wounded dignity, despite the situation.

"Thought so," Jeannie said. "I have a couple dresses like that in my closet. Never hitched a ride in one, though. That's fresh."

"Where are we?"

"Vermont. I'm headed north. To Resolute. Next stop on the tour!"

The girl looked at her, hands clasped in her lap.

"Perilous Between. The band. You know them?"

"A little."

"I follow them. Sometimes. They play Resolute in two weeks."

"Aren't you a little early?"

"I like to arrive early."

"Two weeks early?"

Jeannie shrugged. "Didn't have anything else to do. I'll set up shop, get to know people. It's what I do."

As if she'd grown tired of their conversation, the girl in the bright dress turned away from Jeannie and looked out the passenger window. A white silk flower barrette sagged from where it barely held her hair back behind one ear. She sighed, sounding thoroughly discouraged, and Jeannie felt a little sorry for her.

"You want to come with me, or try your luck on the other side of Route 100?"

The girl whispered something. Between her size and the dress and the night she'd clearly had, the car was filling with an unfortunate odor. Jeannie cracked a window. Outside, a breeze was blowing. On a maple near the side of the road, leaves trembled, alternately showing brightest greens, then dull undersides, then bright again.

"I'm Jeannie."

The girl looked at her, not making any sign that she'd understood.

"What's your name?" Jeannie asked.

"Zibet."

"Sorry?"

"Zibet. It's for Elizabeth. It was my grandmother's name." She recounted this fact wearily, as if for the ten thousandth time.

"Where was the wedding?" Jeannie asked.

"Stowe."

"So you got a ride this far, right? What happened?"

"The best man's roommate offered me a ride back to Connecticut." Zibet looked like she might cry. "I fell asleep. After a while, he woke me up, said he had to turn toward Boston and I should hitch from here. He said I was just an hour from home."

"Wow. Really," Jeannie said. She realized she was still smiling, and tried to smooth her face into something more sympathetic, but it was hard. "So you want to come my way, or what?"

"I must be, like, six hours from home."

"I would think so," Jeannie said. "At least."

"I was out there for like two hours, waiting for a ride."

"Well, hey. Come with me. It'll be fun. Huh?" Jeannie shifted into drive. And when the girl didn't say not to, she stepped on the gas.

The next time Jeannie looked, Zibet had her eyes closed and her head back. Her left ear had five piercings. The earrings were gold moons and stars and one little angel holding a diamond-studded bow and arrow.

The bow and arrow made Jeannie think about Russell, because he was a bow hunter. And also because he was absolutely living in her brain lately. When she'd first met him, she'd thought the bow hunting thing was barbaric. But he'd told her it was more humane than hunting with guns. It was more truly a sport and, by virtue of the challenge, made for a fairer playing field.

When she'd suggested that it wouldn't be fair until the deer had weapons, he'd shrugged, saying if she wasn't capable of intelligent conversation on a subject, he really couldn't be bothered. It had hurt her feelings when he said this. With any other guy, she'd have walked away, ordered a beer, found someone else to talk to. Unfortunately, Russell wasn't any other guy. He was the drummer in the biggest band to ever come out of Vermont. He'd had power over her, emotionally and sexually, even before she met him. Jeannie was never as weak as she was with Russell.

She looked down at her hand on the steering wheel, her ring glistening in the sunlight. He'd given her the ring when they'd hit their first anniversary in October. For them, that had meant five concerts and a sum total of only twelve nights together. But a year was a year, and Russell had given her the ring with a beautiful, serious look on his face. He hadn't gotten down on one knee, but he'd ordered in pizza and sent the rest of the band away from the bus for the night. As a surprise, he'd slid across the table the kind of box that only holds a ring. True, the box was plastic, not velvet, but the lining was satin. The ring was really three rings, one yellow gold in color, one more pinkish gold, the third almost silver, and they were intertwined and never came apart. Like us, she'd thought, desperate for him to say it, but he hadn't. Which was appropriate, probably, because in that scenario, who was the third ring?

She didn't know if the rings were gold. Probably not, because her finger, at the base, had taken on a grayish tinge lately and itched a little. But that didn't matter. It was the thought, the point of the gift, that mattered. It meant commitment on some level, though after he gave it to her, their relationship had continued on much as before, with him on tour, and her in pursuit.

The fact that he hunted still bothered her, but over time, she'd found herself trying to see his point of view on it. Maybe bow hunting was more humane; maybe it really did even the odds a little. She wasn't sure, but she let herself repeat his opinions to her friends when they tried to talk her out of following him.

"I don't follow him," she'd say. "I follow the band." But she knew she was doing both. It was easy to follow someone in a band.

The diner was how Jeannie figured out they were in Resolute. That, and the mileage. It wasn't a town the way some Vermont towns looked that she'd driven through. It didn't have an adorable steeple and a canon or a statue of some war guy. It was a lot like the countryside: weatherboard barns, cows, white houses whose yards were dotted with propane tanks and lawn ornaments. Here, the houses were closer together, and one of them sported a blue USPS post box out front and a flag, which snapped in the wind. They'd passed a thrift shop a mile or so back. In town, there was a church—Brethren United—but it didn't have a steeple and it wasn't white or pretty. It was brown, with a satellite dish bolted over a side door. Across from that was the diner, whose sign read "G&B Diner," and below that, in equal size, "Mountain Dew." Jeannie was hungry, and Zibet would be, too, given the hangover she probably had, having been drunk enough to let some guy drop her off in the middle of nowhere and point her north, telling her it was south.

"Zibet." She shook her shoulder, where a long strand of pink thread hung from the satin cap sleeve. She fought an urge to pull it. "Hey, Zibet. Wake up. You hungry?"

The girl stirred and wiped her mouth. She stared, unfocused, toward the windshield.

"Hungry?" Jeannie asked. When Zibet looked at her, she mimed the act of eating. "You got any money in that little purse?"

Zibet nodded.

Half an hour later, they faced each other in a booth with cornflower blue vinyl cushions. On the table—gray with silver speckles—were chunky cut-glass salt and pepper shakers and a plastic butter dish. From the white shiny menus, Jeannie had ordered scrambled eggs and wheat toast and a large cup of tea, and Zibet had ordered a cheeseburger and coffee and a diet Pepsi. Now she was curled protectively over her coffee cup. After each sip, she'd nod and say, "Better."

Jeannie stretched, then sat cross-legged in the booth, her back to the wall. "So tell me about this wedding," she said.

"Oh, God," Zibet closed her eyes.

"Just give me a rough sketch."

Zibet squinted at her, though the light in the diner was low and fluorescent. "All right. A sketch." She took a sip of her coffee, then a sip of her soda.

Then she sat up a little straighter. "My cousin is 'Cyndi with a Y.' We aren't really close. She doesn't have sisters, so she asked me to be in her wedding. Country club in Stowe. Pillars out front, sweeping staircase." She waved her hand in the air, as if to say, *And so on and so on.* It was a hand that was used to holding a cigarette, a hand that was, perhaps, used to holding court in conversation.

Jeannie nodded. It was weird, watching Zibet come to life over her coffee. She hadn't expected her to become this more confident person, witty and sarcastic.

"Quick ceremony, golfers' lounge. Hunting-dog wallpaper," she grinned meanly, "golf-ball-shaped lamps."

"Huh," Jeannie said. The waitress approached with a pot of coffee, and Zibet stuck out her cup without even looking in her direction.

"The groom has a uni-brow and big ears. Goes by the name, *Wow.*"

"Wow?"

Zibet nodded. Having refilled her cup, the waitress moved on to the next table. From the griddle on the other side of the dining room, a woman shouted, "Order up!"

The diner had few customers, but all of them seemed to be staring. Jeannie became uncomfortably aware of how alien they must seem, between Zibet's bridesmaid dress and her own dreadlocks. She could smell their food being cooked: her own toast, Zibet's cheeseburger, and she immediately became ravenous.

"Cyndi was wearing a pretty dress with sequins," Zibet said. "She had a tan and looked really good, which bothered me." She paused and looked imploringly into Jeannie's eyes, as if they were friends. "Isn't that awful? Because she always used to be fatter than me."

"That's not awful," Jeannie said. "That's just people."

"My mother used to join in when I made fun of Cyndi," Zibet said quietly. "Now she asks why I'm not more like her." She picked up the salt shaker and began to shake it over the table. The grains bounced and scattered.

"What about her does she want you to be like?"

"Thin, mostly," Zibet said. "Tan probably, too."

"Thin and tan? Seriously?"

"Mom's not really a very deep person," Zibet said, holding her fingers up in air quotes at the word deep. Then she leaned back in the booth and closed both eyes. "I drank a lot." She looked up and made brief eye contact. "I do that sometimes."

"Everyone does that sometimes."

Zibet smiled. It looked like a real smile. Like maybe she'd appreciated that Jeannie said this. She swept the salt off the Formica surface with her hand, put down the shaker, then laid her head on the table. "I was a mess. I made out with some repulsive guy." She whispered, "God."

Jeannie realized she was missing the joy she'd felt on the road, just before picking up this person. Zibet was entertaining, but sad somehow, frightening in all her turmoil.

Jeannie leaned forward and spoke quietly. "What can I do to help you? Should we see if they have a store around here that might have some clothes?"

At this, Zibet started to laugh. She had a low, infectious laugh that made Jeannie smile, even as the sadness was still settling around her. "What?" Jeannie asked.

"I am in this dress in some town two hours north of where I was. I'm eating in a diner with a stranger who follows bands."

"Just one band." Jeannie glanced at her ring.

"I'm in a diner with some girl in dreads."

Jeannie knew she should be offended by the things Zibet was saying, but she was swinging back toward amusement again. Being with Zibet was like being on a ride at the fair. The world kept changing, dropping away, then rushing back again, full tilt.

Zibet raised her head from the table and smiled. "Sorry," she said. Several grains of salt were imbedded in her forehead.

"Hey," Jeannie said, raising both hands. "Whatever."

Looking down, Zibet stuck out her tongue and dipped it into the scattering of salt on the table.

"Ooh," Jeannie said, wrinkling her nose. "Don't do that."

"I need my burger," Zibet whispered.

Their lunches appeared less than two seconds later and Zibet raised her eyebrows and said, "Spooky."

The waitress put their dishes on the table then stood a minute, hand on her skinny hip. She wore a yellow and white striped uniform and an apron with the name "Donna" stitched in red near the top.

"So, who are you all?" the waitress asked. She didn't run the words together the way they do in the south. Her *you all* was a northern adaptation of the expression, which came out clipped and a little silly.

Zibet studied her, then picked up her burger as if to dismiss her without answering. But Jeannie was incapable of this kind of rudeness.

"I'm Jeannie, this is Zibet," she said.

"Let me guess," Zibet said with her mouth full. "You're Donna?"

The woman nodded and stared at Zibet's dress. "How come you're all decked out?"

"Fashion show," Zibet answered vaguely. "Can I get some more coffee when you have a minute?"

Donna nodded, but didn't leave. "We can tell you're from out of town. I said I'd ask where."

Jeannie again registered the other people in the diner, who were looking at them. The fry cook had slowed her frenetic pace and was glancing back over her shoulder every so often. Only then did Jeannie notice, the woman was sitting in a wheelchair.

Jeannie opened her mouth to answer, but before she could, Zibet said, "Canada."

"Oh, yeah, we get lots of Canadians," Donna said, her vowels going expansive and worldly. "Quebec?"

Zibet nodded.

"Sure. I'd have guessed that," Donna said. But she eyed Jeannie's hair before leaving the table.

"I guess they don't have hippies in Canada," Zibet said dryly.

"Hippies?"

Zibet pointed at Jeannie's dreadlocks without letting go of her burger. "Aren't you a hippy?"

"That's not really how I see myself." Jeannie took a bite of her eggs, then washed them down with tea.

At the counter, Donna was filling in the gang. One of the men looked over again, his expression so transfixed, he looked almost angry.

The other man said something loudly, but the only words Jeannie made out were "Quebe drivers." Everyone at the counter laughed.

"Why did you say we were from Canada?" she asked.

"None of their business, that's why. Little towns like this, they live off the gossip. Might as well lead them astray. Entertain ourselves. It's what they do."

The eggs were cold, but Jeannie didn't feel like making a fuss. She scooped them onto the toast and took another bite. When she looked up again, she found Zibet staring at her.

"What?"

"Why do people do that to their hair, anyway? I mean, it's not Halloween."

"Funny." They shared an unfriendly smile. Zibet was starting to piss her off.

"Look, I don't know you very well, but I can tell you're hung over and embarrassed about your situation," Jeannie said. "I would be, and I get that. But you don't need to take it out on me. I'm the one who pulled my car over, remember?"

"Let me guess," Zibet said. "Psych major. University of Vermont. You're taking a semester off, but you plan to go back in the fall."

Jeannie sat back, surprised. She half wondered if Zibet had looked through her things at some point, but it wasn't possible. She'd never left Zibet with her backpack or her wallet, and wasn't even sure her life story existed in either of them, anyway.

"Am I right?"

"Dartmouth," Jeannie said. "That's really weird, though."

"Huh," Zibet said. She let her eyes travel up Jeannie's face, then back down again. Studying her. "Leaving school wasn't your idea. Something happened. Also, I think your trip has to do with something other than just following a band."

"Like what?"

"I'm not sure yet," Zibet said. She stared at Jeannie with unabashed intensity. "There's desperation coming off of you, like a smell. I'm thinking probably a guy. Not a nice guy."

Jeannie swallowed against unexpected tears. Who was this girl? When she could speak, her words came out in a whisper. "Where the hell are you getting all this?"

Zibet shrugged. She was finishing her burger now, and looking around as if she wanted Donna back.

"No, seriously. How did you know that, about me being a psych major and all?"

"I'm really good at it. I can read people. Like Donna—did you notice how thin and shabby her apron was? I'll bet she's worked here forever."

"So you're just observant."

"No, it's instinct, too. I'll bet she's divorced with three grown kids who moved away and never visit. Want me to ask her?"

"No," Jeannie said.

"Getting back to you. I'll bet your real name's not Jean," Zibet narrowed her eyes, as if Jeannie's full name could be found on her face.

Jeannie sat perfectly still. She would not reveal it. Let this girl try and guess.

"It's something more formal. Genevieve?"

Jeannie shook her head.

"Jeanette?"

"Nope."

"I'm right, though, aren't I?"

"Imogene," Jeannie said, anxious to beat Zibet to the punch, like this would make her better at the game. Though it was her name, after all.

Zibet nodded. "I missed the Dartmouth thing, though. You don't look like money. But I guess hippies never do."

Briefly, Jeannie considered telling her the whole sordid story of why she'd left Dartmouth. How her roommate's boyfriend had slipped her botany paper out of her backpack while she slept one night and plagiarized three whole paragraphs on polyploidy. How the teacher—who'd always seemed suspicious if not downright offended by Jeannie's hair and clothing—had sided with the boy when he blamed Jeannie, and she'd been suspended for a semester. How her friends, paralyzed by the rift in their circle, had turned to bickering and choosing sides. How awful it had been. How abandoned she felt, and lonely.

But she decided not to share all her history. She didn't know this girl. It had always been her failing, trusting people too quickly. That, and following Russell whenever her life started to fall apart. So she just said, "I'm not a hippy. Don't classify me."

Zibet laughed, a single snort. "Who dresses like that and then says, *Don't classify me?*"

"I'm my own person."

"Sure you are," Zibet said. She'd found another copy of the menu at the table behind them and was running her index finger down the desserts. "Want to split a chocolate cream pie?"

"Don't change the subject."

"Look, I'm sorry. I get mean when I'm hung over and embarrassed. Just like you said."

Jeannie bit her lips. She was beginning to wish she'd left Zibet on the side of the road.

"If you had my talent for pegging people, you'd know that I'm a total disgrace to my mother, who's perfect. I won't be getting into Dartmouth, the University of Vermont, or West Bumfuck Community College. If you had my talent, you'd feel this surge of superiority and pity over what a failure I'm turning out to be. And you'd feel better about all the stuff I said to you."

Jeannie had no idea what to say next. This was a very strange girl.

"So, what do you think?"

"About what?" Jeannie said.

Zibet made a frustrated whimper and bounced up and down on her seat a few times, like an impatient child. "Chocolate cream pie!"

Two hours later, Jeannie stepped out of Thrifty Madge's thrift shop and onto the street. She needed a break from Zibet, who was being falsely friendly to the woman in the shop—Madge, presumably—then rolling her eyes behind her back. The woman was nice, offering forty dollars cash or a fifty-dollar exchange for the bridesmaid dress, which was enough for Zibet to re-outfit herself. Jeannie wondered how long she'd be tethered to this person she had helped. She wanted, in equal parts, to break off their developing friendship, and to protect and save Zibet. Most of all, she didn't want to end up taking care of some sad, obnoxious girl. That was also a part of who she'd always been: caretaker of lost causes. She felt frustrated and confused, and missed the happiness of being alone on the road, headed for Resolute. On the other hand, she thought she could probably come back here tomorrow and convince the woman in the shop to hire her, part time.

Russell arrived on a Tuesday. Jeannie saw the bus parked next door to the G&B Diner. Super-sized and purple, with a black curtain drawn tight over each small window, the bus had wild feathers painted along each side. It would have been hard to miss, even parked as it was, in the McDermott's lot, next to the long row of trucks, each of whose gleaming cylindrical bodies proclaimed, "Vermont Milk—The Real Health Kick!"

It was eleven. Jeannie was dropping off Zibet for her lunch shift at the diner. She now had a part-time job there, working alongside her new best friend Donna, who was divorced from her husband of twenty-two years and whose grown sons never called or visited.

Jeannie had rented a one-bedroom apartment on that first night they'd arrived, then allowed Zibet to spend the night (one night) until her mother came to get her. When Zibet put sheets on the couch that second day, she'd done so without any explanation or fanfare.

"You're not going home?" Jeannie had asked.

Zibet had bent low over the pillow, plumping it for longer than it needed plumping. "I called my mother. She said she was relieved that I'm all right. She didn't offer to come get me, though."

"Did you ask her to?"

"She's got meetings every day. Garden Club, Special Olympics, Socks for Soldiers …"

"Socks for Soldiers?"

She stopped plumping and glanced over. "My mother is all about good causes."

"Oh." Jeannie didn't ask if Zibet wasn't a good enough cause. She wondered again about Zibet's place in her family's universe. It no longer seemed at all funny, that Zibet had been dropped off by some guy at the side of a strange road to fend for herself. What kind of mother wouldn't be out pounding the streets to find her when she didn't come home?

"Long story short, she's very busy." Zibet patted the pillow once more, with sarcasm, if a pat could be sarcastic, then jumped onto the newly made couch and buried her face in it.

"So you'll be staying."

"If that's all right." Floating out from somewhere inside the pillow, her reply was muffled.

Jeannie shrugged. "Of course."

Perhaps to keep Jeannie from throwing her out, Zibet put enough cash on the kitchen table to pay both the security deposit and rent for a month, which was far more time than Jeannie was planning to stay. The apartment was above *Granny Frank's Tender-Hearts Preschool*. Their landlady was Granny Frank herself, a short, squat woman with an enormous bosom and an accent that Jeannie thought might have been French Canadian. Granny Frank asked that they have their own keys made, because she had "only dis one," and said "I don't 'ave de energy t'walk all de way down de street only t'have Sonny Grogan be ridiculing of me." Zibet was having a lot of fun ridiculing of Granny Frank, too. Behind her back, she imitated her. She referred to her as "Granny Spank," and she used frank as an adjective now: "I'm franking tired." "That's franking unfair!" "Frank you."

After leaving Zibet, Jeannie was supposed to go to Thrifty Madge's, where she'd successfully found work. But she knew her boss wouldn't mind if she was a little late. Marjorie ("Madge" only to a few old friends) was as kind and accommodating as Jeannie had suspected on that first day. She'd confided that she had a daughter in a wheelchair, a grown woman who needed help with various domestic tasks every week, and Marjorie was sometimes late herself on the days she helped her daughter out at home.

Upon seeing the band's bus, Zibet asked, "That your boyfriend's ride?"

Jeannie had failed in her quest to not confide in Zibet, and had told her everything—Dartmouth, the polyploidy paper, Russell—on their first night in the apartment. Zibet's advice had been twofold. About Russell, she'd said, "Don't trust him, he's using you."

"He is not," Jeannie answered, too quickly. Zibet just shrugged and drank a shot of tequila. Tequila seemed to be her answer for just about everything.

About the charge of plagiarism, Zibet had said, "Fuck it! You have your brain, he has his. In the long run, you'll get more mileage out of your brain than dick-head gets out of your poly-whatever paper." Which was a truth so wise and obvious that Jeannie had cried with relief, sending Zibet to the kitchen to pour them two more shots of tequila.

"That's quite a bus," Zibet said now. "You think he's in there?"

"He's here," Jeannie said, trying to suppress her wide, stupid smile.

"You've been in that bus?"

Jeannie nodded. "I traveled with them five days last year. Wichita to Columbus and every town in between."

"Woo hoo," Zibet said without enthusiasm, twirling a halfhearted finger in the air.

Jeannie crossed her arms. "You can't ruin my day."

"Not trying to," Zibet said. "I just don't think he's good for you."

They climbed out of the car. Jeannie's pulse had picked up. She rotated the ring, resisting the urge to scratch at the now gray and green disc of color that surrounded the base of her finger. The ring definitely wasn't gold. When she noticed Zibet looking at her, she stopped.

"You should really get rid of that thing. They're going to have to amputate if you're not careful." She'd already pointed out that a rock star should have been able to afford real gold, but Jeannie had told her it wasn't about the value of the metal.

"Then what's it about?" Zibet had asked. A question Jeannie hadn't yet answered.

A long line of mostly teenagers snaked out of the diner and trailed off into the parking lot. Zibet pushed through them, telling them she worked here, and Jeannie followed in her wake, her presence unquestioned.

As she'd expected, the diner was packed. Resolute had started to fill up with other fans like Jeannie—people who followed the band. These fans had also seen the bus, and the counter and every table were full. The locals had been squeezed out, replaced by boys whose jeans hung low, purposefully displaying boxers, boys wearing tank tops and bandanas and puka shell neck-laces, girls in homemade quilted skirts, lip rings, nose rings, and who-knew-what rings. One couple had a little boy, maybe four years old, whose long red hair was pulled back in a messy ponytail and whose tie-dyed shirt hung almost to his knees. The noise was extraordinary—a warm, round drone of excited conversation punctuated by laughter. At a table across the room sat several large men in work boots and jeans and a surplus of Perilous Between T-shirts and baseball caps of all colors and years and tours. Jeannie recognized a couple of these men—Benji and Josh, roadies from the tour—but suddenly worried they wouldn't know her, so she did not wave.

"This'll be a fun shift," Zibet said dryly. "Get your sleazeball boyfriend the hell out of here, will you?"

But Russell wasn't at the table. "He's not here. The band doesn't go this public. They're probably in the bus, waiting for those guys to bring them breakfast."

"Well their transportation isn't exactly subtle," Zibet said. "They must have people crawling up the sides."

"Probably they're desperate. They'll go into hiding once they get their pancakes. "

"Elzybit!" Gil yelled, leaning out the kitchen door. Slick with sweat in his gray apron, he looked surlier than usual. Long strands of thinning hair had fallen from their combed position across his brow and hung gleaming over wild eyes. "Right now!" He pointed at her with a butcher's knife, but probably only because it was what he'd been holding when he spotted her. It could have been a wooden spoon, a spatula, a can opener.

Jeannie and Zibet shared a quick smile. The way he mangled her name changed daily; it was always interesting. Her favorite so far had been, "Bituate." ("As in Barb," she'd told Jeannie.)

"See you later," Zibet said.

Jeannie again considered wandering over to the table of roadies, but decided instead to go to the bus.

A single security guard stood outside to keep people away from the band. Arms crossed, face stony, he wore sunglasses, jeans and a black Perilous Between T-shirt from the Euro-Tour, 2005.

"Hi," she said, kicking up pebbles as she walked toward him, aware that upwards of twenty girls and probably some boys had already approached him today, looking much as she did.

He answered with a lackluster nod.

"I'm a friend of Russell's."

"Popular guy," the guard said. His accent was flat and distinctive, maybe Rochester or Buffalo; she wasn't sure.

"Oh yeah," she said. "Don't I know it. But I'm a really good friend. Can you just ask him?"

"He's sleeping."

The sun was getting high, making her squint. She turned to look at the diner, but only a single girl stood outside now, waiting to get through the door. She had her face turned upwards, her eyes closed to the sun, and was smiling happily.

Jeannie stepped closer to the security guard. "They'll be waiting for breakfast, right? And it'll be out soon?"

"If you're his friend, you'll have his cell number. Call him."

"That's the thing. He must have changed it. I keep getting a recording."

The way the guard looked at her made Jeannie feel small. She tried to imagine what he was thinking. Because he looked sorry for her, but sick of her, too. Sick of her type, maybe—so many kids with nothing to do and no need to earn a living. Kids who idolized drug addicts and followed them around like children after the Pied Piper, snakes after Saint Patrick.

"He has to change the number a lot, because of the fans. But sometimes he forgets to tell me. It's a problem." She shrugged.

"I should have his problems," the man said. She thought maybe he had his eyes closed, like the girl by the door, with her face to the sun, but she couldn't be sure, because of his dark glasses.

"He gave me this ring," Jeannie said, holding out her hand. She felt suddenly pathetic in her insignificance. Not just in this situation, but on the planet.

The man lifted up his sunglasses, held them on his forehead. He stepped forward and looked at her hand. "I have no doubt that's true," he said, then let the glasses drop onto his nose once more.

"You have no doubt what's true?"

"That Russell Maxwell gave you that," he indicated the ring with an elbow, having re-crossed his arms. The name, Russell Maxwell, in this other man's voice, gave her both an unexpected thrill and a shiver of dread.

"So can I see him?"

"I gotta tell you something you won't like now," he said. "You're not the first girl to show me that same ring."

Stupidly, she looked at her hand, as if for clarification.

"You're not even the second," the guard said. "Maybe the third or fourth. I've lost count."

She wished he hadn't said what he'd said. It wasn't that she thought Russell was faithful. She knew who she was: a fan, a pretty girl, one of thousands. But the ring had felt special. The ring had seemed an admission of her uniqueness to him. She dropped her hand and turned away from the security guard.

"Okay, I see," she said quietly, and she started back toward her car.

The door to the diner opened and the roadies emerged, hands full of take-out containers and cups of coffee. One of them yawned widely, groaning at the end until his voice was almost a shout. Behind him, a shorter man who Jeannie knew followed suit, starting to yawn. But when he saw her, his eyes widened. He pulled his lips back, stifling the yawn.

"Jeannie," he said.

"Hey, Benji."

"What's going on?"

"Not much," she smiled, purposefully not watching the security guard for his reaction. The moment felt like a small victory, but the ring on her finger remained an irritant.

"You here to see Russell?"

"I understand he's occupied."

Benji scratched his head under the red cap. *Grave Peril, Vancouver, '04,* said the hat. He was a handsome man, nearly bald, with a big beer belly but otherwise muscular physique.

"Hang on," he said, and he trotted off toward the bus, holding a take-out container high in one hand as he opened the bus door with the other.

As he walked past, another of the men greeted Jeannie shyly, and she returned his wave, suddenly warm with the memory that she'd been well-liked by the band and their crew. One by one, they disappeared inside the bus, leaving her alone with the newly stoic security guard. She smiled at him, and he frowned and shook his head.

After a minute, one of the bus windows slid open and Russell poked his head through. She wanted to fall on the ground with relief when he smiled.

"What the hell?" he said. "Jean Marie, when did you get here?"

"Week ago." She grinned, lowering her gaze and kicking at the pebbles in the parking lot.

"Well, you coming in or what?" Russell said. His face was tan and he hadn't shaved in a day or two. His cheeks were lined with sleep, like a little boy after a nap. She felt his smile move through her. It was wrong to love him this way. She knew it was wrong. Her love of Russell was a love of music and fame and adventure, a love of sex and freedom.

She wanted to get on the bus, but she heard herself say, "I gotta go to work."

"Work?" Russell repeated with a thin laugh. "Since when?"

"I work here part time for this really nice lady. I'm late now." She glanced at her watch. "Really late."

"But you're just gonna quit next week, Jean Marie. We're on the road."

This version of her name—Jean Marie—was his invention. She smiled when he said it.

"She's counting on me."

Nodding, framed in the window, he looked disappointed. "Meet me later?"

"Here?" she asked.

Behind her, she heard the bell on the diner door, then loud, excited voices. It momentarily distracted her. She turned around and saw scores of fans—women like herself, barely more than girls, pushing each other out of the way as they fled the diner, shouting his name: "Russell! Russell!"

She faced the bus again and found him pulling back through the window.

"Dave'll tell you," he shouted, pointing at the security guy. "Give her the lowdown, Dave." And then the window slid shut, and Jeannie was just one of twenty or more women, standing outside a bus, staring at it as if it held answers.

She broke away from the group, not wanting to be one of these girls.

She saw Zibet in the window of the diner. Zibet, smiling at her in a way that wasn't mean. She raised her hand in a fist of solidarity and Jeannie grinned and returned the gesture.

When Jeannie got to work, the thrift shop was already busy for a Tuesday morning. Three girls stood in a cluster, whispering excitedly, browsing skirts and tops, sliding the hangers along the racks. At the register, Marjorie was ringing up another woman. She was talking to herself—something she did when she got flustered.

"Eight dollars," she muttered, holding a slinky orange scarf and punching the buttons on the old cash register. "Orange … scarf."

When she saw Jeannie, she said, "Oh, good."

"Sorry I'm late."

"That's fine, don't worry." Marjorie added a fake fur to the customer's bag.

"Black … stole, twelve dollars," she muttered, punching register buttons, then looking up and smiling. "So that's twenty total."

The woman held a red rubber change purse, which she squeezed now to open. Her fingers were covered in rings —gold bands, colorful plastic rings, a couple with gems.

Jeannie pulled her eyes away and looked at her own ring, her tarnished finger. In her pocket was the information the security guard had given her before the bus had pulled away. She was supposed to meet Russell at ten; the band was staying at an old farmhouse in the woods, several miles out of town. She had an address and a new cellphone number. The guard had written it in neat block print with a gold mechanical pencil taken from the back pocket of his jeans. He'd passed it to her between two fingers with a dismissive flick.

"Jeannie," Marjorie said, heading over to help the three girls by the skirts and tops. "Can you dress Petunia in something new?"

In the window, the mannequin stood topless in a short, black skirt. Like a drugged starlet, she gazed blankly, boldly, at the world outside. Uncovered, her breasts were smooth, molded forms—flesh-colored, featureless. Seeing her so exposed, Jeannie wanted to protect her. She dressed Petunia in a white, not-quite-Chanel jacket with large, black buttons and black trim, then pinned a black silk flower to the jacket from the accessory basket on the counter. The basket held earrings and bracelets and pins, and one lightweight fake-gold tiara studded with red and clear crystals.

"That's good," Marjorie said, appraising Petunia's new outfit. She came over and fluffed the petals on the silk flower, then went back to the register to ring up purchases for two of the girls. The third, a heavy teenager with dyed red hair that was almost purple, was fingering Zibet's bridesmaid dress, which hung on a formals rack near the front of the store. She looked outrageous enough to match Zibet's personality, and maybe Jeannie should have wanted her to have the dress. But she had a sudden urge to keep the girl from buying it.

"Sorry," she said, walking over. "That one should be out back. It's been sold."

She felt, rather than saw, Marjorie's eyes lift and look over when she said this. But Marjorie continued with her task and said nothing. Jeannie lifted the plastic hanger off the rack with an apologetic smile, then carried the dress to the back of the store.

She took it in place of payment that day, along with the little gold and crystal tiara. Marjorie had smiled and raised her eyebrows when she saw Jeannie trying on the tiara, nestling it into her dreads.

At the apartment that afternoon, Jeannie found Zibet lying on the living room floor in her underwear, playing solitaire. She was drinking white wine out of a faded Flintstones Jelly Jar glass that had to be thirty years old. The fan in the yawning, paint-peeled window was running full speed, but the heat was still unbearable.

"Hot," was all Zibet said when Jeannie came in.

"I have a date tonight."

"The band?"

"Not the whole band."

"Oh yeah, sure."

"That's not funny."

"It's a little bit funny," Zibet said, turning over a card.

Jeannie took her garment bag back to the little bedroom they shared. She'd been surprised at how well she could sleep with Zibet in the double bed.

Despite her unpredictability during the day, Zibet was a quiet and deep sleeper.

Jeannie put on the bridesmaid dress and the tiara, taking her time, checking her reflection in the mirror as she went. She put on makeup, decided she'd applied too much, and washed it off in the tiny bathroom sink. Then she put on just a little eyeliner. Zibet appeared in the doorway, jelly jar in one hand, half-full bottle of wine in the other.

She leaned against the door jamb and said, "Why are you wearing that?"

Jeannie shrugged. "I like it."

"It's too big."

Jeannie had belted the dress with a length of black organdy from the scarf rack at the store. It wasn't really a scarf, it was a scrap from another dress that had been altered, so Marjorie had let her take it for free rather than paying the three dollars on the tag. Using safety pins, which she hid well inside the fabric, Zibet tacked up the bottom of the dress at eighteen-inch intervals, which changed the look entirely.

"Thanks!" Jeannie said.

"Too bad you don't have a crinoline. What happened to the crinoline?"

"Someone bought it separately. But that's ok. I like this as it is."

"Kind of a Morticia-meets-Cinderella look," Zibet said. She poured more wine into her jar, then took a long sip.

"You all right?"

"I drink, therefore I am." Zibet raised her eyebrows mysteriously, then turned and wandered back to her solitaire game.

"You want to come with me? It'll be a party, I'm sure. They have a party every night."

She turned. "Party?"

Jeannie said, "But you have to be good."

Zibet smiled.

It was hard to shift in the dress, and the heel of her boot caught a seam and ripped something as she braked to turn into the private road marked "Zucker."

"That's like in *Charlotte's Web*," said Zibet. She was wearing jeans and a purple T-shirt—very understated next to Jeannie's dress and tiara. "Zucker.

We're like living *Charlotte's Web*."

"I think that was Zuckerman," said Jeannie.

"If I married whoever lives here, I'd be Zibet Zucker."

Half a mile or so along the road, a guard stopped them. Not *Mean Guard Dave*, as Zibet had dubbed him when she heard the story of the bus, but an equally quiet, unsmiling man. He stood in front of a makeshift blockade: a long board over two sawhorses. He asked their names and flashed a light around the inside of the car before removing the board from the sawhorses and waving them on. It was dark, and in the headlights, Jeannie could make out thick woods on either side. She followed the line of the road, first right, then left, until they finally faced a large, yellow farmhouse. Beaming out at the night, every window held a lamp, or candles, or a string of Christmas lights. Colorful Japanese paper lanterns decorated the front porch. Jeannie saw the bus and six or seven cars pulled up near an old barn, so she drove that way and parked in the grass beside them. When she opened her door and the dome light came on, she checked her reflection in the rear view mirror.

"Trust me, you look great," Zibet said. "A little weird, with the crown thing and all, but very pretty."

Jeannie smiled, still looking in the mirror. She almost said that she felt really close to Zibet at that moment—close like a sister—but decided it would sound mushy and make Zibet uncomfortable. So she said, "That's the first nice thing you've said to me."

"Don't go frankin' weird on me now." Zibet got out of the car and slammed the door.

They entered the house through a side screen door that had been propped open, wide, with a brick on the top wooden step. Jeannie didn't want to think about how many mosquitoes had made their way inside, guided by the bright, outdoor flood lights. She nudged the brick with a toe and it fell to the ground. Following Zibet into the house, she let the screen close behind her. Jeannie heard music coming from down a hallway. Not Perilous Between, but The Beatles. "Rocky Raccoon." It was off *The White Album*, she thought, but wasn't sure. She used to know all the albums, all the songs. How had she become disconnected from the music she'd loved as a younger girl?

She would have thought that spending so much time around a band would have fixed these things in her mind, but her love of Russell had emptied it instead: cored it out, like an apple.

A farming family must have surrendered the house to the band. Everywhere Jeannie looked, she saw the strange combination of unsophisticated charm and decadence. On the antique kitchen table stood three empty quart bottles of Jack Daniels. On the arm of a faded flowery couch balanced an ashtray with a burned-out cigarette—its ash, three-inches long. Someone had taped a picture of Kennedy Jackson to the face of the grandfather clock; the big hand jutted from under his chin, with its little goatee, and the little hand was barely visible above his forehead.

10:30. She needed to find Russell.

When she started toward the stairs, Zibet paused, watching her, and said, "Hey."

"What?"

"He's using you."

"So you've said."

"I can feel his vibe, in this house." She looked genuinely concerned. "It's bad."

"You don't know him," Jeannie said. But then, seeing Zibet's expression turning from sympathy to anger, she said, "I'll be careful."

Zibet nodded and started to walk away, toward wherever the music was coming from.

"See ya," she said over her shoulder.

"Where are you going?" Jeannie asked.

"Kitchen," Zibet said. "The bar will be in the kitchen. I've been to parties before." She disappeared down the hall toward the sounds of voices and laughter, and Jeannie turned and started climbing the stairs, toward Russell. Her sense of him was strong tonight, like gravity. He was definitely upstairs. As she went, she held her skirt daintily in both hands.

At the top, on the landing, Kennedy Jackson stood with his arms around a skinny girl who looked about seventeen. Her eyes were red-rimmed and shiny, and she was asking him who'd written each of the band's songs.

"What about 'Rush Forward'?" she was asking. "Who wrote that?"

"Me," he said.

"How about 'Paloma Roja'?" She had the breathless voice of a fan who can't believe how close she's gotten to the object of her affection.

"Me."

He looked just as he always had—his long black hair, straight and glossy like a Native American's, now showing a few gray strands here and there. He kept it tied back with a leather band. His eyes were large and brown, and his nose was crooked from being broken at least twice. Jeannie had heard the stories—something about a bar fight, she thought, and something about a horseback-riding accident. He wore a faded blue shirt, unbuttoned and open, baring his muscular, hairless chest. On his wrist, he wore a black leather bracelet that stayed in place with a big brass snap.

"Did you write 'Creeping Sleep'?"

"Nope, that was Russell," Jeannie called from behind them.

Kennedy looked up, saw Jeannie and smiled.

"Heard you were in town," he said, in his signature rasp. "That's good. Maybe Russell will start acting his age now."

Jeannie didn't know what he meant, but she smiled and walked on. After she'd passed them, she heard the girl giggle and say, "Did you see that dress?"

"Real pretty," Kennedy answered, not picking up the bitchy snag in her voice. Or maybe just choosing to ignore it. Kennedy Jackson was not capable of cruelty, but he was capable of ignoring it.

Jeannie didn't care if she looked weird. She'd looked weird all her life.

He stood with his back to her. On a chair. On a balcony that had been tacked onto the back of the house at some point. The room was dark, and he was lit by the glow of the moon. At first she didn't wonder what he was doing. Russell was close, her heartbeat was one of his instruments. He looked magical, all lit up like that. Strong and important and alone. Probably he was admiring Mount Witness, which rose up behind the woods, immense and impressive. Soon the moon would disappear behind it.

The sounds of the party drifted up from somewhere below and behind them, from another part of the house, another country. It was still The Beatles on the stereo: "Don't Pass Me By."

"Back up!" Russell shouted, making her jump. The chair he stood on was an armchair, soft and deep, and his feet fought for purchase. He swayed slightly. "No, more! Much more!"

"Russell?" she said.

He turned his head to look behind himself at her, and his eyes were empty. Not only did he not recognize her, he didn't really see her there, offering herself to him in the tiara, the beautiful dress. She could tell that he was drunk or stoned or both. He was everything intoxicated. And the magic drained away and the moon was suddenly just a spotlight on her shame—on all that she'd allowed herself to lose in the name of this man.

Downstairs, Ringo sang, wondering why he was alone.

Russell turned and looked out from the balcony again.

"I'm going to call you Newton," he shouted. Outside, the yard was a wide expanse, pale yellow-gray. "Is that all right with you? Can I call you Newton?"

He began to laugh, and Jeannie wondered if he was seeing things out there, imaginary people to shout at. His body went slack with laughter and he bent at the waist, so that Jeannie dashed forward, worried he would sink off the armchair and tumble from the balcony like a frat boy. But he regained control and stood again, stable somehow, on the chair.

Ringo begged not to be made blue.

Jeannie saw the bow in his hands then. The arrow. She saw the girl below, a young, pretty girl, holding an apple on top of her head. The girl was laughing more than Russell even, and Jeannie decided she was very high on something—maybe a few things.

"You won't really do this," Jeannie said.

Russell looked at her sideways, squinting in his effort to focus.

"Jean Marie?" he said.

Someone turned up the music downstairs. The house shook. Ringo was sorry for doubting. Downstairs, people sang along with him, all of them, sorry for having been unfair. This was how it had always been. Music all the time, and joy and parties and sex and fun.

"This is too dangerous." She indicated the bow.

"Yes," he said. Then he shook his head. "I mean, no. I won't really do it."

Jeannie looked down at the lawn, at the girl who was waiting for further instructions. "She's very pretty."

"It's too dangerous," he said in a sing-song, mocking voice. Downstairs people were shouting the song, so that it broke into nonsensical lyrics and general hysteria.

"Who is she?" Jeannie asked.

"Who are you?" Russell started laughing again.

Jeannie took a step back and he reached out to her, fumbled his fingers inconsequentially in her hair so that the tiara slipped sideways. "Don't get mad, baby. I'm just fuckin' with you."

"I'm not mad," she said, and it was true. This was not anger. It was everything else: hurt and sorrow and self-loathing. She considered trying to explain all that she felt—the disappointment that he would never love her, the sadness and ache of it—but was overcome by the truth of how little it mattered to him. She repeated what she'd said, if only to keep his eyes turned in her direction a moment longer. "I'm not mad."

"Good." He nodded, winked at her mechanically, then looked back out at the lawn. The girl had backed up, as he'd asked her to. She stood in the shadow of the woods, barely visible now, the white undersides of her arms the only indication that the apple was being held tight to the top of her head. Jeannie heard something new downstairs. Felt it in the floor beneath her feet. A buzzing static. The CD had been started over. Or maybe it was the original record and it had been turned over. She heard a plane landing. "Back in the USSR." The old house filled with sound. It shook with it.

"Nice!" Russell shouted to the ghostly shape of the girl. "Stay like that." But she'd never hear him now. He lifted the bow.

"You said you wouldn't. It's too dangerous," Jeannie said. "You're drunk."

"Baby," he answered, his feet sagging forward in the armchair, his toes fighting gravity. "I'm a drummer. Drummers always find the center." And he let his arrow fly.

She was running. Running down the stairs, holding the skirt of her dress up high. Running along the hallway to the door they'd entered just twenty minutes earlier. Punching it open with both hands, then running into the yard. Just as he'd shot the arrow, the girl had stepped backwards into the woods. Or had she been hit? Jeannie couldn't see. She ran out from under the balcony and looked up and thought he was gone, but then she saw the outline of him, a golden filament of shape sitting in the armchair.

"You worry too much," he shouted. "I missed her by a mile."

She ran, terrified. Ran as if he might aim at her next. Where had the girl been standing? She'd been at the edge of the woods. Under what had looked like the biggest tree, but from down here, they were all big. All the same. Enormous. She did not see the girl.

"Hello?" she shouted. "Are you all right?" Behind her, the music erupted from the house. "Hello? Are you here?"

It was too dark to see. She dodged in and out of the trees and Russell shouted directions to her. "Left! Right! No, left!" But laughing, too. Amused at her concern. Maybe he was right. Maybe he'd missed her by a mile. But where was she then, the girl?

Jeannie stopped running. Looking down at the grass, she put a hand to her ribs and tried to catch her breath. From the balcony, the girl had been straight back, just at the edge of the woods. So the balcony would be directly in front of where she'd been. Jeannie turned and faced the balcony. It was to her left a little. So she side-stepped until she was in line with it.

She felt the woods behind her and the mountain behind that. She felt the enormity of the earth turning, herself turning with it. Rotating. She looked into the darkness. Nothing. No one. At her feet, then, she saw it: the apple. So this had been the place, but the girl was not here. Maybe she'd gone into the house while Jeannie was running outside. She'd see her at the party. Or she'd never see her again. That was the nature of these concerts. People came, people went. Community drifting in and out of her life, braiding around her. She shook her head, then realized she'd lost the tiara.

Before heading back to the house, she picked up the apple. When she turned around again, she saw that Russell had climbed back into the chair and was standing as before. He raised the bow and pointed another arrow at her.

"Put it on your head," he shouted.

"No."

"Come on, Jean Marie. I won't hurt you."

"That is not my name," she said, shouting. "And don't point that fucking thing at me."

He dropped his hands and watched her walk toward the house. "You coming back inside?" he asked.

"I'm going to find Kennedy," she said.

"Kennedy?" he asked, jealousy coiling around the word. "Why? You going to tell on me?"

She ignored that. "And then I'm going to find my friend and leave."

"What friend?"

The one who knew what a snake you are. The one who warned me. "Goodbye, Russell."

As she passed under the balcony and reached to open the screen door, she heard the sound of the arrow leaving the bow, swishing above her head and out into the woods. She heard it strike, turned, and saw it jutting from the tree where she'd been standing just a minute ago. Perfectly centered.

"Told you," he said, his voice a throaty whisper floating down through wide-set balcony floorboards above her head.

Christine Wheeler

August 2010

"You know the route?" Martin said, his Jamaican accent a soft, almost-undetectable lilt.

"I have the GPS."

He nodded. "But you've looked over the route?"

"Yes."

"It's not good to rely on the GPS."

"I know," she said, itching to get on the road. Dreading it equally. "I know where I'm going."

He checked his watch. "What are you guessing, three hours?"

She knew that if she let him, he'd start going over the route with her, questioning her choice of roads and shortcuts, offering advice that might take twenty minutes.

"Hey, Martin, if I wanted a husband, I'd have gotten married."

"Someone straight, I'm guessing."

She laughed and grabbed his dark, wide hand fondly. Sometimes she wished he were straight. Large and bald and handsome, he was her house-mate and her friend. He loved her more than pretty much anyone ever had, except maybe Stella, whose love was a shifting thing these days, hard to see through the thick mist of adolescence. He was older than Cricket: fifty-three to her forty, and played big brother when she needed that. He knew she'd had a rough childhood and was estranged from her family, but never asked for the details.

"I'll call you from the road," she said. "When we stop for lunch."

Stella pushed between them and walked to the car without a word.

"Goodbye!" Martin called after her. She twitched a hand over her shoulder without a backward glance. Cricket would have been hurt, if she were Martin, but he was more sensible than she was.

"You remember how to set up the tent?" he asked.

Cricket put her hands on her hips. "Excuse me?"

"All right." He smiled and pulled her in for a quick hug, then stepped back. "See you Sunday," he said, suddenly brisk, knowing how she felt about goodbyes.

It happened then, as it always did. The tightening in her throat. The tears. Every goodbye of significance was always this way for Cricket. Even if she was coming back in a day, she'd brace herself for forever.

"See ya," she said. Trying not to cry, she turned to the car, silently cursing her cowardice. Martin knew how to listen. He knew when to give a hug, when to sit back and say nothing, when to disagree, when to interrupt. She'd really meant to tell him everything before she left.

Stella was wearing ear buds and had her eyes closed and her seat reclined. *Little Princess,* Cricket thought. She started the car, waved to Martin, who'd bent over to pull weeds and didn't see, and began to back out of the driveway.

"Hey, Stel?" She touched her daughter's pale, freckled arm.

Stella pulled one ear bud free but did not turn to look at her or even open her eyes.

"I don't intend to drive all the way to Vermont with you not speaking."

Stella squinted at her, removed the other ear bud, and pushed the button on her seat until she was up straight.

"Thanks."

Stella shrugged. "It's fine."

Cricket turned onto 25, trying not to dwell on how the past year had transformed her daughter. Stella had come late into her teenage moods and my-mother-is-the-devil attitude, but with impressive vigor.

"What were you listening to?"

"The band."

"The Band? Really?"

Stella looked at her. "Not a band called The Band. The band we're driving to hear."

"Oh." Cricket glanced at the GPS. Her turn was in seven miles. "Remind me what they're called?"

"I can't believe you're asking me that again. Why are you even coming?"

"It's not the easiest name to remember. And stop being rude."

"Perilous … Between," Stella said, gesticulating with both hands and inserting a long, sarcastic pause between the words.

"Like I said, hard to remember."

"It's an adjective and a noun. Just like Grateful Dead."

"Between is a preposition," Cricket said. She didn't look at Stella, who would probably be rolling her eyes. "Can you plug it in so we can listen together? I want to hear some of their songs before the show."

Stella nodded and plugged her iPod into the car jack. Music bloomed out of the speakers. Too loudly, but Cricket didn't say anything. After a minute, Stella leaned in and turned it down.

"Thanks," said Cricket.

"It's fine."

A part of Cricket was looking forward to the show, just because she'd lived that kind of life for so long. This would be her first return to the sights and smells of a concert ground since the days, so long ago, when she had lived on the road, following The Grateful Dead. She hadn't been a passionate Dead Head, not at first. She'd followed the band because it had swept through Philadelphia and saved her. That was how she'd learned that you could live in buses and vans, you could sleep in trains and on hotel room floors without having a name, a social security number, a story. You could melt away, simply disappear. Stop being Andrea Kozlowski, and reinvent yourself.

Now, driving to Vermont to see a band, she felt as if she were traveling back in time. It was her daughter's favorite band this time, not hers. Perilous Between. She liked the name, even if she couldn't keep it in her head.

Stella had wanted to go to the concert with friends, but Cricket felt she was too young.

"I'm sixteen!" Stella had shouted.

"Which is too young to drive to another state without *adult supervision,*" Cricket had retorted, hating her use of the words adult supervision.

When she'd heard exactly where the concert was to take place, she hadn't believed it. The coincidence was too strange, like something from a mystery novel. She'd googled it to be sure Stella hadn't gotten it wrong. But sure enough: Resolute, Vermont. A tiny town she'd never been to, but had read about time and again.

"I'll take you," she'd said to Stella.

"And Missy? And Angelina?"

"No, I don't think so," she'd said. "Let's go just you and me."

At this point, as he so often did, Martin had quietly broken in to say how nice that was of Cricket, to offer to take Stella. And not wanting to disagree with Martin—who Stella sometimes called Daddy, even though she knew he wasn't—she'd thanked her mother, then made her promise not to change her mind.

"I promise," Cricket had said. "I'll get time off work, and I'll take you. We'll have fun."

She'd held up her cup of tea and clinked Stella's seltzer to seal the deal, knowing as she did so that the trip might help her keep another promise she'd made—if only in her heart—year after year after year.

On the road, when she forgot herself, Stella sang Perilous Between songs, alternately sucking on the tootsie pop Cricket had brought for her.

"So what song is this?" Cricket asked.

Stella brightened. She had a huge crush on Kennedy Jackson, the lead singer of Perilous Between, and talking about the band was the surest way to get her to drop her moodiness. Sometimes, when she talked about them, she almost seemed like the sweet little girl she'd been not so long ago.

She leaned forward and turned up the song. "This one's 'Sleepy Sponge.'"

Cricket listened for a minute. The lyrics meant nothing. *Walk sideways and watch for toes. Dine on urchin in the murk below.*

"What's it mean?"

Stella grinned. "It's a kind of crab," she said. "Sleepy Sponge Crab."

Cricket listened some more. *And then the sand fills your ears. Washed clean, a thousand years.* All these rhymes. Did her favorite songs always rhyme? *… to do, to do, to see you through?* They did. Of course they did.

"The best thing about this song," Stella was saying, "is that they never mention it's about a crab."

"So how do you know?"

"You just do." She shrugged. "That's the brilliance of it."

Cricket put on her turn signal to merge onto 93.

"Like when you were a kid, you probably listened to The Beatles, right?"

"They were a little before my time."

"You never listened to The Beatles?" Stella looked at her, daring her to answer.

"Yes, I did. Of course I did."

Stella looked away again. "Well," she said, "They had songs like that. Where no one really knew what they were singing about."

"Like what?"

"Like that one that goes, I am the egg man," Stella said. "That's some reference to a party they were at—like an orgy?—where some guy was breaking eggs over this naked woman." They looked at each other. Stella made a face and Cricket said, "Eww," and then they both started laughing.

The fun moments, like this one, were so precious now. Cricket wanted to stop the reel, freeze the frame. She wanted to cling to their shared laughter, hold it close, the way she used to hold Stella close as a baby. Winters, Stella in soft pink fleece, staring up at Cricket, blue eyes wide with awe and adoration. Summers, Stella in a soft white cotton onesie, the two of them rocking in the chair for ages until Stella fell at last into bottomless, sweaty sleep. Even then, Cricket would stay there, studying the baby's thin, muscular neck, smelling her milk-and-powder smell.

It had been a complete surprise, when she'd gotten pregnant, years after leaving home. She'd always assumed her father had ruined her in some way. In every way. Ruined her inside and out, so that she wouldn't be able to have children. She'd never told anyone about how he used to sneak into her room in the night. She'd come close so many times with Martin, only to chicken out in the end, like this morning.

During what she'd come to think of as her middle life—that time between childhood and parenthood, when she was following The Dead—she'd had a few affairs. Not terribly many. There had been a kid named Jimmy who'd liked to leave the tent flap open, and Vishnu, a piano player with an opening band, and Bob, a roadie.

She'd been afraid of sex. Desperately afraid. And so she'd forced herself to seek it out, try to enjoy it. Of course, she hadn't enjoyed it. Every time had been painful, emotionally and sometimes physically. In these relationships and one-night stands, she'd been inconsistent about birth control, but had never gotten pregnant. She'd decided she couldn't. That her father had taken that from her as well. It was a shock, then, when Stella announced herself by turning the tip of a wand blue, not long after Cricket had been with a guy named Bill, a graduate student at Berkeley. They were introduced as The Dead had finished up "Iko Iko." Bill had handed her a beer during "Looks Like Rain." And by "Stella Blue," she'd been in his arms. She never saw him after that night, but she thought of him often, wondering if she'd stolen from him by having his child.

Ever since then, it had been Cricket and Stella (named, of course, for the song). Cricket had given up the campgrounds and the tents and the drugs and the miserable sex, and had settled outside of Portland, Maine, eventually allowing a gay man to become a housemate for financial reasons. She and Stella and Martin made up a strange little family, but it was the right family for her.

Stella and Cricket arrived in Resolute a little before five and drove straight to their campsite. She'd reserved a 200-square-foot patch of field from a farmer who'd let his crops go fallow for the year. He'd marked off campsites with small wooden stakes, and set up fire rings inside crowded circles of sites. They drove slowly, bumping over uneven ground and watching for the number that would indicate their patch of earth: 333. All around them, other cars and vans bumped through, and people who were already settled gathered in small, friendly groups, talking, cooking, drinking, dancing. A bare-chested, barefoot man with a lavender towel wrapped around his waist walked in front of their car, smiling and holding open his hand, shaking a thumb and pinkie finger in their direction.

"He's hot," Stella said.

"He's naked," said Cricket. Stella looked at her and raised her eyebrows meaningfully, making Cricket laugh and shake her head.

They parked, and then Cricket set about putting up the tent while Stella unloaded the car, complaining all the way.

At the next campsite, a mother called to her little boy that supper was ready.

"In a second," he shouted back. "I just want to unroll my sleeping bag."

He unzipped their tent flap and backed inside, pulling his sleeping bag along with him. Cricket had one of those familiar but unexpected stomach-punching memories from her past. Her brother Chris, backing into a new doghouse he'd built with their father, yanking their dog, Bardzo, on his leash.

"It's a nice house, Bardzo!" he'd shouted to the reluctant dog. "Come inside, you'll see."

Pulling on the leash while the dog dug its feet into the soft dirt, Chris had made Andy and their mother laugh out loud. The old man, standing to one side as always, had tried to catch Andy's eye. She thought of him fumbling with his pants in her room at night, forcing himself on her, into her. Her throat filled with bile and she looked away. Her mother's hand had found Andy's shoulder then, as if to reassure her—something that hadn't made sense at the time. It was only later she'd figured it out; her mother had known. All along, she'd known that Matthias was assaulting their daughter, but had been too shocked or ashamed or cowardly to do anything about it. Knowing this had helped with the guilt when Andy ran away. Her mother should have stepped in, done something. Her mother could live without her.

But nothing helped the guilt she felt about abandoning Chris.

After Cricket cooked burgers for them, they ate sitting outside the tent, watching as more people arrived and found their campsites. Everyone who walked by offered a friendly greeting, a raised mug, an invitation.

"Check us out later at 244! Big party," said a girl in a red floppy hat.

Cricket remembered this camaraderie among strangers at The Dead concerts. She remembered, too, the way the world reassembled itself from one town to the next, like a puzzle that's been broken up, then pieced back together on a new table top.

"Can I go?" Stella asked excitedly.

"Maybe we'll both go."

Stella frowned. "Mom, I'm almost seventeen. I'm old enough to walk three hundred feet and meet a few people without my mother."

In many ways, she was right, Cricket knew. But Cricket had learned how to parent in reaction to her mother's see-no-evil speak-no-evil hear-no-evil style. With Cricket's mother, if you ignored something, it went away. Or worse yet, it never existed. Doing the opposite—seeing evil everywhere— was Cricket's mothering style.

"You're too young," Cricket said softly, reaching for Stella's hand. "I'm sorry, but—"

"What is it with you?" Stella pulled her hand away. "I'm not five anymore. I get that you think I'm too young to be here without you. But why can't I walk over there," she pointed to where the floppy-hatted woman was now sitting in a circle of people, "and have a little fun?"

"Honey," Cricket started to say.

"No, seriously! You're always right on top of me," Stella said. "Exactly what do you think will happen to me over there?"

Someone will get you drunk. Slip you pills. Hurt you. Rape you. Steal you away. You'll disappear forever. With a jolt, not having understood this before, Cricket realized that her fears for Stella were a mixture of the terrible things that had happened to her, and the terrible thing that had happened to her mother.

Stella glared at her, maybe sensing her distraction. "My friends all feel sorry for me, do you know that?"

Cricket looked down into her crossed legs and counted to five in her mind. Then she said, "But none of their mothers brought them here, did they?"

Stella put her unfinished burger onto her paper plate and threw it in their trash bag.

"Maybe Missy's and Angelina's families knew it wouldn't be any fun for them to be here with their mothers," she said. She crossed her arms over her legs, propped her chin on a hand, and looked away. If they were home now, she'd storm from the room. Here, she didn't have anywhere to go but inside the tent.

Cricket had never told Stella about her life following The Dead. The reason she'd left home, and the age she'd been when she ran away, had seemed like good reasons to keep Stella in the dark. But now it felt like a window of opportunity had come and gone. She had no idea how she'd ever tell her the truth, or what Stella's reaction might be. Maybe hearing that her mother had left home at fifteen would make Stella leave home.

This fear brought on other feelings of fear and guilt. Her brother would be thirty-three now. If she found him, would he remember her? Would he forgive her?

Stella said, "I've smoked pot, you know."

"You have?"

"And it's not the big scary drug everyone makes it out to be."

Cricket was tempted to agree, but stopped herself. A thousand joints passed themselves back to her across time, across a thousand campfires just like this one. She told herself not to lecture Stella right now, but heard herself starting up against her will.

"Did you know the pot that's out there now isn't like the pot that was around when I was young?"

Stella shrugged and looked away, chin back on her hand.

"It's much stronger, Stella. You have to be careful."

"Are you saying you smoked pot when you were a teenager?"

Cricket nodded and Stella smiled, incredulous. "You did not."

"You really have to be careful," Cricket said again.

Stella huffed and shook her head. "You make like you want us to talk about things, but then you won't talk. You just ..." She let the words fade out as she held up a hand and made a "yak yak yak" gesture with her fingers and thumb.

"I worry about you."

Stella uncrossed her legs and started to crawl into the tent. Then she paused. "Can I be by myself for a while?"

"Sure," Cricket said. "I'll stay out here."

"Fine."

Later, in the tent, she called to say goodnight to Martin, then lay awake, wishing she and Stella hadn't argued, listening to Stella's soft, regular breathing. To listen made her appreciate the mechanism that is life. Such steadiness comforted her: one breath after another after another, keeping time with the singing insects, and breezes stirring long grass, the gentle cows lowing in their sleep within the whispers and creaks of a farmer's barn.

Her father was dead. She knew this because, years before, in an effort to follow her family's news, she'd subscribed to *South Philly In Passing*, a little weekly paper. Through it, she'd read about her mother being named treasurer of their church. And about Chris becoming an Eagle Scout. She'd read that her former English teacher, Mrs. Sedgwick, had been named National Teacher of the Year by Bill Clinton. And about how her old boyfriend, Brendan Monroe, and her best friend from the tenth grade, Charlotte Douglas, had gotten married the week after they graduated high school. And then one day, the girl who used to be Andrea Kozlowski read that her father had died. Until that moment, she'd never understood that this was the reason she'd subscribed to the paper—wanting to know when it was safe. Matthias Kozlowski was dead, and she was safe.

Cricket awoke to the gentle patter of rain. Her first thought was childish and petulant: the forecast hadn't called for rain. It wasn't supposed to rain! She'd checked the weather a few times, but not in the last couple days. She opened her cellphone and found the time. 4 a.m. Next to her, Stella slept on top of her unzipped sleeping bag, covers thrown aside as if she'd been very hot. Cricket rolled onto her back and closed her eyes, but nervous fists pressed in on her temples and she knew she wouldn't be going back to sleep. All she could think about was her brother.

In the past, she'd planned many times to visit Chris. Or not to visit, necessarily, but to see him. On the day of his high school graduation, she'd almost driven to Philadelphia from Portland. Her plan had been to slip inside the gym, watch Chris graduate, then slip out. Her only thought, before changing her mind, had been that, with their father dead, she'd be safe. Hours before leaving, though, other possibilities began to occur to her. She imagined recognizing old neighbors and teachers—walking shoulder-to-shoulder with them as they flocked toward the gymnasium's orange double doors. Worst of all, she imagined seeing her mother. Seeing her, and being seen. So she had unpacked her bag, pulled her car back into the garage and stayed away. Until now.

The line to get into the concert wasn't really a line but a mass of wet people in every imaginable outfit—from jeans and T-shirts and beads, to cotton dresses sticking like Saran Wrap, to running shoes and rain slickers. Their campsite was only halfway back in the line, and after they left the car by their tent, Cricket and Stella had to backtrack to get to the end and begin waiting.

"We should have started earlier," Stella moaned, standing on tiptoe to see better, then falling despondently on her heels.

Cricket left a message for Martin, telling him they were fine but it was raining. Before hanging up, she had the mad impulse to tell him everything. Right now, on a voice mail. Tell him and get it over with.

Martin, my real name is Andrea Kozlowski. My father used to come into my room at night. He used to rape me. I ran away. I left behind a younger brother. I haven't seen him since he was eight. For years, I've wanted to reach out to him. I think he lives in this town. Maybe he'll be at this concert. I want to find him I wish you were here to help me.

Imagining such a message, she ended the call quickly, worried she might actually say this crazy thing, then slipped her cellphone into her back pocket.

Cricket and Stella hadn't talked about their argument from the night before. Each was acting cautiously—very polite. Now, Cricket took out some gum and held it up as a question to Stella. When she nodded, Cricket popped a square of it into her daughter's palm and they stood quietly together, chewing gum and watching the world around them.

A group of girls ahead had their arms strung over each other's shoulders and were singing a song Cricket recognized from the Perilous Between music Stella had been playing in the car the day before.

"Oh, I know this one," she said to Stella. "It's … Wait, I'll get it …"

Stella pressed her lips together, as if trying not to say the name of the song, and then it came to Cricket.

"'Bendy River,'" she said happily, looking at Stella for confirmation. "Right? It's called 'Bendy River'?"

Stella bit her upper lip and nodded, smiling. Cricket tried to make a high five, but Stella's eyes grew wide with horror and Cricket stopped.

"Sorry," she said. She thought about putting an arm around her daughter's shoulders, but knew she'd be frozen out, and changed direction, light bumping Stella's shoulder with her own instead. "I was right though, right?"

"Yes, Mother. 'Bendy River.'"

"Don't call me Mother."

It took forty minutes of waiting before they were finally in sight of the concert grounds, an area enclosed by high fencing. Cricket shifted her backpack from one shoulder to the other and tried to get a look. The whole place was more like a refugee camp than anything else, except these refugees were having a great time. Several young men behind Stella and Cricket had been openly smoking pot for the last hour, and Cricket was glad the subject had come up already. The boys were probably around twenty. Stella glanced at them from time to time, and smiled broadly when one of the boys said hello to her. They talked in loud, loose voices about the music, and the food they were going to have. *I hope Sammy Samosa is here. I need a potato cheddar one BAD.*

A handsome man with a sad face and downcast expression walked alongside the line, handing out fliers. His bangs fell over one eye and his short-sleeved white shirt was damp and yellowed with sweat beneath the arms. He was muscular and had callused hands. Cricket wondered if he was a farmer or a laborer. What did people in Resolute, Vermont, do for work? Stella took one of his fliers and smiled, saying, "Thanks," and he nodded but would not meet her eye.

"What is it?" Cricket asked.

Stella handed it to her and said, "Religious stuff."

"We are the Commonwealth of Israel," announced the flier in bold black letters across the top. **"And we want to teach you about Yahshua."** Cricket slipped it into the outside pocket of her backpack.

The rain was constant, an annoyance. Its patter tapped relentlessly against rooftops and windows of surrounding cars, and against the thin plastic of her red raincoat, and Stella's yellow poncho, and into puddles on the ground. Her exposed face and hands and ankles were cold and her teeth chattered. But the rain helped to calm her somehow, hypnotizing her with its beat.

The line to get in was organized chaos: thousands of people massing toward a few breaks in the fence, where security guards took tickets, checked IDs, went through bags. And all along, more cars were pulling into surrounding fields. As she'd expected, they were beginning to slide and slip and get stuck in the mud. She told herself not to worry. One way or another, she'd dig her car out at the end of the weekend. At least they had reached their campsite. Cricket noticed that some people had begun pitching tents right alongside incoming roads, in the rain. But the police were making them move. There were two kinds of police, from what she could see: state troopers and sheriffs. It was the troopers she watched most closely.

You could find out anything on the Internet. It had become Cricket's lifeline, her link to a world she'd left behind. She'd been surprised to learn that her brother was a cop. But nothing had shocked her like the Google search that informed her he'd moved up here from Philadelphia. Wouldn't that have meant a big pay cut, a huge lifestyle change?

Whenever she saw a trooper, she peered hard, studying his face under the big green hat. But none looked familiar, and she was both disappointed and relieved each time.

A makeshift shelter had been created at each fence break. It felt good to stand there, out of the rain for a few minutes, when they finally got to the security checkpoint. The man who went through their backpack did a thorough but unenthusiastic job, looking like he'd had just about enough of these people and this weather. As he handed the pack over to Cricket again, a girl in the next line slid in the mud and went down on her behind. She laughed as she pushed herself up, not seeming at all bothered by the fact that now she was covered in mud.

Once inside the grounds, the crowd mutated and thinned. There was room to move, and Cricket could breathe. The band wasn't due to play until four, so she and Stella began to wander, seeing as much as they could through the rain, which let up from time to time. Everything inside the site seemed full of color: people's clothes, their phones and purses and backpacks, even the food. Vendors sold hats and T-shirts and necklaces and posters. They sold Belgian waffles, the smell of which—warm and sweet and tempting—pervaded the cold and damp. They sold candy corn wrapped in red, shiny cellophane, because this was supposedly Kennedy Jackson's favorite treat.

Despite the weather, the people at the concert were mostly cheerful and excited. To Cricket, they seemed incredibly young.

"Dude, did I sleep in your car last night?"

"Not mine, man."

Stella glanced at her sidelong, looking unsure about whether or not to establish détente, and laugh with Cricket at these people. Cricket grinned at her, but looked away quickly in case Stella didn't smile back.

"I can't remember where I slept. I have absolutely no idea!"

"That's hilarious, man!"

At this, they did laugh together, breaking the discomfort.

"These people are so funny," Stella whispered.

"They probably come to every concert," Cricket said.

"I've read about that. Some people live out of their cars and follow this band."

"A lot of them used to follow The Dead," Cricket said, not quite making eye contact.

It seemed impossible to her that she'd ever lived this life. But she had, of course she had. And certain sights and sounds reminded her of what that had been like.

She could hear Jackson Browne at full volume—"You Love the Thunder"—competing with all the other noises in the field: conversations, laughter, barking dogs.

Someone called out "Who wants a foot job?" and a girl shouted back something unintelligible, laughing too hard to be understood. These were the happy people—the elated teenagers throwing Frisbees and singing in groups and wrapped in blankets, noisily gossiping and shouting. Then there were the ones who were all about the music, comparing playlists on iPods in small, serious clusters under cover from the rain. There were quiet couples, leaning into each other, talking in hushed whispers, stopping every twenty feet to kiss deeply. And then there were the displaced: loners wandering, arms crossed over chests. A girl with stringy black hair standing in the middle of a crowd, smoking a cigarette over a torn square of foil and staring around blankly. Her nervous-looking friend hovering at an elbow, asking from time to time, "Sharon, are you sure you're all right?" All of these people reminded Cricket of herself, of her transition from one person into another—all the stages she'd gone through to leave behind Andrea Kozlowski and her sad story.

She'd been fifteen when she ran away. She packed one afternoon and left very early the next morning. The middle of the night wasn't a safe time. Her father might slip into her room at midnight to discover her packing, or even climbing out through a window and onto the roof. Instead, she had come home from school, kissed her mother's cheek, and done her homework at the dining room table, as usual. Later in her room, she'd taken all her books from her backpack and pushed them far underneath her bed, behind the floral dust ruffle. Then she'd filled the backpack with clothing: jeans and shirts and socks, but also shorts and T-shirts and a baseball cap, because it wouldn't be cold forever. She'd taken a blank journal she'd never to that point had the courage to write in, and a picture of Chris—toothless, smiling madly, holding a hose and filling a baby pool. This picture she'd tucked into the front cover of the empty journal, and wondered, what words would fill these pages, how would her life read in a year?

If her father came to her room, it would be for a short time only, between midnight and one. He was always gone by one. But she didn't want to chance it, so she set her alarm for three-thirty and tucked it under her bed by the books. In the end, he never came to her room that night. And, too frightened and excited to close her eyes, Andrea Kozlowski never did sleep. She turned off the alarm before it ever made a sound, crept from her bed and dressed silently in the warm, shimmering darkness of a room she'd loved at the age of twelve and hated by thirteen. She slipped her backpack over her shoulder and walked to her window. At the last minute, she changed her mind about the roof, and the ten-foot drop into the tall cedar bushes. She might twist an ankle or worse, and there was no guarantee that leaving this way would be any quieter than going down the stairs, slipping out the kitchen door. Her parents slept at the front of the house, and the kitchen was at the back. She put her robe over her sweatshirt and corduroys in case anyone might catch her going down the stairs, then left her room. The house accommodated her; it didn't make a sound. Through her door, along the hall, down the stairs, around the banister and down the longer hall with the wood floor. Her sneakers never squeaked. The boards didn't groan, the window in the kitchen door didn't shake. She was out on her back lawn into the chilly night without having made a sound. She left her robe on the patio, swung the backpack over her shoulder, and jogged out of the yard and into the night.

She walked to the bus station, then waited until she could take a nearly empty bus to the Spectrum, where The Dead had played that night and would be playing once more before moving on. On that bus, she met Beatriz, who'd left the concert to visit a friend who lived near the bus station, and was on her way back now. One of only four passengers, Bea had asked her for a cigarette, and Andy said she didn't have any. Then, seemingly without irony, Beatriz offered her a cigarette from a full pack she pulled out of the breast pocket of her denim jacket. They spent the short ride talking. When Beatriz heard this would be Andy's first concert, she took her under her wing, sharing a flask of schnapps with her. The driver yelled at them about drinking on the bus, and Bea yelled back that it was coffee. They got out at the Spectrum, and Beatriz took her to meet her friends, Paolo and Gordy Z, who were camping out in the parking lot in a battered brown van with no back doors. The three of them had been traveling together for four months, following The Dead, and they invited Andy to join them as if it were nothing, as if they were offering her a sip of Coke, or another cigarette. They spent that next night at the concert, dancing and singing along with the band, talking and making plans. The van was Paolo's. Where the doors had fallen off, he'd hung a voluminous black curtain across the back, which he kept anchored at the bottom with hooks and grommets. It seemed so exciting that here, just a few miles from her house, Andy could get into this stranger's van and disappear. A whole new world seemed to be unfolding, and she embraced it, resolutely emptying her mind of her high school friends, her mother, her little brother.

The next day, Andrea Kozlowski got left behind at the Spectrum, and

Christine "Cricket" Wheeler, named for the brother she had left behind and the wheels that would carry her to safety, drove away with her new friends and her new story in a brown van. The curtain flapped, lulling her to sleep beside Beatriz on blankets thrown over a large rectangle of carpet. They lay under quilts, to keep warm despite the relentless, whipping air. Up front, Paolo and Gordy Z had shared a cup of sweet coffee with cream and played cassette tapes of The Dead and Jimi Hendrix and Jackson Browne. From inside strange dreams, Cricket had heard the two of them, crooning "You Love the Thunder." The van had made its way to the first of many campgrounds where they would stay on their long way to California for the next concert, and then the next, and the next.

Stella wanted a T-shirt, so Cricket bought her an orange one with dark blue lines that looked like clouds, but spelled out Perilous Between. On the back they spelled *Shape of the Sky.*

"What's Shape of the Sky?" she asked.

"It's what they're calling this tour," Stella said, shouting, because the rain had picked up again.

"Kennedy Jackson said Vermont changes the shape of the sky. The mountains and all that. I think you have to lie down to really see it."

An hour later, they found themselves standing under cover of a booth that belonged to a hairdresser from Resolute. The woman had a sharp, skinny face. Cricket found it strange that this woman was in the beauty business. Her booth smelled of cigarette smoke, and her own hair was thin and pulled back in an unimpressive ponytail. Who would want a haircut from this woman? She was charging five dollars to braid beads into people's hair, and ten for a cut. As an odd sideline, she was trying out a new kind of "home-made massage" that involved running an iron over a blanket settled onto the bare backs of people who were willing to give it a try: three dollars for ten minutes. *Don't Worry: Set to Low and Dryer Than a Popcorn Fart,* said the hand-lettered sign in red magic marker. This sign is what started Stella laughing.

"Oh my God," she said between giggles. "Look at that."

"Shh," Cricket said, but she also started to laugh.

"She is ironing people's backs," Stella said, a little too loudly. "With an iron."

"Shh!" Cricket was having trouble keeping her laughter quiet. She covered her mouth and gave Stella a look, but this only made it worse, and Stella raised her voice another notch.

"Please, Mom, can I have my back ironed?"

"Don't be mean," Cricket said, trying to get herself under control.

Stella snorted. "If she doesn't burn someone, she'll electrocute them. It's raining."

Cricket put an arm around Stella and steered her away from the woman's booth so they wouldn't be heard.

"Seriously, why would anyone do that, when they could iron themselves at home for free?" Stella said.

The two of them got hysterical together, egging each other into uncontrollable laughter, bending over and nearly falling down with the silliness they felt.

That's actually when she first saw him—her brother, Chris—right in the middle of all that laughter. Which was surely why he was watching her. Not watching with recognition, but with appreciation: a slight grin on his face. He was enjoying her happiness—the happiness of a stranger. He glanced at her, then away, then back. Not as though he knew her. He'd have no reference to recognize her face or know who she'd become. Not like Cricket, who had followed his life, tracking him on the Internet, reading his news, studying his pictures when they were available. High school graduation, first job at Philadelphia Parks & Rec, police academy training, Philly cop, homicide detective, and then this, his curious move to Vermont to become a state trooper. Even having seen his pictures, though, she'd been unprepared for how very much he looked like their father.

Cricket looked away sharply and removed her arm from Stella's shoulder. She turned her body away from where Chris stood and looked around wildly for the best escape route.

Stella noticed her change in mood. "Mom?"

She glanced back at her.

"What's going on?"

Cricket shrugged, but couldn't say anything for the moment. When she looked around, Chris was still there, but he wasn't watching anymore. He must have been off duty, because he wasn't in uniform. He was with a woman in a wheelchair. Pushing a woman in a wheelchair. He had Matthias's eyes and the straight, tight line of his jaw. He had the dashing smile. The smile that, in Matthias, could turn down at the edges and become something dangerous in less time than it took to move out of the way. Cricket swallowed and tried to relax.

"Sorry," she said to Stella. "Something … I didn't feel well for a second."

Stella watched her with an expression somewhere between suspicion and concern.

"Let's go check out the sculptures," Cricket said. She hooked a hand under Stella's arm and started in the direction of the tall, brightly lit sculptures that Stella had said were always part of Perilous Between concerts. After a moment, perhaps having waited to see if Cricket might faint or throw up, Stella pulled her arm away, but then bumped into her side in a friendly way.

"I'm all right," Cricket said.

"That was weird."

"It was," Cricket agreed, looking at her.

"You were just really strange back there. It was kind of spooky."

"Sorry."

Stella shrugged. "It's fine."

Cricket was annoyed with herself for having behaved this way. She had not expected he would look so very much like the one person she would have run from. But now she realized how unrealistic it had been, in any case, thinking she could approach Chris at this concert. What did you say to someone after twenty-five years? How did you start?

Four o'clock came and went without music. Four-thirty. Five. Finally, at five-thirty, an opening band of local high school students came out. Some woman introduced them and said that Kennedy Jackson himself had chosen them after auditions. People were so wet and tired and ready for entertainment that they went wild for the high school students, screaming and clapping and calling out encouragement. And the students were good. One kid in particular played the guitar as if he'd been doing it for twenty years, though as a high school student, he couldn't have been more than seventeen. The music was strange and beautiful—both romantic and sinister. Moody. The kids were mostly following this guitar player's lead, trying to keep up with him. If they were doing covers, Cricket didn't know them. The music was unfamiliar to her, and really wonderful. It had a desperate, raw quality. She felt like she was hearing something new, something not quite ready, but still forming. Maybe, in years to come, the members of this band would recall sharing a stage with this boy on lead guitar. They'd tell their friends they'd played with him back when he was still perfecting his sweep picking.

Stella danced in a small self-conscious square of ground. She kept looking around, checking that other people were dancing, too. Cricket decided not to join in, because that might embarrass Stella. She closed her eyes, though, and tried to let the music carry away all the worry she'd felt earlier.

After about half an hour, the music finished. People started shouting and cheering. A man had joined the group of high school students. Cricket glanced at the large screens that flanked the stage. He was handsome, with long dark hair, and he wore a leather vest, but no shirt.

Stella told her what she already knew. "That's Kennedy Jackson!" She was jumping up and down, looking younger and more unashamedly excited than she had in months.

Jackson took the mic and said something, but he couldn't be heard over the rain and the cheers from the crowd. He held up a hand and the audience quieted a little.

"All right!" he shouted. That started the audience again, so he held up his hand a little longer. "When I was a kid, somebody helped me out once. Changed my life. So now I like to pay that person back.

"These guys are from here, they're students from Resolute, " he said, indicating the band. "And a couple other towns. I forget the hell where." He smiled and there were more screams, with names of towns.

"I can't believe I'm here," Stella said. She looked at Cricket and maybe the expression on her face was a little bit conciliatory. "Thank you so much!"

Up on stage, Jackson was introducing the members of the band. People kept clapping and whooping, cheering for each name. Cricket didn't hear any of it. She put out her arms and Stella laughed and walked into her hug like she meant it.

"Thank you for saying that," Cricket said.

"You're welcome." Stella's mouth was pressed into her shoulder, and her voice came out muffled and funny. They laughed together and Cricket let her go.

"All right," Kennedy was shouting. "You give us fifteen minutes. We'll finish setting up, get the rest of the band out here. First, how about a hand for these guys?"

The crowd erupted, screaming, shouting, and pumping fists. Kennedy Jackson walked off, surrounded and finally swallowed by the small, excited group of high school musicians.

It had stopped raining. The sun never came out fully, but the air warmed and steam rose from the ground. Cricket and Stella took off their rain gear and stuffed it in their pack. They bought ice creams and ate them at the edge of the great, excited crowd, nudging forward to get closer to the stage.

The band started for real just after seven. Cricket was glad she'd heard their music in the car.

"That's not the right drummer," Stella said, pointing with her ice cream stick.

"No?" Cricket looked up at one of the enormous screens. The drummer was a beautiful woman with wild, black curly hair, wearing all-white clothing.

"No. The regular drummer is a guy named Russell. He's really hot."

A girl standing nearby seemed to have heard them. She pushed in and shouted in Stella's ear. "Russell's not playing."

Stella made a face. "Why?"

She shrugged. "He got arrested! It's all over the website. He's not even here."

Stella opened her mouth in surprise.

"Yeah," said the girl, nodding and dancing at the same time. "There's all kinds of rumors. Someone said he killed somebody." She danced away.

"Oh my God," Cricket said. She realized that she hadn't read a paper since leaving home, hadn't listened to the news.

"That's probably just rumors," Stella said. "He's supposed to be this really great guy."

"And he's hot," Cricket said, smiling.

"Yeah!" Stella said, not picking up on the sarcasm.

Cricket found herself being transported by the music once again, newly entranced with each song. From time to time she recognized one from the car ride. And as the first hour passed, she began to have a sense of the band's overall sound, which was dark and kind of swampy, with entertaining lyrics that were often funny. Their proficiency showed up what the high school students had done, but didn't erase her feeling that she'd seen the first performance of an enormous talent when that one kid played guitar.

She let the music take her. For the first time since arriving, she remembered how it had really felt to follow The Dead. It had been an experience of the body—a physical marvel—as much as anything else. She closed her eyes and danced with abandon, swirling and letting her arms float in the air above her head. Once, when she looked around to track where she was and where Stella was, she found her daughter staring at her, looking astonished. Probably she was embarrassed. But Cricket closed her eyes again, not letting Stella in. This moment was about Cricket. And maybe, just a little, it was about Andy.

At ten, they wandered away to find real food. Cricket kept a careful eye out for Chris, but didn't see him again. Stella didn't say anything about her mother's dancing. Instead, she talked nonstop about the music: what had sounded different from the albums, and how she hoped they would play something called "Velvet Glove in an Iron Fist," and that "amazing" transition from "Safety in Numbers" to "Monkey Out of Me." She seemed to have forgotten that she was too cool to be with her mother and too old to express her emotions.

They ended up having tacos near the entrance to the concert grounds. And then, because it was too hard to push their way back through all the people, they decided to just head for the tent. It was Stella's idea, which surprised Cricket.

"I want to lie on my sleeping bag and listen," she said. "We can unzip the skylight and watch the stars."

"I like that idea," Cricket said, noticing for the first time that Stella's eyes looked heavy, and that her steps were dragging a little. She decided not to remind her about the cloud cover, the unlikelihood of stars.

They left the security checkpoint and started back toward their campsite. After a minute, Cricket reached over and took Stella's hand. Maybe because it was getting dark, Stella didn't pull away. Cricket squeezed her fingers, and then let go, just in case Stella was uncomfortable.

"I didn't know you could dance," Stella said.

"A little," said Cricket.

The walk back to the tent was, of course, much faster. She realized they were less than half a mile from the stage, and the music could be heard perfectly well, though with an occasional distortion brought on by who knew what—the mountain? the farmer's field? the shape of the sky?

They crawled into the tent and lay there, listening, whispering, commenting on the songs. After another hour, once the band had started playing something that sounded a lot like The Dead's psychedelic improv, Stella's words took on an exhausted breathiness. By twelve, she was asleep. For a while, Cricket stayed, thinking she'd go to sleep, too. But then the band took a break. She heard the high school kids start up again. The change in music distracted her and woke her up, and she decided to take a walk. She eased out of the tent, and closed the flaps, but did not zip them, for fear of waking Stella.

The night was warm and overcast. A few stars were visible from time to time through thready clouds. People stumbled between tents, slipping some in the mud, laughing and singing and drinking. Here and there the fire rings had been stoked into larger bonfires, and people gathered around them, partying. She'd just resolved to stay close to the tent, not let it out of her sight, when she saw him again—her brother. He was talking to a young man some thirty feet away. She walked closer, slowly, trying to stay in the shadows. The young man was the person who'd handed her a religious flier in the line that morning. She was able to crouch beside a tent and listen to their conversation. She didn't care, particularly, to know what was happening, but mostly just wanted to hear Chris's voice, maybe know what kind of person he was. She wanted to dispel the feeling that he was the embodiment of their father.

Chris was saying, "I hear you went back to live in the Community."

"That's right," the other man said. He had a boyish voice, and Cricket peeked around the corner to look at him again. She wondered if he was a friend of Chris's, or if he was in trouble, maybe.

"You heard about that woman who was found, right?" Chris said.

Cricket shifted, trying to change position and stay quiet at the same time.

The young man answered, "Woman?" His voice sounded tight and worried.

"Yes, Zedekiah. Fisk Endicott found a woman's body in the ravine."

"I did hear about that," the man said quickly. "I did."

"We know who killed her. The weapon was found on the floor by the bed where he was passed out."

"What was the weapon?"

"Crossbow," Chris said. "I guess it could be called an accident. He was drunk."

They were quiet for a moment. Cricket was holding her breath and her heart was beating too loudly, and it was just the way it used to be, when her father's footsteps approached down the hall.

"He'll go to jail?" asked the man named Zedekiah.

"Oh, yes, he'll go to jail," Chris said. "The thing I don't understand, though, is that he seems to have had some help."

Zedekiah said something she couldn't make out.

"I'm off duty here," Chris said. "We're just having a conversation, Zedekiah."

"I know," the man answered. "I know that."

"The accident happened at a party," Chris said. "And the man's confessed, as I told you. There's no doubt who did it."

Zedekiah sniffled loudly. Was he crying? Cricket pictured him wiping his nose with a hand. Why was he crying? They weren't talking like he'd known this girl.

"People at the party say he never left. But the woman's body was dumped in the ravine. He says he doesn't know how that happened. How she got there."

"She was dumped in the ravine?"

"Or maybe not dumped. Maybe just left. Left in the ravine. Some people even think she got there on her own."

Her brother had a calming voice, slow and gentle. His voice was nothing like their father's.

"Do you think that?" Zedekiah asked, stuttering on the last word. "That she got to the ravine by herself?"

"It would have been a long walk, hurt like that," Chris said. "We found traces of lime in the parking area above the ravine. And also on her clothing and in her hair. As if maybe one of the local town garage trucks had taken her there, wrapped in a tarp, the way you pick up the animals."

"Not just me," said Zedekiah.

"No, I know," said Chris. She liked her brother's voice. He sounded compassionate.

"Whoever got her to the ravine, I have to figure, they didn't mean to cause her any harm," Chris said.

Zedekiah made a mournful sound of agreement. "Maybe the person really wanted to help her, but couldn't because it was too late."

"Maybe," Chris said. "We're probably not going to be able to work it out very easily."

The two men stood in silence for so long, Cricket had to look around the tent again to check they were still there. Her knees ached from crouching, and she eased back and sat with her legs crossed, only remembering the mud as a cold, damp ooze began to seep through her jeans.

Finally, Chris said, "It would be helpful if the person who brought her to the ravine came forward. That would help a lot."

"He'd be punished," Zedekiah said.

"Maybe," Chris said. "But not so much that it wouldn't be worth getting it off his chest."

They were quiet again. And then Chris changed the subject. Smoothly, kindly, he said, "I'm glad you're back in the Community now. Maybe it's a better place for you to be."

The other man said, "I think so, too."

"I wish you good luck with that," Chris said.

She imagined them shaking hands, then heard footsteps walking away. Her legs ached. She uncrossed them and stood, then abruptly found herself face to face with her brother, who'd practically walked into her.

"Whoa!" he said, surprised.

She reared back, heart pounding, then turned and ran. Behind her, he called out, but she didn't slow to hear his words. She ran around campfires and tents, sliding into a half-split at one point, but recovering, swerving around drunken boys and stoned girls. She was off-course, and had to follow the campsite signs to make her way back to 333. Out of breath and irrationally terrified, she dove into the tent, and then lay there, panting, trying to stay quiet.

"Mom?" Stella whispered.

"Shh," Cricket said. "Nothing's wrong."

"Are you all right?"

"I went for a walk and got lost. I was a little scared."

"You smell like mud."

"I fell."

She could hear Chris's voice, calling out from far away.

Stella chuckled. "There's a lot of drunk people here," she said sleepily. And then her breathing turned steady again.

Chris's voice was coming closer. Other people were shouting back at him now. She heard them first.

"Hey, man, keep it down! We're trying to party over here."

Laughter, and then his voice. "Andy?"

"Quiet, man!"

"Andy? Andrea Kozlowski?"

He wasn't in her row, and it sounded like he was going away, walking in the wrong direction.

"Andy Kozlowski!" His shout was desperate, lost.

She closed her eyes very tightly. Still her heart hammered. She told herself he was not her father and this was not her bedroom. This was not Philadelphia, not 1985. He wouldn't hurt her. But it did no good; she couldn't move. She was trapped in an old nightmare. Trapped and paralyzed and silent. She tried not to cry, not to answer, not to breathe.

The best she could do was make herself a new promise. Tomorrow morning, she would tell Stella everything. She wouldn't ask for forgiveness or sympathy; she wouldn't tell Stella how to feel about her story. She'd just ask her to listen. In some ways, Stella was stronger than Cricket. She was definitely stronger than Andy. So maybe she'd understand. Maybe, when they went back to hear the second day of music, Stella would help her find Chris again. They could talk to him together.

Rita Frederick
August 2010

The dishes have piled up and the mail has piled up and the laundry has piled up and none of it feels like Rita's fault or job, but somehow she is the only one in this family who's going to do anything about any of it and sometimes she wonders how it came to be this way, since she's not a naturally neat person. Her mother kept a perfect house, never a wrinkle in a dust ruffle, every window cleaned and shining without a smudge even at sunset in summer, and she misses her mother bad, because her mother used to come over and help Rita out a bit, knowing that keeping a clean house was never easy for her the way it seems to be for some women. She's even forgiven her mother for always being after her to lose weight, to stop talking so much and so fast and be a better listener, because it's no good holding a grudge against a dead woman, and anyway it wasn't like her mother was mean to her, because after all, she always backed down when Rita would shout at her to "Just quit!" She knows that if anyone came into this house they'd be surprised and probably would talk about her afterwards, because the dining room table is covered with papers and old lamps Howard says he'll repair and file folders of taxes going back ten years at least and a bowl of old candy and also several baseball caps and a box of sneakers someone—maybe Rita herself—bought two years ago and has never worn. The papers are knee-deep in the den and there are piles of magazines lining both sides of the stairway all the way up because she doesn't want to throw them out; that would be such a waste since she hasn't had time to look at them yet. Also Rita has a special fondness for collectibles, the only joy in her life since her mother passed, and she's special proud of her Hello Kitty! collection, in particular the small patent leather purses and the lunch box full of Pez dispensers and the seven-piece makeup brush kit. Her collectibles are an investment, even if Howard and Polly laugh at her when she says this, but it's true. She's taken real pride in finding these things and buying them at a good price and keeping them just as they were when she got them, because if you don't tear off the cellophane or cut through the plastic tape, these things stay worth more—anyone with an eBay password knows that. Except she's running out of places to put them and so they build up and keep her from being able to get to the dryer, for example, which is why the laundry has piled up. She can get to the washer, so she does manage to wash the important things and hang them. But it's harder to wash the jeans and get them dry, or the towels, and she wishes her mother was around to help like she used to. Even considering the way her mother used to suck in air as if she was surprised by the mess every time she came over, as if this wasn't exactly how Rita's house has always looked, and her mother's reaction was over the top considering that it's never been Rita's fault anyway, she has a whole family that won't pitch in. Polly can't be bothered to help—only ever talks about how she can't wait to turn eighteen and move to Burlington where her boyfriend goes to college—and then there's always the real big pause where Polly tries to make Howard and Rita feel guilty for not having the money to send their daughter to college, and Howard does feel guilty but Rita does not. Because if a girl wants to go to college, she should get a job and save her money and get a few loans or maybe even a scholar ship if she'd ever cracked a book—which Polly never did—and then go to college. But instead she just comes and goes and complains and looks down on Rita for not being like the mothers who bake oatmeal bars and organize shopping trips to Saint J. and campouts in the Willoughby State Forest and clean their houses top to bottom. Rita never signed on for this job of cleaning up after everybody, she never wanted to spend her life that way—who would? Anyway she can't invite people over because the truth is her house would do more than surprise people—it would shock them and give them more to gossip about—and she doesn't want to be the talk of the town. She doesn't even have her dad over anymore, though he doesn't bring it up and she thinks maybe he's relieved not to have to try to make conversation with Howard on a Sunday night while she cuts up the roast and heats a can of green beans and salts the Tater Tots and sets the table and every other thing in the house that needs doing. She feels a little guilty about her dad—how he's alone all the time and she should get over there more often, because he's an old man without help—but she's just too busy here with the laundry and the papers and the dishes and everything else, and mostly she just wishes he'd agree to move into a nice nursing home where trained people could keep an eye on him. But that new policeman won't help her convince her dad where he needs to be, where he'd be safest, and she doesn't like the new policeman at all because he's been rude to her at least two times.

It's when her mother was sick that it all got away from her. She used to keep on top of it, at least as much as some of her neighbors did. But her mother got sick and Rita was at the hospital every day for near to eight months, and the house just up and filled with things. Howard's terrible with the mail, never gets around to reading all the bills and newsletters and ads that come for him. Every few months he pretends to try to get on top of it, reading some things, filing some things. It's a miracle they haven't had a bad credit report or gone bankrupt, the way Howard does the books. He's a *furniture man, not a paper-pusher*, he likes to say, which has to do with his work selling antiques out of a storefront in town, which is how they make their living. It's also why they have some nice pieces under all the papers and clocks and old records and radios and that globe with the flaking gold stand, that used to belong to Howard's father but now sits at an angle like it's really spinning away in space instead of holding down at least four years of credit card receipts. Howard's just as bad about organizing the barn as Rita is about keeping up the house. She gets on him for that sometimes, but he insists it's different because it's his business and where else is he going to put the new pieces he hasn't had time to research or price or fit into the store, which is little and can only handle so much. Plus, he says, he leaves *passages*—that, his very word and it makes her laugh—*passages*, he says, between all the furniture in the barn so he can move around out there and find what he needs. Which she supposes is sort of true, because she can always walk to where he is if she needs him when he's in the barn. For a while she started making passages in the house, too, parting all the paper and pillows and sleeping bags and vases so she could make her way down the hall between things. But she's not a small woman, as her mother never tired of telling her when she was alive and would come over to help out a bit, and it's not easy to make enough room all the way through the house, and her mess isn't neat rectangles like Howard's furniture out in the barn, so this didn't last long, and Howard never noticed anyway, and now she's back to having to move things in order to get from one side of a room to the other. For example, just this morning, she had to move a stack of board games—even though they don't play board games and it's beyond her how they came to own these—and a Casio electronic sixty-one-key keyboard (no one plays that either) from the couch in the TV room to make space to sit before turning on *The Today Show*. Not that she watches TV all day, but just for a little while in the morning, while she has her juice, though she watches a little more since they got the new TV, which is a fifty-inch by Panasonic that makes Rita feel happy every time she looks at it.

And so now she's on the couch and, miracle of miracles, has the remote in her hand because it was right where she left it for once—on the coffee table beside a stack of photo albums that she's planning to organize at some point before Polly graduates so she can give her a gift of memories. There's a spot about that black weatherman who used to be so fat but now is thin, finishing the New York City Marathon, and then a commercial comes on so Rita changes to the Shopping Network just to see what they've got this morning, and they're showing a Sterling Silver Zambian Emerald Bamboo Ring for the one-time-only price of $49.97. Rita is trying to imagine that ring on her own hand, or a hand very much like hers but with long and graceful fingernails, when she catches movement in her side vision out the window. She looks and there's nothing there, but she knows there was something just a second ago, so she gets up to investigate.

She steps around the box full of all her mother's old Tupperware, and a velvet-lined boxed set of nice segregated steak knives sitting on top of the microwave oven they replaced last spring when this one broke. She sees a scurrying something at the few exposed inches of baseboard under the window, and thinks how, on top of everything else, the mice are getting worse and really will need to be dealt with soon. But this is not the movement she saw a minute ago, because the mice are inside the house and this movement happened outside.

Rita hovers behind her faded blue lace curtains and watches the barn, each of her hands clutching fabric at the sides of her robe. Sure enough, a minute later, a man walks around from the back, easy as you please. Brazen! He's dressed in jeans and a T-shirt, and his brown hair is long and tied back in a ponytail like a girl's. He's got dirty bare feet, and she knows what he's doing here. He'll be one of those people she tried to warn everyone about—one of those concert types with their drugs and their pipes and tattoos and loud music, and with too many earrings and toe rings and nose rings and belly rings. She told everyone; she promised these types would show up and make trouble if Resolute allowed this concert nonsense to happen with the so-called famous band. The man tries the barn door but doesn't know how to operate it because the handle is tricky, so he takes a minute to get it open. When he glances around, she feels as if their eyes have met, but they mustn't have, because without a smile or a shrug or a wave, he disappears into the barn and pulls the door shut behind himself.

A hot spike of pain makes her realize she's been biting at her chapped lips again. She forces herself to stop. She needs to figure out what to do.

The barn is very large and—she has always thought—stands too close to the house, throwing the TV room into shadow by two o'clock, even in summer. She doesn't like the barn, and Howard's mess is the least of it, because it's creepy out there, too hot in the summer and too cold in the winter and creaky all the time and old. It's very old. Also because she saw a show once where an innocent girl was hung in a barn, and the barn became haunted and the woman who lived on the property was the only person who could see the ghost—a terrifying transparent gray child in a nightgown, whose noose still dangled from her neck. And so Rita avoided the barn when Howard wasn't around. Going in there now—with a dirty drug addict—does not feel safer than going in alone. She considers but quickly rejects the idea of calling that stupid new policeman because of how quick he was to interrupt her at the town meeting when she'd tried to be heard. And won't he be sorry now! Won't they all be sorry now! She could call Howard, but it's the time he's usually at the diner, having his coffee, reading the paper. He won't go in to work before ten without an appointment. She could call the diner, but Gil would answer, and she won't talk to Gil, not since he made fun of her for the two desserts last time she had dinner over there. It wasn't like she ordered two ice cream sundaes. She ordered cherry pie, which is her favorite, and she ordered strawberry cheesecake, which is a different thing and he should be happy for the business instead of rotten to his customers. *Got enough to eat, Rita?* With his snide expression and nasty smile. *Wouldn't want you to waste away.* Now she never eats at the G&B while Gil is working. If she sees his car in the lot, she just turns her own car around and drives back home. And no, she won't call the diner. So the only thing to do is go out there herself and take care of business. All she really needs to do is open the barn door, and shout the man outside.

She leaves the TV room and shuffles toward the front door, then loses her balance stepping high to get around the box of clothes she picked up from Goodwill on her last trip to Burlington. She pulls on Polly's purple flip-flops. And because her robe is torn in the back—she really needs a new one—and she's still in her pajamas, which are lightweight and a little see-through, she tugs on a black nylon raincoat that almost covers the robe but doesn't hide her bare ankles, thick with veins. When she opens the front door, she tries not to make any noise, then wonders why, since the whole point is to alert him to her presence and scare him off. So she slams the door shut behind her.

The walk is about thirty steps—that's how close the barn is to the house—and she arrives at the barn door and is swallowed in shadow before deciding what she's going to do. It's probably in the 80s already, and the raincoat is feeling like a mistake, but she leaves it on because it's a layer and it feels like protection. Without planning to, she reaches for the barn door handle. She leans left on it, and then presses her thumb on the latch and pulls the door toward herself so that it swings open with a groan. Rita freezes, expecting the man to be standing just inside, ready to rush her with an axe or a knife or even a noose, but there's no sound and no movement. Inside is swimming darkness and she can just make out the yawning entryway to one of Howard's first passages in front of herself. And although she'd been going to shout the man out, she is now struck by the urge to watch him—to see what he's doing in there—before alerting him to her presence. It's a crazy thing to do, and she experiences a kind of out-of-body awareness of herself moving into the barn. The door closes and she stands in the darkness a moment until she can see the ribbons of light streaming in between gaps in the old boards, and soon it's enough light to see where she can step, so she starts to walk soft along How-ard's passage. It smells pleasant in the barn, but unlike most times when she comes out here to find Howard if she needs him, today the thought of cows living in here a hundred years ago, perfuming the boards with their breath and their milk and their powerful sweet stench doesn't actually make her smile. She's too scared to think of anything but where the man is lying in wait. Her coat makes noise, swishing around her muscular calves, and she wishes again that she hadn't worn it, because it's so hot. It's too dark in here for him to see what she's wearing anyway. Every few steps, she stops and listens, and after a couple minutes but no more than twenty steps, she starts to hear music. It's coming from up ahead and up the ladder, and while this is kind of a relief, because it means he's probably up there and not down here with her, it's also a disappointment. She won't be able to watch him without going up that dam-nable ladder in the dark, and no way in hell is she doing that. And so Rita is making to turn around and head back for the door, where she can shout him out like she'd planned, when she hears a voice calling from outside the barn. It's a girl's voice, calling soft in a kind of excited whisper. The door to the barn rattles, and Rita's arms fly up in fear, crossing over her chest so that her hands clutch opposite shoulders. She is only steps from one of Howard's intersect-ing passages, but it crosses under the ladder, and she is scared to pieces of being seen by the man in the loft. Still, she knows whoever is outside is about to be inside, and Rita will be directly in her line of light when the door opens.

The girl calls out again, and Rita hears the word she's saying: "Kennedy?"

Up in the loft, the man makes a noise that sounds like a growl. Like a werewolf growl, Rita is thinking, except that she recognizes his tone as one of aggravation, which probably isn't how a hungry werewolf would sound.

"What?" the man says then, almost a shout.

And Rita near to shouts back, he startles her so, but, like her arms, which are still crossing her chest, her throat seems to be paralyzed. The door behind her is rattling, and the man shouts "CHRIST," real loud this time, not seeming at all worried about anyone who might live in the house—which takes some gall, she thinks—and Rita's out-of-body personage uses the opportunity to dart under the ladder and along the passage that leads beneath the loft. She does it just in time, too, because the door opens then and a beam of light shoots down the first passage like in that science fiction movie where aliens burst out of astronauts. Rita can see bits of dust and very old hay fluttering in the light and then she sees the man's bare feet making their way down the ladder, and by the time she realizes he'll be facing her when he gets to the ground floor, he's already made his way down, but his head is turned toward the door and she's safe. Her heart is pounding hard enough that she briefly wonders if this is what will kill her—a heart attack brought on by this stupid dirty drug addict and this stupid concert that she warned everyone about. And wouldn't that show them all! Wouldn't they all be sorry! Then she realizes that the barn door has shut and there's still light, and they must have a flashlight with them. She presses against a tall dresser and hears them making their way up the ladder. The girl says, "I can't see anything," and she giggles, and the man says, "How did you find me?" and then the girl says, "I followed," in a low whisper that has a grin behind it, like she's real proud of herself, and Rita thinks the girl must be a moron because it's clear even to her hiding in the dark that the man named Kennedy isn't happy about her appearance.

"Oh," he says, and he sounds so put out that Rita snorts without being able to stop herself.

The steps on the ladder pause.

"Did you hear something?" asks the man.

"No," says the girl, who has reached the top; Rita can hear her moving around up there.

So he keeps climbing the ladder.

"Look at all this stuff!" says the girl.

"Some kind of furniture freak lives here," says the man. "This here is his stash."

Rita feels a twinge of irritation at hearing the man call Howard a freak, even though she might have said similar things herself in moments of anger.

Then the girl says, "And this here is my stash!"

"What?" he says, and his irritation seems to be rising.

"I thought you might want to get high," she says.

He sighs then, sounding resigned about her being there with him, and says, "What's your name again?"

"Maggie," she says, sounding hurt, like maybe she already gave him everything he asked for and now he can't even bother to remember what to call her. Rita clamps a hand over her mouth to keep herself from giggling or snorting again in her flighty state of nerves.

"Well, Maggie, I don't know what you know about me but I don't get high anymore."

"Oh," says Maggie. She sounds as disappointed as a child who missed a birthday party.

"But you go ahead if you want," he says. "Just don't burn the place down."

Rita's glad he says this, because she was just thinking the same thing. And if the barn caught fire, the house would take about a minute and a half to light.

The girl called Maggie makes a satisfied sound and Rita imagines her getting down to work heating some drug in a spoon like that Richard Pryor who set his face on fire, though she never quite understood how, or rolling up thousand-dollar bills to snort something, like the people in that movie about the stock market. But then she smells sweet smoke and knows it's marijuana they have up there, and her panic wanes as she remembers what it was like to be nineteen years old and going out in Howard's friend Michael's car, because Michael used to smoke marijuana—though Howard and Rita never did, they never would have—but still, it makes her smile to remember being nineteen and so pretty and round and smooth, and so excited to be in the presence of something wicked.

"So how come you're up here in this barn?" asks Maggie. She is sucking in air while she talks, same as Michael used to, and she doesn't know she's not wanted in the loft by the man named Kennedy. She's a clueless dirty drug addict.

"It can be hard to get a little peace," says that Kennedy person.

"Peace like what?"

Rita was wondering the same thing.

"Peace," he says, "from the traffic."

"Traffic? There's no traffic in this little shithole town."

Again, Rita is irritated. She does not like the girl named Maggie and she hopes the little tramp gets her butt kicked out of the loft.

"Traffic as in noise," he says. "The noise of being Kennedy Jackson." His voice sounds like it's coming out through a smile now, like maybe he's forgiving her for being so stupid about not understanding he didn't want her to follow him.

"What kind of noise is that?" asks Maggie. And Rita's glad, because she wants to know, too.

"It's the noise of being wanted," he says now. "The noise of fans and friends. I have so many friends these days, more than you'd want in a lifetime."

"I still don't get it," says Maggie.

He whispers now. "Following me, that made noise. You see?"

She must be shaking her head, because it's quiet and Rita senses in the silence his out-and-out misery.

"It's the noise that comes with being famous," he says.

It's at this point that Rita figures it out. Where she's heard the name before. Who he is. The lead singer of the band that's drawing hundreds of thousands of drug addicts to Resolute is in her barn.

The girl named Maggie is quiet at last, and Kennedy Jackson sighs heavy-like.

"Why don't you put that thing away and come over here?" he says.

There's rustling, and then Rita hears Maggie laughing a lot and more rustling.

She knows what's happening now. And while she's curious to stay and listen, she thinks the temperature and the old cow smell and the excitement of having a famous rock star in her barn might just make her pass out, and she wonders if this would be a good time to leave, while they're busy groping each other. The music is still going, and she decides that between that and their groping, she'll be able to sneak out. So she takes three steps back into the main passage, and she's about to tiptoe toward the door, where she'll feel safer to shout them both out, when the girl named Maggie says, "Hey!"

Rita looks up and sees nothing—only the beam of the flashlight pointing right into her eyes. She turns to make her way out but now is blinded and sees only darkness again. She stumbles into a low table and trips forward into some other taller thing, and cries out in pain. Behind her she hears fast sliding steps on the ladder and in less than a second, the man has the back of her coat, so she wrestles out of it, rights herself, and runs down the passage in the dim beam of the flashlight, which the girl must be pointing down from the loft.

"Hey," she shouts again.

But Rita's at the door now, and she smashes it open and daylight has never felt so good or safe or beautiful, and she wheels around and shouts into the darkness behind her, "Get the hell out of my barn!"

Then she turns once more and hobbles to the house, cursing the pain in her shin and hoping they're not running after her, because they could surely outrun her, and what would she do if they caught her? Because while they're definitely two of those dirty concert drug addict sex maniacs, the fact that he's supposedly the most famous member of the band makes her think he wouldn't actually murder her, but who knows with these people? And she runs into her house and slams the door and wades through the hallway papers all the way to the kitchen in an attempt to get to the phone. She has to lean over the card table, where she's been piecing together her Blossoming Courtship 500-Piece Puzzle, and she manages to get hold of the phone and she dials—missing digits and having to start over twice—heart threatening to quit her all over again. Out the window she can see the girl running, running crazy fast—and the man, following slower, shoulders slumped and hands in his pockets. The girl named Maggie is thin and blonde and leggy, and she's wearing a shirt that shows five inches of tan back above her tight denim cut-offs. She turns her pretty face to glance over her shoulder to the house, eyes wild with fear—which is something anyway. But that means they'll be gone when anyone gets here, and will people believe her, that Kennedy Jackson was in her barn? That anyone at all from that concert was here, let alone the most famous person? Rita knows with painful certainty that they won't believe her—no one will—and she falls in a chair, not even brushing off the Hello Kitty! greeting card set that was on it, so the card box gets crushed under her bottom, and when he answers, she starts to cry and it takes what feels like a long time to make any sound at all.

"Howard?"

Guy Masters
August 2010

Everything is in place. The auditions are slated for six p.m. Kennedy Jackson will be there. Guy Masters makes himself say this out loud. "Kennedy Jackson will be there." Saying this does nothing to ease his anxiety. Jackson will stand in that same room with Guy and a handful of others, and vote about which kids should open for the band. Guy and Kennedy, casting votes as if they were equals. On his bike, Guy laughs harshly at this idea. Then he pats his breast pocket, checking that the note is still there. He doesn't want to think about the auditions. He doesn't want to think about shaking the man's hand, trying to grip it with anything like strength—that same large hand that plays all those chords for millions of fans— and speaking to him, pretending to be his equal. Most of all, he doesn't want to think about passing him the note.

The day is overcast and cool, not quite fifty-five degrees. On mornings like this, the mist around the top of Mount Witness is stunning and a little ominous. The trees are flush with summer; from this distance, the mountain is steeped in dark green, and the swirling clouds near the top hint at secrets. Feeling inspired, he decides he has enough time, turns his bicycle, and takes the long way to school.

As their music teacher, Guy helps high school students learn how to listen to music, read music, play music. He teaches them scales, dynamics, and harmony. He teaches them the circle of fifths, that visual representation of the interrelatedness of the major and minor keys. He conducts their band. Guy loves his kids. For him, it's probably as much about the kids as it is about the music. He knows that this should be good thing. In the life he leads, the actual life he ended up with, this is a good thing. But sometimes old fantasies of a different life keep him from seeing his achievements.

A few of his students show promise. Christine Humphrey plays piano beautifully. Guy teaches her every Saturday morning in her home, where she learns on a cockeyed Casio with too few keys and her mother hovers anxiously in the doorway, as though worried he'll do something improper. Christine is a memorizer. She learns a piece, gets it into her fingers, performs with something like emotion, and then forgets it and starts on something else. If you produce the sheet music she knew by heart three months ago, she'll have to start from scratch.

Louisa Shortsleeve is a whiz on the clarinet. She never misses a note, though her delivery is wooden and shows no real feel for the music. Louisa is a mathematician, a perfectionist. Not a musician.

Carter Akyn, though, he's a musician. The boy can play anything on the guitar. And it takes him about half a minute to figure out how to play it: fast or hot or sultry. He's a natural. Unfortunately, he's a natural who dropped out of school five months ago. Carter still plays guitar. Guy's heard him in the unfinished house he's been working on, just north of town. It's why Guy is biking to school that way. Because before Carter's work day starts, and on lunch breaks, and after work sometimes, Carter plays his guitar, looking out an unfinished window toward Mount Witness.

Thinking about Carter reminds Guy of the note in his pocket, and the task he'll face later. He does not want to fail, but he is afraid. Afraid of making a fool of himself, afraid of breaking rules. It has always been this way for Guy. It is why he has this very safe and pleasant life, and not the one he used to envision.

He pedals for ten minutes, then takes the old logging road out to the growing development called "Abnaki Forest," named for the two things it has displaced. He checks his watch as he coasts down the long, sweeping bend that brings him to the small ring of new houses. It's 7:15.

Guy stops, then quietly walks the bike into the circular dirt drive connecting the four houses. Carter's car is the only one here. Easy to spot, with its green body and junkyard-find white hood. Guy leans his bike against Carter's Honda, then walks around to the side of the second house on the loop.

He hears a ballad being played on an acoustic guitar. It's a song he has never heard—probably one of Carter's own. The notes nudge up with hope and longing, then fall into despair, changing keys with heartbreaking effect. This is not a happy song, but Guy is smiling.

Maybe Carter will make something of his music; it does seem to be his passion. But in this town, dropping out to get a job working construction seems to Guy a pretty fine way to stop showing promise. Without an education, Carter can't even become the local music teacher.

A car drives in, followed by another. Guy knows the drivers' faces, but not the names. The men are from nearby towns. As they unload materials and tools from the backs of pickup trucks, the music stops. Concerned he'll embarrass Carter if he realizes he's been listening, Guy walks back to his bike. He has a long day ahead of him, a lot to do before the auditions. His hand floats up to his shirt pocket again, fingers the note so that it crackles.

In a sense, the concert started in the waiting room of Guy's dentist's office, where he'd read an article in *The County Record* about bands who feature local kids as opening acts. He called the author of the piece to ask about the promoter who'd been quoted so widely. The journalist told him that the promoter was, in fact, now scouting Vermont towns on behalf of Perilous Between, one of the few successful bands to come out of the state in the last twenty years. Then—and this was uncharacteristic for Guy—he'd called that promoter. Mentioned Resolute would make an excellent concert site, if the opportunity arose. The promoter's assistant took his name, thanked him for his time, and hung up, leaving Guy to believe that would be the end of it.

He's pleased to have been the catalyst for the concert, but worried about being able to fulfill the role he's been given. Kennedy Jackson, widely known for helping musicians get a start, asked Guy to come up with a list of kids who could audition to open the concert. It's exactly like the article said. As the band tours from state to state, they give kids a chance. When they played in Poughkeepsie last year, over three hundred kids showed up to audition. Five of them got spots. But in Resolute, there aren't five kids good enough to be offered this kind of chance. Guy said this to the manager, who called him.

"One kid is great, but he dropped out of school this spring. And I know of a couple kids from Johnson that are pretty good; can I bring in kids from other towns?"

The manager was a busy woman who didn't sound like she cared one way or the other where he found musicians. She just wanted to hang up and tick him off her long list of things to do.

"I think that'll be fine," she said. "But not the boy who dropped out. We need to encourage kids to stay in school."

"The thing is," Guy said, "he's remarkably talented."

She didn't say anything.

"In fact, he's the only student I've ever had who showed this much promise."

"But he's a dropout, right?" she asked. Her voice was clipped and hurried. She just needed to know which box to check.

"He dropped out in the spring."

"So I'm going to have to say no."

That'll teach him, Guy thought.

Dozens of people are cramming into the gymnasium, where the auditions will take place. This, despite the fact that Guy tried to tell Principal L'Ecuyer that the gym has the worst acoustics of any space in the building. He watches as other teachers race around, trying to make people leave. Their shoes squeak on the slick wooden floor. Their voices bounce around, full of excitement and self-importance.

By the time they empty the gym of bystanders, Guy is sitting on the bleachers with nineteen students from Resolute, Johnson, Coventry, and Newport. Standing at the exits with their arms crossed and their shirt sleeves rolled back, a number of other teachers watch, intent and curious. In the center of the floor sit three people on folding chairs: the band's manager, whose name has turned out to be Holly Lockwood, though Guy keeps remembering only "Hollywood," and so does not address her directly; Martin L'Ecuyer, the school principal; and Kennedy Jackson himself. He slipped in just as the exits were secured, having been kept safely in the music room until then.

Guy wishes he weren't so impressed, seeing this man. There was a time when he'd have feigned disinterest. But at that time, Guy thought he himself might one day be touring on a big black bus, playing his own compositions all over America and Europe and Asia, often having to slip into dark back rooms to avoid fans. Now he is a balding, middle-aged man in a white-and-blue striped shirt from Sears.

Kennedy Jackson walks toward Guy and his students. He's a tall, strong man, with ropy arms that are usually exposed. Guy knows that, in concert, Kennedy Jackson wears leather vests that show off the workout he gets when he plays guitar. Today he's in faded jeans and an orange T-shirt with dark blue lines that spell out Perilous Between in a cloud shape. His long hair is pulled back in a ponytail and he wears a silver bracelet on one wrist. As he approaches, he puts out his hand for the inevitable handshake. There's a two-inch hole in the seam under the arm of the T-shirt. Guy wonders if Jackson knows about it. For a ridiculous second, he thinks of telling him.

"You're Mr. Masters?" asks Jackson.

"Guy, please," he says, accepting the handshake nervously. He grips, shakes, lets go. The handshake has gone all right. He wonders if it's bad form, the music teacher going by his first name at these auditions. He wonders also if he seems—overall, on first impression—as preposterous as he thinks he does.

"All right, Guy. I'm Kennedy."

Guy nods and smiles, hearing all his students say "duh," in a ghostly chorus inside his head.

"Teachers are vital," Jackson says. "Mine—the one who inspired me to play guitar and is sort of responsible for my success—was Mr. Anderson."

"Mine was Miss Wilt," says Guy before he can stop himself. And then he feels so stupid. He's not successful. It would be an insult to suggest she got him here. Or back here, really, because he grew up in this town.

He takes a deep breath and starts introducing the students who are seated behind him on the bleachers.

The auditions last almost three hours. By the time they finish, Guy knows which five students have been chosen, though they do not. He could have hand-picked them and saved everyone the trouble. He'd have chosen the same five. Not if Carter were here, though. If Carter Akyn had been allowed to try out, one of these kids wouldn't be getting good news tomorrow.

The students leave, and Jackson and the manager spend a little time conferring in their folding chairs. Excitedly rubbing his hands together, Principal L'Ecuyer looks on, uninvolved. From his seat on the bleachers, Guy tries to think of a way to talk to Jackson alone. He's irrationally terrified at this prospect, and is sweating through his shirt so badly, he wonders if the ink on the note will run. He stands shakily from the bleachers and walks to the small group in the middle of the gym.

"Mr. Jackson?"

"I thought we were doing the first name thing," Jackson says.

Guy laughs a brittle, artificial laugh. "Right." He nods. "Kennedy, I wonder if I could talk to you."

Jackson looks wary, and Guy knows right away that he thinks this will be about Guy's own music, his own great potential. He laughs the brittle laugh again and shakes his head. "It's not what you might think."

"What might he think?" asks Hollywood. Guy doesn't let himself look at her. She's the one who put the kibosh on Carter because of his status as a quitter. If Guy looks at her, he'll chicken out. He knows he will. At heart, he's a rule-follower and always has been. When a clerk hands him too much change, he returns it. He unplugs every appliance in the house if there's lightning. He parks legally, always uses turn signals, pulls over to receive cellphone calls. Now, hands in his pockets, he remains quiet, hoping something will change the tension that has built up. He thinks about how strange they must look, the four of them, clustered in the middle of this enormous space.

Finally, Jackson says, "Well, I've got to get going. Why don't you walk me out?"

Guy nods, feeling such relief that he'd be embarrassed if anyone knew.

They walk out of the gym and down a long, dark hallway, toward the back door of the school. Behind them, walking at a not-quite-respectful distance, L'Ecuyer and the woman don't even pretend they're not trying to listen.

"What's up?" Jackson asks finally, because Guy seems not to be speaking.

"How long are you in town?"

Jackson smiles uncertainly. "Leaving tonight. I've got meetings all—"

"Right, okay, sure. But for the concert. When do you come in?"

The man's smile fades, but he looks more confused than unhappy. Like he's trying to work out what Guy is getting at. "I'm not entirely sure. Other people organize the schedule. They just tell me where to be."

"I heard you'd be staying out at Darren Zucker's place," Guy says.

Jackson nods. "That's right. The Zucker farm. Nice family, letting us stay there."

Guy takes in a breath, licks his lips. "There's two ways to get out to that farm from here. The fast way is a straight shot on 105. But there's a back way, too. It takes you past some new homes being put up. They look out at the mountain."

Jackson shrugs. "Yeah?"

"If you go that way, and I've written it down for you. It's not hard, but …" He's feeling foolish again. This wasn't the way to go about the thing. "Anyhow, if you go that other way, you should stop. Sometimes, in one of those houses, there's a kid who plays guitar. You should stop, listen."

Jackson's eyes lose their concern and he smiles. "Your kid?"

In a way, yes, Guy thinks. *One of mine.* But he shakes his head. "I don't have children. It's not for me."

They stand, regarding each other silently. L'Ecuyer and the manager finally walk forward. She looks like she might say something, so Guy pulls the note from his shirt pocket. He decides not to think about the way his hand is shaking as he gives the paper to Jackson.

"I wrote the directions and drew a map. Go first thing in the morning, or after five at night."

Later, at home, Guy is exultant. He did the right thing. It wasn't easy, and he was worried, but he did it. He has a beer in one hand and a plate of leftover sauerkraut pork chops in the other, and he's walking toward the TV as if that might be the way to celebrate at the end of a very good day. But instead he veers off from the den, goes around the grandfather clock that actually did belong to his grandfather, and into the living room. He puts his dinner on the coffee table between the couches and collects his old guitar case from where it sits in the corner behind his mother's piano. Opening the case, he swipes at dust and a few cobwebs. Then he takes out the guitar. It's a beautiful thing: a Martin D-28, still in its original hard case, given to him by his parents on the day of his high school graduation.

He remembers leaving Resolute at the age of nineteen and taking a bus to New York. He found a job clearing tables in a busy bar near Broadway, and felt like he'd made a start. But after seven months, he'd had only four auditions, and had never heard another word about any of them. He'd been turned down by several agents, and had watched three friends get gigs with small bands. So he gave up. He took a bus home, placed his guitar in its case, and went to UVM for a teaching degree.

His is not a sad story and he knows it. He loves the kids, loves his job. Guy was right to credit Miss Wilt; she taught him how to be a good teacher.

He picks up his beer, takes a sip, replaces the bottle on the table. He turns the guitar in his hands, making mental notes about how he could restring it and polish it. So many great things were going to happen with this guitar. Maybe they'll happen for Carter. The thought makes him smile. Guy settles back into the deep, soft couch. He lets his guitar rest on his knee, and enjoys the weight of it there.

Lexie Quinn
August 2010

Lexie walked along the dirt road and a pebble made its way into her sandal and under the arch of her foot. She put up with it for a few steps, then stopped, remembering the princess and the pea, bent down, and whisked it out with a finger. At the side of the road, a rabbit bolted from a hiding place, seeming to think she'd bent over for a slingshot or a stick or a brick. Anything Lexie could wield might be a weapon to a rabbit. Standing up, she watched the strong legs propel him over some farmer's field, large white tail wagging up and down at her like a finger.

"Weapon to a rabbit," she said, thinking of her dad. She said it again twice more, fast, until the letters confused in her mouth and she sounded like Elmer Fudd. Not the way her dad could sound like him, though.

"Be werry werry quiet … I'm hunting wabbits!" He could do the voice just about perfect. Of course, now his girlfriend Angela tried to do it, too— the way she inserted herself into every moment, every family tradition—and couldn't. But Lexie's dad found that somehow charming, and he laughed anyway.

Lexie looked after the rabbit again, but it was gone. She wondered what the farmer was growing. The plants were short and round, evenly spaced balls echoing the rabbit's tail in neat rows on both sides of the road. Cabbages, she decided.

The car that offered her a ride ten minutes later was a little scary. There was a stern-faced woman driving and, next to her, a skinny younger man who stared with a crooked smile that made Lexie think of Sylvester the Cat staring at Tweetie Bird. She got in, just to be polite, but the smell in the car was very bad, strong like Febreze, and underlying that, a settled-in smell like over-cooked potatoes and milk gone bad and sweat left too long between folds of flesh. The skinny man stared at her boobs over the back of his seat the whole time she was in the car. She knew her fiancé, Keith, would be upset about this later, if she told him. He always told her to wear clothes that downplayed her figure. She'd gotten her mother's large chest and thin waist, and Keith said she needed to cover up so men wouldn't be tempted to bother her. Sometimes she wished Keith himself would look at her with playful lust. So far he only ever looked at her with a stern kind of protective love. But once they were married, that would change.

In the car, to try to make the man stop staring, she'd talked about Keith. How he'd gone to Vermont for work.

"This cousin of his got him a job up north, at the border. Not as a border guard, you need school for that, but he's a maintenance mechanic."

The woman grunted something, which Lexie didn't understand, and the man licked his lips, still staring at her boobs, so she crossed her arms and kept talking.

"I'm not sure what a maintenance mechanic does. He said that so far it just meant he was painting a hallway."

The man laughed at this—an unattractive adolescent-sounding guffaw—and Lexie felt offended.

"Working for the government means decent money and good benefits," she said to him. "We'll have medical, and we'll be able to use the gym."

"How come he ain't driving you, then?" asked the ogling boy-man. The woman slapped him, but the question was out now, so Lexie answered.

"Working for the government is pretty hard," she said. "They couldn't let him off to come get me." She didn't mention how he didn't have a car.

"I took a bus and a train as far as Stowe. From there, I had to hitch. No bus service to Resolute, the town where I'm meeting him."

The woman let out a long, bored sigh and pulled the car to the edge of the road.

"Well, we're not going nowhere near there," she said. "We live two miles up this road, here." She pointed to a rutted stone driveway disappearing up a hill into the woods.

"Okay. Well, thanks," Lexie said, wishing they'd let her out back at the turnoff from the main road. She'd have to backtrack from here probably a good mile before she found a stretch where another ride might come along.

As she reached for the door handle, the woman pushed a button and all the doors locked. Lexie felt a bolt of fear.

"I need some money for gas," the woman said. "Ten dollars seems fair."

"You only drove me a little ways," Lexie said, pressing her hand protectively over the little leather purse at her waist.

"Gas is expensive, and I ain't got money to be giving rides to strange girls just 'cause they make big eyes at my boy." She glanced at her son, then looked at Lexie again in the rear view mirror. " 'Sides, your boyfriend got that great government job, so you can afford it." She said this last part in a sarcastic mean voice.

Lexie handed over ten dollars just to be let out of the car. Ten dollars of only a hundred and forty: forty of her own, and a hundred that Keith had sent to help her make the trip.

She started walking again.

She could feel the crackle of paper in her jacket pocket, where she'd put the letter. She'd mail it in a few days. Then her dad wouldn't have to worry about her, but he wouldn't have time to come here and haul her back home before the concert.

Dear You:

I'm meeting Keith and we're getting married. I love him and he loves me. I know you don't like him. But he's good to me and that's important. Mom was never good to you. I watched her tromp all over you when I was little before she finally up and left you to take care of me and Greta all by yourself. Keith would never do that. Even with Greta being the way she is he would stay by me. I'm hoping you can understand, now that you've found someone who's like that too. Good to Greta. (Angela, I mean.)

I'm on my way to Vermont for that Perilous Between concert you forbid me from coming to. Forbade me to come to? Don't know. I hate English, I swear. Really glad high school is over. As soon as I get home, I'm getting a job where I don't need to write anything at all. Anyway, I know you didn't want me coming here because Vermont is where Keith is and we'll see each other. You were right about how I'm not even a big fan of the band. The truth is, they're fine and all but I don't really know their music. But they're Keith's favorite and I'm planning to be the kind of wife who takes on what her husband likes. Sort of how you've taken on macramé for Angela, and she's going bowling now for you.

I'm meeting Keith on Wednesday and we're getting married here at the concert. I had the idea after I heard a girl at the mall asking her mom if she'd let her go with friends to see Perilous Between. They were sitting next to me in the food court, eating lunch. This girl and her mom reminded me of me and you, sort of, because they seemed close, like friends, even though they're mother and daughter. The girl kept asking in this high, pleading voice, could her mom please, please let her go to Vermont!? And her mom started laughing and said she'd see, and to stop pestering her and eat her lunch! It seemed like fate, me hearing that conversation. And it felt like a sign that you'd forgive me if I decided to come here. Because I know you love me and you won't be mad forever.

Me and Keith will come back home after some time together. I want to be with him for a little while, feel like a married wife, maybe get a job somewhere and make some money. That would be good, wouldn't it? You're smiling now, I bet. Anyways, then we'll come back home and help you and Angela with Greta and we'll be like a really big family. I know it's hard. Harder without me there to help. I'm sorry about that. But I'm going to have my life. You'd want me to. You'd want me to be happy and have my life if I'm going to stay in that sad little town with all those fake people who can't be bothered to look our way when I walk down the street holding Greta's hand.

Anyway, you have Angela now. So that'll help.

That's about it. I love you. And you still love me. Even if you're mad, I know you still love me. But don't be mad.

Love, Me

"You" and "me" were what she and her dad always called each other in notes.

Dear You,
Buy Milk
Love, Me

Dear You,
Be home by 12 and NO LATER!!
Love, Me

Her letter was straightforward. He'd want that. He'd respect that. "Be frank with me, Lexie," he'd always said to her. "Give me the up-front." And that's what this letter was: the up-front. Or mostly. She didn't say she was in a hurry to get married so she could finally have sex with Keith, because that would sound really stupid and young—not something a mature person would say before making a big decision. And she wasn't exactly up front about how in love she was with Keith. It was hard to know how much you'd love a man before giving yourself to him. That would come, though, soon enough. In the meantime, Keith loved her. He was kind and smart and handsome. He wanted to marry her and support her and take care of her. And he was kind to Greta, Lexie's "Irish twin," as her nana used to say.

Lexie's dad and Keith had never gotten along much. Not after that first little while. They'd liked each other well enough for a month or so. Keith was kind to Greta, never uncomfortable or unsure. He'd jump right in and finger-paint with her or dance. Keith would jiggle around playing the goofball, just for Greta, and Lexie's dad had liked that. Here was this sixteen-year-old woman with Down's Syndrome, sewing yarn into farm animal cards, making pictures like a three-year-old, and Keith just plunked down and asked her to pass the cow, please.

But when her father found out Keith had failed out of school four years ago, at sixteen, and had been charged with possession at seventeen, Lexie's dad had stopped liking him. Never mind that Keith didn't have a drug problem anymore. He'd gotten straight before she met him, and now he was a really serious guy: hard-working, and super into his new weird church with all its rules about don't eat this and don't dance like that. (The rules actually kind of bothered Lexie, but she didn't say so.) Keith was straight-edge, and she had to accept that. So straight that they hadn't even had sex yet. She wanted to, but he said they should wait. How many men were willing to wait? Wasn't this another sign that he loved her and was looking out for her?

Not a lot of cars came by, and the ones that did whizzed past, probably not even noticing her outstretched thumb. Lexie was bored. When she was little and feeling bored, her nana used to say, "Can't dance and it's too wet to plow!" Lexie had never understood this, but it had made her laugh. Her nana also used to say, "You made the bed, now take your medicine," and "Who's a rascal?"

She missed her nana, who'd moved in to help after Lexie's mother left, but died five years ago. She also missed Greta something terrible, and hoped her sister would forgive her for leaving without saying goodbye, the same way their mother had left them.

Greta had Angela now, so that was something. And anyway, Lexie would be home soon, a ring on her finger and Keith by her side. Greta loved Keith enough to forgive anything. Lexie just hoped that she herself would come to love Keith as much as Greta did.

Now she was almost back at the road they'd turned off from. She breathed the fresh air deeply, trying not to worry about money and feeling lucky to be out of that car.

She heard the sound of something big coming along the road at the inter-section up ahead, so she started to run in case it might be someone who'd give her a ride. It sounded like they were coming from the right direction, heading north. She needed to go north.

It was a bus. Like the one she'd taken from one train station to the other in Boston, but much more stylish. Where that one had been white with ugly green trim, this one was purple with silver feathers painted all along the sides. It looked like a really nice tour bus, and she almost didn't stick out her thumb, because tours would have policies about hitchhikers. But at the last minute, she made a half-hearted gesture, just in case. And though the bus swept right on by her, it did slow after a second and pull to the shoulder. Lexie bent low over her knees, breathing heavy. She stood up and started walking then, one hand pressing against the cramp in her side, her big yellow-and-white striped duffle bag slung over the other shoulder. As she approached the bus from the back, a door whooshed open at the front and a man stepped out. He was very handsome, with long black hair and large, muscular arms. He wore a leather vest and looked familiar. He held on to the top of the door that had opened, and Lexie stopped walking at the sight of him.

"You need a ride?" he asked. His voice was whisper soft and deep.

"Yes, please," she said.

"We're going north. You headed north?"

She nodded.

"Well, come on in." He motioned for her to step up. She did, and had to duck under his arm to enter the bus. "I'm Kennedy," he said.

"Lexie," she said, just to be polite. But her mind was churning and she was trying to decide if the name meant something important that she hadn't worked out yet.

Inside, the bus was cool and dark, like a cave. There were leather couches facing one another, and a desk set up with laptop computers. She realized, as her eyes adjusted to the dark, that there were a lot of people on the bus. Mostly men, but some women. Their voices were loud, but in a strange, murmuring way that seemed to gather and recede all around her like surf. This was not a normal tour bus. This was some sort of group. A group of very wealthy friends or something. She felt like she should understand what was happening, but she did not.

Feeling him at her back, Lexie moved out of Kennedy's way. He took his seat, which was in the middle of one of the black leather couches, totally surrounded by people.

"Sit anywhere you like, Lexie," he said quietly. She looked around; all the seats were full, so she started toward the back of the bus. By the time she passed him, Kennedy already had his eyes closed, and an angel-faced girl next to him had her head on his shoulder. Another man was talking in low tones to two others on the couch across from him. They seemed to be discussing something important. Because, although they paused, none of them looked up as she walked through the middle of their conversation. The man who was talking was using his hands to show something to the other two. She heard the words *scaffolding* and *crazy at that height*, and another man said something about chains. A girl sitting alone on a smaller plush couch near the laptops smiled at her, so she almost sat there, but at the last minute realized there was a small, delicate-looking baby on the seat next to her. The baby was wrapped snug in a purple and blue blanket, and the girl held a tiny protruding foot in her hand.

"I'm Carrie," the girl said when Lexie paused. She nodded and smiled. "And this is Francis."

"He's sweet," Lexie said. The girl nodded, then looked out the window, so Lexie kept walking. She walked away from the leather couches, through the small kitchen area and into a passageway lined with bunk beds and hung with dark curtains, for privacy. No one was in bed. Incredibly, the bus kept stretching back away from her. Behind the sleeping area, she saw more leather couches and noticed a few open seats, so she walked back there, aware now of the deep, soft carpet under her feet and the bass-heavy music coming out of speakers in the walls. No one seemed especially curious about her, or why the bus had made such an abrupt stop.

At the rear of the bus, a man played darts. This section looked more like the real thing, with soft leather seats in rows and an aisle running down the center. Kneeling backward in his seat, he threw the darts over four empty rows into a dartboard firmly attached to the back wall. He aimed with troubling intensity, not glancing over to acknowledge her presence, his hand in constant motion as he felt out the next move, passing each dart slowly back and forth through the air several times before letting go. Worrying about his accuracy, Lexie sat across the aisle, behind a balding man with two silver hoops in one ear and a small patch of black beard centered under his bottom lip.

He twisted around and reached over the top of the seat to shake her hand. "I'm Benjamin. Sometimes Benji."

"Alexandra," she said, shaking his hand. "Usually Lexie."

The way he'd twisted around reminded her of the skinny man in the bad-smelling car. But Benji was smiling kindly and she didn't feel afraid. He wasn't staring at her boobs at all. He was making eye contact. Benji had blue polish on the thumbnail of his right hand and Lexie wondered if this meant anything significant, or if it was just his way.

"You a fan?"

"A fan?"

"Of the band."

Lexie's thoughts moved slowly forward as she understood at last why the bus looked the way it did and why the name Kennedy meant something to her.

"Oh my gosh, I'm so stupid," she said.

"You didn't know?"

She shook her head and beamed at Benji. "Are you guys Perilous Between? 'Cause if so, then yes, I am a fan. Or well, I like the music, but my boyfriend is a total freak for you guys."

"Not me," Benji said, putting the blue-thumbnailed hand to his chest in a gesture of denial. "I'm not in the band. I'm a technical consultant. Sort of like a roadie, but I get to ride on the bus, where they can keep an eye on me."

He laughed then, and the man with the darts glanced sideways and hissed, "Shut the fuck up, Benji. I'm trying to concentrate."

"This is Russell," said Benji, neither lowering his voice nor acting remotely insulted. "He's a drummer and an asshole. You want to stay away from Russell."

The other man tightened his jaw but did not look over again. He closed one eye and threw a dart with a red-feather tail. It landed in the center of the dartboard with a small *phop*. Lexie noticed then that all the darts had landed at the heart of the board. They crowded out one another around the bull's-eye. Russell cackled like the Joker in *Batman*, then leveled his gaze at Lexie and said, "Drummers always find the center."

His face relaxed then, and he seemed to notice her for the first time. Now when he looked at her, she felt a pleasant little smack of something in the pit of her stomach. He tucked three remaining darts into the breast pocket of his shirt—a grey and black plaid shirt with the arms ripped off—and swung himself toward her over the empty seat to his right like a monkey on a tree limb.

"What'd you say your name is?"

"Lexie."

"You have a boyfriend, I heard."

She nodded, thinking about saying how she and Keith were going to get married at the concert, but it was hard to say anything at all, the way this Russell was watching her. She remembered in high school reading *Les Misérables*, a book whose title she couldn't pronounce, and how a man was described as devouring a young woman with his eyes. She'd remembered that expression—he *devoured* her—and while she'd found the words kind of sexy but also strange in high school, now she knew what they meant. The way Russell looked at her made her feel naked. Naked as in sex, but not just that. Also as in meat. The way uncooked steak is naked, or liver. The way oysters shiver on crushed ice, their pale obscene insides exposed. She looked away, worried, because she felt a distinct attraction to him. It trembled inside her and quickly spread to touch the places Keith refused to go.

"So maybe not such a boyfriend, after all," Russell said softly. He reached over and ran his fingers lightly down the pale, smooth underside of her wrist. And then he was gone, across the aisle again, kneeling backward in the seat and pulling the last three darts from his pocket. She shuddered. When her nana used to shudder, she'd say, *Someone's dancing on my grave,* pulling her cardigan tighter around her shoulders.

"Fucking weirdo," Benji whispered, and Lexie smiled nervously.

She scooted over one seat to look out the charcoal-tinted window.

An hour later, the bus driver announced they were almost to Resolute. The three men who'd been talking about scaffolding and chains started shouting things about getting food, and practically everyone else called out in agreement. So the bus pulled into the parking lot of a trucking company and stayed there while various people unloaded and went next door to a local diner. Benji and Lexie moved up front, and he quietly pointed out who was who in the band, so she would know faces and names. She thought about going for food, but then stayed on the bus at the last minute. She was hungry, but she didn't have a lot of cash. If she pretended the ten dollars she'd lost that morning had been spent on breakfast, she'd come out even and she'd feel better. She took a spot up front, on the smaller couch, because no one was in the back anymore.

Benji went into the diner, asking three times if she was sure she didn't want anything. The members of the band gave their food orders to Benji and another guy. Everyone wanted pancakes. They all wanted bacon, too, except Kennedy, who was a vegetarian. Russell wanted both bacon and ham.

The mood on the bus changed with half the people missing. The driver turned off the music so Kennedy and one of the scaffolding guys could have a meeting up front. The other band members went to lie in their bunks. The girl named Carrie and baby Francis were both asleep. Lexie thought about trying to sleep. She tilted her head back and closed her eyes. But instead of drifting off, her thoughts returned to home. How home had changed, and was changing again. It used to be a place for her family: Mom, Dad, Greta, Lexie. Then her mom left and it was a place for just Dad, Nana, Greta and Lexie. That had been nice, for a while. Now it was a place for Dad, Angela, and Greta. Maybe Lexie would have a place there again someday. She wasn't sure, and this made her enormously sad.

Her father sometimes had a hard time handling Greta out in public on his own. It was how he'd met Angela. He and Greta had been in the market for some butter and sugar and chocolate chips, to make Tollhouse Cookies, which were Greta's favorite. She was allergic to nuts, though, so they never had nuts.

"No nuts, Dad! I can't have nuts, you know."

Anyway, her dad told Lexie they'd been standing together in line to pay, and then Greta wasn't there. It was hard for Lexie to understand this; Greta wasn't exactly quick. But her father swore he'd turned around, and she'd been gone. He'd had to leave his grocery cart at the checkout and start searching the store. He'd called up and down each aisle, "Greta? Margaret, where are you?" And then he came upon her in the ice cream section, pointing out her favorite—chocolate chip cookie dough—to a "pretty young woman in a blue dress." That's how Lexie's dad had described Angela to her later: a pretty young woman in a blue dress. Which was probably more or less accurate. She wasn't young, but she was in her forties, and he was in his fifties, so she was young to him. Pretty? Maybe. But with lines around her mouth and hair she had to dye black "every five minutes" to control the steely gray that she said had appeared in her thirties. As for the blue dress, Lexie had never seen it.

Angela was a loud-mouthed, confident, fast talker with a Boston accent.

A woman who talked so much that, if she had just taken a bite of bread or meat or vegetable, she would poke the food into her cheek with her tongue in order to tell a story. She actually did this a lot, and thinking about that ball of hot, wet, chewed food always made Lexie lose her appetite.

At first Lexie had liked Angela. It was nice to have another woman around. And despite the fact that she grew to resent her, she had to admit to herself that this was not an unkind or spiteful person. Lexie's dad had fallen hard for Angela, and she for him. When she moved into their house after only two months, Lexie had a hard time with it. Hard to watch the three of them becoming some kind of family without Lexie. By this point, her father had told her to break up with Keith, and she and her dad fought all the time, so that she herself could no longer find the place at home where she fit.

Angela had taken to sitting on the other side of Greta. And when Greta was upset, it was Angela's hand she reached for. Angela could calm her in a way that only Lexie used to.

The door opened with a rasp and a bang, and a breeze sifted through the bus, which felt nice. Lexie stretched and opened her eyes, and then she jumped, because someone was there, and she hadn't noticed him taking the seat beside her: Russell.

"I could feel that you were awake," he said. He was touching her knee very lightly, and she felt it on her skin, but also deep inside.

"You could?"

"Can I ask you something?"

She was tempted to say, *You just did.* It's what her father would have said. But somehow that didn't feel like the right reply, with Russell. So she just looked at him and waited.

"Do you feel it?" he passed a hand back and forth in the air between them. His hand was large, with a number of hard-looking calluses. She remembered that Benji had said he was the drummer.

"Feel it?" she repeated.

"There's an electricity running between us. Don't you think?"

She looked at his hand. She didn't really believe that he meant this, but the pleasant nausea she felt in his presence could have been electricity running between them. She wasn't sure. She'd never felt anything like it before.

"Maybe."

Standing up, he blew out slowly and shook his head. "I sure do." He bent over and cupped her face in a palm. She could feel the calluses now, hard bumps like stones against her cheek. "I'll see you in a little while. Don't go anywhere."

Lexie nodded. He walked down the aisle and disappeared behind a curtain, into his bunk.

Outside, a few people had left the diner to come over and look at the bus. The driver closed the door again with another rasp and bang. People stood back from the bus like it was radioactive, but they seemed to be studying it— *Casing the joint*, Nana would have said—trying to figure out how to see inside the dark windows.

One girl was talking to the security guy who'd climbed down from the bus to keep people off. She was showing him a ring on her hand, and frowning. She reminded Lexie of a lost child. The security guy was shaking his head. She looked at her own hand again, at the ring.

Up front, a few people were narrating the scene, doing it wrong for laughs.

"Sorry, miss, but we don't know where you left your virginity," said one of the men from the scaffolding conversation.

"But officer," said another, his voice pitched high and shaky, "I'm sure I left it right here."

People laughed, but then Kennedy got up and swung around, not smiling. He stalked back to the bunks and pulled open a curtain.

"Deal with your woman," he said.

Russell came out of his bunk, looking tired, but angry, too.

For a second, Lexie thought Kennedy must have meant her when he said "your woman," because he glanced at her. But Russell didn't seem confused in this way.

He just said, "My WO-man?" imitating how Kennedy Jackson had pronounced it. "You want me to deal with my WO-man?"

Outside, the girl was turning away from the security guy. Her head was low on her shoulders, and Lexie could feel how disappointed she was about something. Benji and the others came out of the diner just then, holding

Styrofoam containers and steaming coffee cups in cardboard holders. Benji, who'd been yawning, stopped when he saw the girl. He turned his yawn into a grin and said something to her.

"Fucking Benji," Russell said, shaking his head.

"You need to talk to her," said Kennedy Jackson.

"Why?"

"You have no moral compass, you know that?"

"Yeah, yeah," said Russell.

Benji was stepping up onto the bus now, followed by several others who'd gone into the diner for food.

"Did you see Jeannie out there?" he asked, smiling wide.

Russell flipped his middle finger but otherwise ignored Benji. He was kneeling again, this time on a seat up front. He popped one of the emergency windows over the shouted protests of the driver, then called out over the security guard, "What the hell?" He said, "Jean Marie, when did you get here?"

"Week ago." She grinned, lowering her gaze and kicking at the pebbles in the parking lot.

"Well, you coming in or what?" Russell said.

Lexie found herself fighting down disappointment, hoping the girl wouldn't get on the bus. Outside, she was saying something else to him.

"Work?" Russell said, chuckling. "Since when?"

After a second, he said, "But you're just gonna quit next week, Jean Marie. We're on the road."

Lexie watched the girl's smiling mouth form words, but didn't try to understand. She thought about Keith and wondered why she'd never felt about him the way she suddenly seemed to feel about this man, a stranger, and not a very nice one.

Now Russell was saying, "Meet me later?"

The girl said something, then swung around because, behind her, other girls were flowing out of the diner, shouting. Lexie could hear them. "Russell! Oh, My God, Russell!"

The girl faced the bus again. Russell was pulling back through the window.

"Dave'll tell you," he shouted, pointing at the security guy. "Give her the lowdown, Dave."

He tried to latch the window again, but couldn't get it, and he shrugged in the direction of the bus driver. "Sorry there, Clarence."

The bus started up and began to inch out of the parking lot, not hitting anyone, but definitely not stopping either. People stumbled backward to avoid getting in its way, and soon they were back on the road.

The driver was muttering loudly to Benji over his shoulder about "those windows" and something to do with a "readiness checklist."

Kennedy looked at Russell and shook his head. "Very classy," he said.

"Everything's under control," Russell said, smiling. He walked to Lexie's seat and plopped next to her.

"Was that your girlfriend?" she asked.

"Used to be," he said, shaking his head. "It's kind of a sad story, actually," he whispered.

To her immense pleasure, he took her hand, put his head on her shoulder and closed his eyes. She knew she should push him off, knew that even this small sin was unfair to Keith, but she found that she didn't want to. Benji glanced disbelievingly from where he stood at the front of the bus, talking to the driver. But when he walked by a minute later, on his way back to the back seats, he didn't make eye contact.

As the bus rumbled from one dirt road onto another, Russell ran his callused thumb over Lexie's palm and she found herself going all soft, as if she were melting into the seat. She told herself it was just a few days until she and Keith would be married, and then he would touch her this way. But something inside felt different with Russell. Keith would want to make love. Even when they finally married, Keith would never want to show her any rougher side of himself. Their love would be sweet and slow and beautiful, like harps playing. Not passionate or exciting. With Russell it would be drums, pounding and thrashing like an angry heart that can never stop, no matter how desperately it wants to.

The bus pulled up at an old farmhouse with a garage that was attached by a walkway with a sagging roof. Russell stirred in his seat, then stood and helped Lexie up. He carried her duffle bag off of the bus, then slung it possessively over his shoulder.

"Do you know where we go?" she asked him uncertainly.

"Upstairs," he said, with a tilt-a-whirl kind of smile. "Always upstairs."

He leaned down to kiss her then, hard and deep and slow, and she closed her eyes to the bus and Benji and Kennedy and the other members of the band and their friends. Russell caressed her wrist and slid his hand along her arm, and under her blouse. He slid two fingers into the edge of her bra and caressed the curve of her breast. She kept her eyes shut to the world, and the world went away.

Zedekiah
August 2010

In life, the animal had been a rabbit, but it was not a rabbit now. Gently, Zedekiah shoveled it from the gravel at the side of the road and slipped its limp corpse into the first plastic bag, which was blue. He said a prayer for the animal, knowing even as he did so that it had no soul, and the prayer was simply a gesture. At the back of the truck, he knotted the top of the bag, then pulled the second one, which was white, from the truck bed. He put the blue bag into the white one, the way they wanted him to, and knotted that. From the outside, all these bags looked the same: white over blue over a soft lump that bled red or purple. Zedekiah tried to remember that each of these, even the most horrible, had once been a creature of God. And that made the job easier.

At the Resolute Town Garage, where he picked up the truck every morning, the manager had nicknamed him "Earth Zed," and Zedekiah liked that. At the garage, they didn't know anything about his past or the Community. They only knew who he had become six months ago, when he'd moved here from Island Pond: a thirty-one-year-old man living alone in a cabin off the grid. Leaving his home required a half-mile trek through thick woods to a dirt road which led another mile to a paved road which led in one direction to Island Pond, in the other, to Resolute. Or, as Zedekiah thought of it, in one direction to his past, in the other, to his present. His future was out there too, but he wasn't sure where.

A few farmhouses were accessible on foot. Their pebbled access roads meandered through these woods, but Zedekiah had never felt comfortable to walk along private property to more easily reach the cabin. And so his was a solitary life deep in the woods, full of long walks and plenty of time for prayer and contemplation.

He placed the rabbit's shrouded corpse into the back of his truck, next to the raccoon that had been in the middle of Parson Road and the mass of feathers he'd bagged out on 5A. Usually people didn't report birds; he'd come across this one on his own. He started up the truck, then sat a little while, deciding whether or not to put on the radio. In the end, he left it off, because it wasn't company, the way music should be. When he thought about the Community, what he really missed was the companionship. His former life had been full of people and activity: singing and dancing, prayer services, sharing meals, talking about Yahshua. He missed the Community, but he'd found he could not stay there without Casiphia. And he could not stay there and pretend to be someone he no longer seemed to be. Sighing, he put the truck in gear and drove back to work in silence.

At the Town Garage, as he unloaded the light, bagged bodies into a small cart, the manager, Niko, waved to him from where he stood smoking outside the office door. He wore a soiled and sweat-soaked uniform with a name patch on the breast pocket that read, "Nicholas."

"Earth Zed," he shouted, waving the cigarette through the air in a torpid gesture meant mainly to convey exhaustion and dissatisfaction. Niko did not like his job. He said so often, and his every movement was designed to reinforce that message.

"Got a call about a deer."

Deer were heavy and awkward, all limbs. Two people went on deer calls, and as Zedekiah was working alone today, Niko would have to help him. Niko's face—the squinted eyes, the pushed-out lips, the thin stream of smoke blown out the side of his mouth—expressed an intense dislike of the task before them. Zedekiah nodded, to indicate he'd heard, then pushed the cart to the small building in back of the garage where they incinerated the animals every other day.

After he'd returned the cart, he went into the garage to find Niko, who had finished his cigarette and returned to his desk. The Town Garage was very old and hadn't been painted in a long time. Thin streaks of red on the wood let you know what its color had been, years ago. Inside, the floorboards were worn and wide-spaced. The building smelled of dust and oil and the camphor gel that Billy Birk rubbed on his hands when his eczema flared up. Billy was off today. He'd be hunting coyote up in Warren's Gore.

Niko sat at his desk, a rolltop with a short leg that had been lengthened by a diaper wipe box, into which he'd poured excess concrete from a sidewalk repair job. Papers fluttered freely around the desk when anyone came into the building, but Niko never seemed to be straightening them. At work, he was in a near-constant quest for handwritten notes on minute slips of paper.

"We need to head out 105," Niko said, not looking up as Zedekiah approached. "Lady who called it in said it was off the road, like it had been thrown. She says it's past the Smiley Farm on the right."

In his second or third week on the job, Zedekiah had figured out that when Niko said, "the Smiley Farm," he meant the Community. Also, when he said, "those cult whackos," or "Jonestown, Vermont." He wondered what Niko would think if he knew that Zedekiah had lived at "the Smiley Farm" all his life. That he'd never known any existence but the Community until four months ago. Probably Niko would ask the same two questions everyone else always asked. *Did they keep you there against your will?* And, *Were you one of the children who the state police took?* The answer to the first question was *No.* The answer to the second, *Yes.*

"Where the hell is that piece of paper?" Niko lifted a tea-stained mug, then a metal box, then an old phone that didn't work. "Too much crap in here," he muttered. Then he said, "Here it is," and picked up what looked like a corner of newsprint torn from the *Buyers Guide* or the *News & Citizen,* covered in his small, square writing. He held it out to Zedekiah between his index and middle fingers, like one more cigarette.

"You drive," Niko said as they walked to the truck. Upon hiring him, Niko had just assumed that Zedekiah had a driver's license. In fact, this was not true. In the Community, Zedekiah had driven from the age of twelve. He'd learned from his father, then had driven loops around the compound for a year before starting to help deliver furniture to the outside world. He was a good driver. He started every round trip with a prayer. Back in the Community, this had been a public prayer in the presence of any passengers and, usually, clasping a hand with his front seatmate. Now, in the company of strangers, it was a private, quick muttering under his breath or even just inside his head. He never skipped the prayer, though. Partly this had to do with habit, and partly with a hope that his faith would come back if he kept acting as if it hadn't left.

Now, as Niko waited for him to start the truck, he bent over and pretended to tie his left shoe, whispering silently into his knee, "Thank you for this opportunity, Yahshua. Please help me to drive well and return myself and my passenger safely." He cleared his throat before sitting up, then shook his head to toss back the hair that always fell into his eyes.

"All right there, Earth Zed?" asked Niko, smiling as if he knew a secret.

And Zedekiah said he was fine.

They drove northwest, and he wondered, as he always did when he neared Island Pond, if he'd see anyone he knew. So far, he hadn't. His brothers and sisters didn't leave the Community much. In fact, other than the time that they had both been taken away—along with all the children—Casiphia had never left at all.

"So how's the cabin working out?"

"It's fine. I feel lucky to have it."

"Last fellow who had your job wasn't real big on the outhouse once it got cold." Niko snorted a mean little laugh. "'Course, you moved in there in February, so you know all about that."

"I didn't mind. I found it a matter of preparing myself and dressing right, mainly."

"Preparing yourself," Niko said, smiling. "What's that like? You lined up your *People Magazine* and flashlight ahead of time, did you?" He took his cigarettes out of his breast pocket, shook them until one popped out the top, then grabbed it between his teeth. "You mind?"

Zedekiah shook his head. He did mind, actually, but not in the way Niko meant. He imagined how it would go, trying to explain that Niko would be stronger for denying himself this addiction. He would actually feel better if he quit smoking. Just as it felt better to Zedekiah to use the outhouse in winter, to deny himself comfort in the interest of becoming stronger. In the Community, conversations about self-discipline had gone on everywhere, all the time. Brothers and sisters would help each other to be cleaner, stronger, free of addiction and idle habits. But out here, people did not like being told what they could do better.

"You don't mind being all alone in them woods at night?" Niko asked. "You don't find it too far out?"

Zedekiah shook his head, then ran his fingers back through his bangs, resituating them.

"I haven't had any problems," he answered. Although in fact, he did get frightened in the cabin at night. It was a point of some embarrassment for him, but nothing he could control. He'd always lived with people; now he lived alone. And in the absence of what had once been an unyielding faith in God's protection and love, he could find no solace from strange noises outside at night. In the first week, he'd hardly slept at all. Prayer no longer helped, though he kept trying. What did help a bit was to isolate the sounds and identify them for himself—*that's an owl, that's a mouse, that's a squirrel on the roof.* When he did this consistently, his fears lessened. Occasionally, he'd see people in the woods—nearby neighbors, hunters, campers. They pretty much kept to themselves.

If he did have any problems, he'd use the shotgun. He was not adverse to defending himself. The Bible was very clear on this point: "If a thief is caught breaking in and is struck so that he dies, the defender is not guilty of bloodshed."

When they got to the place, he drove slowly, looking right and left, even though the message had said the deer would be on the right. Sometimes people got it wrong.

"There she blows," said Niko, flicking the half-burned cigarette out the window in the direction of a small tawny deer in the grass. "No antlers. That's a plus."

Zedekiah pulled over and parked.

As he got out, Niko said, "You wear them gloves, Earth Zed. Got that?"

Zedekiah nodded. Niko knew he did not like wearing the gloves. They were supposed to protect him from diseases the animals might have carried. But mostly they reminded him of the ambulance workers—how they had snapped on tight, powdery latex gloves before they'd taken Casiphia away. He had never understood that.

They opened the tailgate. Zedekiah unfolded one of the large white tarps and laid it out across the truck bed. Then he removed a plastic tub, dug out a scoop of quicklime, and set it on the ground. After they moved the animal, he'd sprinkle the lime in the grass where she'd been. All around them, insects filled the air with noise, a mass of sound in which no one song was distinct. The deer was a young doe. Flies buzzed around her torso, where the car had hit her, tearing a gash in her side. The blood was black now, the gash dry. From the neck up, she was as pretty as a living deer—gentle and vulnerable, her large, bottomless eyes rimmed with dark markings. Zedekiah thought this might be what an angel would look like, placid and delicate, waiting to be of help. And not for the first time, he hoped that the angels had been there for Casiphia when her time had come.

They put on their worn leather gloves. With a groan, Niko bent down to take the back feet. He waited, doubled over, holding the small cloven hooves, while Zedekiah moved around to the head. Her eyes were open, forever watching. He closed his own as he lifted and said a silent prayer for her.

The cabin in the woods had come with the job, in place of other benefits which, being a town employee, Zedekiah should have had. But Niko owned the cabin outright, and his budget at the garage was whistle-thin.

"You take a place to live, I put your health plan into a new bathroom for the office. Complete with shower. Huh? That way, you have a free place to stay and a shower every afternoon."

This was a selling point, as the cabin had no running water, no electricity. Nodding, Zedekiah had agreed to what Niko wanted. He didn't mind about the health insurance, being a strong and hearty young man, having always been a healthy child. Not like Casiphia, who had fallen ill with every cold or virus that passed through the Community. She was a delicate thing, pale and thin, with translucent fingernails that went nearly blue in the winter. She was allergic to everything from bee stings to tomatoes, and she'd had to carry an inhaler for asthma. When she'd been pregnant with their first child, she and Zedekiah had visited the doctor twice a month, whenever he came to the Community. It had done no good, though. She'd lost that child, a girl, in the fourth month, and the second, a boy, in the fifth. Nothing to be done about it, the doctor had said. She couldn't keep a pregnancy on her own.

That evening, as sunlight faded through the snarl of leaves and branches surrounding the cabin, Zedekiah gathered wood for a fire. Even in summer, nighttime was still cool enough for a fire to be a welcome thing, particularly in a dark cabin so deep in the woods. Normally, he didn't mind being alone. On the contrary, solitude was the closest thing he'd found to familiarity since leaving his own world, settling into this other. Although the Community had been full of music and conversation, prayer and love, there had been pleasant stretches of solitary time when they worked. Zedekiah had taken on his father's trade—making furniture—which they sold in specialty stores in Burlington and Montreal and Boston. He'd liked the work, which required strength and skill, preparation and an eye for detail. He'd passed many a private hour planing lumber, ripping straight edges, sanding the wide arms of a chair until they gleamed and felt like silk to the touch. His had not been one of the social jobs—the cooks, the plumbers, the electricians—and now he was glad for that training in isolation. He didn't mind being alone. It was the depth of the dark woods at night that gave him pause.

By sundown he had a good fire going and dinner cooking above it in the old black pot he'd found at a yard sale in Resolute. Over the fire, the pot swung from a pivoting metal arm he'd devised himself. Every night, a different mixture: beans, chicken stew, seared beef. Tonight he had a fish soup in the pot—sole with potatoes and carrots and peas and butter. Zedekiah would sit on the edge of the cushion in Niko's brown corduroy armchair and check his meal every ten minutes or so. He didn't know much about cooking beyond what Casiphia had taught him. But he knew enough to put a little salt and pepper and a lot of vegetables into whatever he cooked, and to pivot the pot out of the fire and add a little water if his dinner smelled like it was burning. That had been enough to keep him fed.

Before he ate, he knelt on the hard, wooden floor and clasped his hands in front of him. "My Lord, you have given me another meal and another day of life. Thank you for this providence and please help me to continue to serve you as best I can."

From outside the cabin, he heard something that might have been the snap of a branch. This was not unusual. The night was full of bumps and creaks and gusts. But the sound he heard felt wrong to him, tentative or accidental. Something sneaky and distinctly human. It did not repeat, though he waited, hands still clasped together, for close to a minute, heart pounding. Drawn over the windows were curtains Niko had fashioned out of cut-up brown blankets and safety pins. Zedekiah considered looking outside but was afraid of what he might see. Finally, he decided he was acting like a child. He finished his prayers, then quickly added a personal supplication: "My Lord, I am frightened here in the dark, alone. I miss my friends. I miss Casiphia. Please help me to find courage. A man should not live in fear." He waited then, holding his breath, hoping as he so often did that Yahshua might send him a sign. But there was nothing.

She had died giving birth to their son, who would have been called Shem. She was only five months along. Zedekiah had not been in the room. It was not their way. The doctor said that Casiphia's bleeding got out of control. Zedekiah saw the blood, after they took her. It was everywhere: in their bed, on the floor. But also, somehow, on the wall behind the bed. And in the bathroom on the floor. He wished he knew how the blood could have traveled so far, but he never saw that doctor again to ask him.

She died in an ambulance she hadn't wanted to get into, on the way to a hospital she'd always been terrified of. Zedekiah and his brothers in the Community buried the baby next to her. They had left room for one other grave, Zedekiah's own. He had not known at that time that he was leaving, that he would not be able to live here, in the Community, without her. That Yahshua would turn away from him in his time of need.

Every person here was family to both of them, in a sense. He could not look at Leah without seeing Casiphia's closest friend. He could not turn to Enoch, his own friend, without seeing Casiphia's brother, her face recognizable within his. When Jared brought food from his wife, Abigail, to help Zedekiah out, he'd tasted only the herbs—rosemary and oregano—that Casiphia had given to Abigail as a gift a few weeks before. He prayed for strength and hope and recovery, but received no answer. His God, like Casiphia, had been taken away. A month after she died, he packed a small bag in the dark of an early morning and walked three miles along Route 105. Niko happened along in the truck and stopped, introduced himself. He asked if Zedekiah wanted a ride, and took him as far as Resolute. Zedekiah had meant to go farther, but had fallen into this job and this life without even trying.

He lay in bed. There hadn't been any more snapping branches, no new strange noises. In fact, he heard fewer sounds than usual. And as he dropped off to sleep, he felt on the verge of understanding something important. But its meaning remained obscure to him, and soon he was in a dream that he would not remember.

"Shick and futt," wheezed Billy Birk, shaking rain from a red umbrella no larger than a dinner plate. "Fitt and shuck."

"Will you learn to curse like a man, for Christ sake?" said Niko, squinting at him and shaking his head.

"Raining like a bitty bit out there." Billy ignored Niko. "Morning, Earth Zed," he added.

Zedekiah nodded at him and filled a blue mug with boiling water for tea. He made his own—Casiphia's apple chamomile recipe—from ingredients ordered out of a health food store in Burlington. He had the muslin teabags she'd made and he kept a stash of these in a small box under the coffee filters. His tea filled the garage with a sweet, flowery smell that lasted only four or five minutes against all the other, less appealing garage odors, but it helped him begin his days.

"What the hell's a bitty bit?" Niko asked.

"Don't start with me," Billy said. "I'm wet and old and cranky."

Billy walked to his desk and fell into a heavy wooden chair on rollers, which then propelled him backward across the cement floor to the coffee area. Steeping his muslin teabag with gentle dunks into the boiling water, Zedekiah stepped to one side to make room for him, and Billy smiled amiably. He was in his sixties, but had the face of a little boy—his ears were small, his eyes, large and bright. When he smiled, his top teeth bit down on his bottom lip, and he looked like he'd just told a naughty joke.

The coffee area was a makeshift counter, fashioned out of a long, wide board which Billy had rescued from the old town library when it was demolished. Billy reached up, grabbed one of a line of mismatched, chipped mugs, then rolled his chair along the counter to the coffee, where he drained all the regular into his cup and replaced the empty glass pot on the burner so that it sizzled. He rolled back to his desk, creeping his chair forward with heel-to-toe footsteps along the floor. Zedekiah reached over and turned off the coffee maker.

Across the room, Niko picked up two sheets of paper. "Earth Zed!" he shouted.

Zedekiah spilled tea from his cup, burning the fleshy part at the base of his thumb. He put the cup down and put his hand to his mouth.

"You want a different job today? I got no dead animals for you. Just dead people."

"Beware the generous manager," said Billy in a loud, raspy whisper.

"Shut it," said Niko.

Billy glared at him.

"There's a big funeral tomorrow. Llewellyn Bergeron. Heard of him?"

Zedekiah shook his head.

"He was a Resolute bigwig in the fifties," Niko said.

"Only he's been in the nursing home down Johnson for about five years," said Billy.

"We need everything in order," Niko said. "His widow still has some pull around town—"

"She's about 112," Billy broke in.

Niko nodded. "But we'll sure hear about it if everything's not shipshape."

Zedekiah stared at him.

"You up for the job?" Niko asked.

"What is the job?"

"Cemetery work in the rain!" shouted Billy. "I tell you, with a boss as fine as Nicholas Stephen Takis, the streets are ever paved with gold."

"*Shut. It.*" Niko jammed his index finger on his desk with each syllable.

Billy glared at him again.

An hour later, Zedekiah stepped out of the truck into a light rain. The cemetery was four miles out of town, spread over the side of a hill. From where he stood at the top, Zedekiah looked down the slope at the final resting places of the many people whose lives had played out in Resolute, Vermont, through the years. The graves disappeared toward the bottom, engulfed in a thin mist. He sighed and pulled his coat tighter around himself. The Bergeron mausoleum stood behind its own set of angel-flanked iron gates. Back in Island Pond, Casiphia's grave was simple, barely noticeable. Her stone lay flush with the ground—one foot by two feet. It said, "Casiphia. Wife of Zedekiah. Mother of Shem."

The angels at the mausoleum doors watched him. One of his chores today was to sand a patch of rust from the metal leaves decorating the gates, which would be messy work, if not impossible, in the rain. He looked up at the gray sky, then closed his eyes to stinging raindrops. Rather than putting his hands together in prayer, he hugged himself.

"Thank you, my Lord, for this opportunity to serve you." He opened his eyes, looked around at the gravestones and lush, soaking greenery. Strangely beautiful, for all the sorrow of the place.

Shivering, he remembered the warmth of his cabin in the woods the night before, the soup boiling in its pot, the deep, soft chair he'd sat in to cook. He remembered the heat of the fire and wondered at the fear that lately affected him, even in such a cozy cabin. Now, as he walked among the graves of the cemetery in the raw, wild air, again he felt afraid. He had trouble envisioning any violence coming to him. The fear was not a rational thing, but a force within, like his heartbeat.

Down the slope, within the mist, he noticed movement. But it was just an old man, visiting a grave. Zedekiah recognized him as Fisk Endicott, a man he'd met in town. Fisk had known Zedekiah lived in Niko's cabin and had introduced himself and asked if he liked hiking the woods. Zedekiah had said he did, and Fisk Endicott went on to tell him about a number of favorite hiking routes not far from Niko's cabin. Now Zedekiah was grateful for that advice, because some of these had become his favorite spots for peaceful contemplation and fervent, if distracted, prayer.

The man held a large, green umbrella. He walked slowly but with a certain upright bearing and strength that made him look younger than his eighty-odd years. He was probably there to visit the grave of his wife. Thinking of them, how they'd had so many years together, such a lifetime of providence, made Zedekiah feel envy, and this was a sin. He looked away, not wanting to invade Fisk's privacy.

From the back of the truck, he took the shovel and made his way carefully through the wet grass and slippery stones to the mausoleum. The first chore Niko had assigned him was to scoop out some of the surrounding earth and smooth it over the cement anchors in which the iron rails of the entrance gates were sunk. From the sides, the angels scrutinized his work blankly. Beyond them, from the door of the mausoleum, a third angel stared out from what Zedekiah realized, with a jolt, was a door knocker. A door knocker on a tomb. The angels' eyes were blank, forever staring, and they seemed closer in depiction to their fallen companion than to the heavenly Gabriel. As always, thoughts of Satan sent a shudder across Zedekiah's shoulders and into the tender muscles of his neck.

The angel in the knocker looked out at him, around him, over his shoulder. Zedekiah suddenly felt a prickle of dread and a strong desire to turn around. As children, he and Casiphia had played a game called Lot's Wife. Each had to stand perfectly still and not turn around as the other, hidden by the terms of the game, walked up slowly. As soon as the order was given, Zedekiah had always longed to turn his head, peer at whatever might be approaching from behind. He understood Lot's wife's fear, her inability to trust. And now, unable to resist, he did turn around.

Behind him stood the old man. Zedekiah started and dropped his shovel, even though he'd seen Fisk just minutes before.

"Did I spook you?"

"You're a quiet walker, sir."

Fisk smiled. "Soldier's training." He nodded toward the Bergeron mausoleum. "Llewellyn Bergeron was a son of a bitch. I won't miss him and I don't mind sayin' so."

Zedekiah nodded, unsure of an appropriate response.

"Visiting Rebecca," Fisk said, and he gazed up the slope for a beat, presumably toward his wife's grave.

"That must bring you comfort."

Fisk squinted at him. The rain pattered his umbrella in a steady rhythm. "Suppose it does," he said. "At first, I did it for her sake. 'Case she was watching from heaven, looking to see if I remembered. But now, I suppose you're right. It's mainly for me."

"I was married once," Zedekiah said in a quiet voice, but his words were drummed out by the rain, and Fisk had chosen that moment to look up at the charcoal sky.

He gave a little shake and pulled his raincoat tighter around himself. "Well, you take care. Keep that coat on, son. Catch your own death out here today."

"Yes. Thank you, sir."

The old man walked the path toward the road. Halfway down, he moved his umbrella aside, as if to test the day, though the rain was still coming hard. He quickly moved it back and continued, disappearing around a corner.

Zedekiah closed his eyes and wiped the rain off his face.

"I know a secret," a child's voice whispered. He opened his eyes, but no one was there. Just the watchful angels. Zedekiah wondered if his faith was being tested, then remembered Job. He stared down at his work, fighting further urges to look up or around. He had to find his faith again.

"Please, Yahshua, help me to be strong."

His first test of faith had come at a very young age. June 22nd, 1984. The date was etched hard—harder than the details. And because he'd heard so much about the day the state police tried to remove the children from the Island Pond Community, he had memories he wasn't sure were his own. Zedekiah had been just five. Yet he remembered being taken out of his warm bed by his mother and a strange woman with short black hair. It was wrong for ladies to have short hair. Even as a child, he'd known that. He remembered being on a bus, crying. The seat was red leather—or red plastic that looked leathery, maybe—with white piping. His mother had been there, too, her arm around his shoulders, but still, he'd been crying. He didn't really recall being prodded onto the bus by a state trooper who'd been forceful and rude, his comments terse and clipped, but he was quite sure that had happened. He also knew his father had given him stern, grown-up advice about doing what he was told and being strong and saying prayers to Yahshua. And he did pray, on the bus. Sitting next to his mother on one side and the lady with short black hair on the other, he'd put his hands together and cried and prayed.

In the courthouse, he sat with the other children on a long, hard bench. He was very tired. Enoch was there. Enoch would have been eight at the time. And Casiphia had been there, too. She'd slept on the bench, slumped against one of the other women who had come with the police. On a wall above their heads, a clock ticked. Down the bench, a little girl cried for her mother. But most of the children were very quiet. As frightening as this was, it was also the biggest adventure.

The police were stern and serious. Their uniforms and weapons were frightening, though years later, Zedekiah would admit to himself that these men had been gentle, if not outwardly smiling or kind. On that day, however, they had instilled in him a panicky sensation that set acid to turning in his stomach—a paralyzing fear of police that would never quite resolve. He and Enoch stared at the state trooper standing near them, arms crossed, outside the room where a judge was said to be working. The state trooper met their gaze steadily. He was very tall and hard-looking, like pictures Zedekiah had seen of cowboys on horses. But this man's hair—Zedekiah saw, because the man removed his hat to scratch his head—was cut almost to his scalp.

One by one, the children were led away into a room. A large door opened and closed as each child went. Eventually, Zedekiah was called. Enoch's eyes widened in fear as Zedekiah stood to follow one of the state troopers into the room. And Enoch's dread had deepened his own.

His parents were in the room with the judge. He was told this later, but did not remember it. Surely they must have been with him in that hallway, too. She'd been on the bus. Had his father been on the bus? He wasn't sure. He only remembered that the judge was thin and kind, and that he looked very tired. His father told him, later, that Zedekiah had made him proud when the judge asked him what his parents did when he was bad, because Zedekiah had answered, "He that spares the rod hates his son: but he that loves him chastens him."

"And they hit you with a rod?" the judge had asked.

"Maybe they would, sir, if I did bad things," Zedekiah had said, shrugging. He could remember being spanked. Spanked hard. But hugged, too. Hugged hard. He had told the judge all of this, and eventually, he had been allowed to return home with his parents.

After he finished cleaning up the Bergeron gravesite, Zedekiah drove back to the Resolute Town Garage. He wasn't sure, but he thought he might be getting sick. He felt hot and cold all at once, and his arms prickled with goose flesh. His eyelids burned whenever he closed them, and he had a dull headache behind his left eye. When he walked in, Billy said that Niko was out for lunch. Then Billy looked hard at him.

"You all right there, Earth Zed?"

"I'm very tired," he admitted.

"You should go home. I can't drive you. Gotta make a presentation about speed bumps to the dratted town board. But don't walk. You take your truck—I'll square it with Niko. Drive as far into them woods as you can and walk the rest. Then get some sleep. You got something to eat out there?"

Zedekiah nodded. His teeth chattered and he wrapped his arms around himself. Billy put a hand to his forehead. His palm was cool and pleasant, and Zedekiah felt a rush of emotion: a mix of loneliness and gratitude. Tears threatened. He had not been touched by another person in a very long time.

If Billy noticed, he did not let on. "Got any cold tablets?"

"I'll be all right." Zedekiah had never taken medicine. He had never needed it.

"The hemp with that." Billy opened his top desk drawer and shoved around a collection of bottles. Finally, he picked one and opened it. He shook three orange pills into Zedekiah's hand and said, "Take a few of these before you go to bed tonight."

Zedekiah parked the truck in the snowplow turnaround that sat empty all summer, then made his way through the woods to the cabin. He heard sounds in the woods. He said to himself, *That's just a low-flying blackbird,* but he imagined the angels from the mausoleum flying above him, doing tricks in the air, rolling and laughing. Lucifer. Because he wasn't feeling well, he said to himself, *This is just what a fever does,* but he was frightened.

He'd planned to lay a fire, for the comfort of it, but by the time he got back to the cabin, he was sweating and hot. The sun was still bright in the western sky, but the woods hampered the light and he was able to darken the cabin easily by pulling Niko's homemade blanket blinds. He drank a glass of water and then another. Before falling into bed, he took the three pills Billy had given him. In another frame of mind, he might have taken only one. But he wasn't thinking straight, and he decided that, never having been sick, he would know less about medicine than Billy. Then he fell into the bed, and into an unnatural sleep in which the inside of his head felt dry and empty, like an oven. He slept hard, having forgotten to pray.

The next part, the terrible part, happened fast, as terrible things often do. Someone was outside his cabin. And there had been a frightening part of his dream—someone crying—that tied neatly into the moment. He was asleep, and then without warning, he was awake and someone was walking around on the ferns and sticks and rocks outside. Remembering the angels, he jumped out of bed, moving fast, still not fully awake. Someone was wailing, keening like a spirit who can't rest. The shotgun over the bed was an old 870 of Niko's. Zedekiah had it in his hands, just as he'd imagined doing if someone wanted to hurt him out here. The gun was on his shoulder by the time he opened the door to the night. A figure slumped on his porch in the dark. The figure said something. Zedekiah thought of Lucifer. He aimed without seeing—no time to think. No time to ask for strength and guidance. Just his heart beating very fast, and the trigger.

The gun popped up off his shoulder, as if pulled high and away by an unknown presence. He missed her—shot the air above her head. She did not fly at him with otherworldly intentions. She was not a devil, not an angel, but a girl. He lowered the gun and saw her clearly for the first time. A young woman, younger even than Casiphia had been. She was bleeding from the lower left side of her body, so that at first, he thought he must have hit her after all. But then he noticed that she had, of all things, an arrow clenched in her hand. She'd lost a lot of blood and her breathing was shallow and pained. He wondered how far she had walked with this injury and where she had come from. She tried to speak, and her eyes rolled back and she fell.

Zedekiah made a strangled noise as he knelt and tried to speak to her. But her eyes were open very wide, forever watching, and he knew she was gone. Kneeling on the ground, hands on either side of her thin shoulders, he tried to make sense of what he was seeing. Pressing two fingers to her neck, he prayed to find a pulse, but there was none. The medication was still making him feel strange and empty and dry. But he was no longer shivering. He wept.

"Help me, Yahshua," he cried out. "I don't know what to do." Zedekiah's nose was running and he was crying and he could not see.

He knew the place from his conversations about hiking with Fisk Endicott. Down a ravine, a pretty little creek. He'd sat there many times, listening to the birds and trying to pray. There was a gravel turnaround on one side, something to make life easier for the big snowplows on the mountain road during a storm. He carried her out of the woods toward his truck. It was dark, but he was not afraid. Yahshua had come back to him. He had laid his hand on the gun before it fired and kept Zedekiah from further harming the girl. And now he was helping him find a resting place for her. He placed her in the back of the truck and covered her over with a tarp. He would drive to Fisk Endicott's pretty ravine. He would leave her there. Someone would find her Someone else would call the police. Zedekiah could not. The police would have come. Troopers, with their grim expressions, their brusque formality and shaved heads. It was too late to help her now. All he could do was leave her in a pretty place until someone came.

He placed her in the icy cold water, hoping it would help to preserve her until she was found. He did not wear the gloves. As he moved her into the water, he prayed to Yahshua to be merciful to this innocent soul, and to forgive him his own powerlessness to help her. It was like baptism, the way he eased her into the water, praying. He stood, looking down at her, then said, "I'm sorry."

He rinsed his hands in the cold water, then pushed them through his hair, plastering it back on his head, out of his eyes. He picked up the large white tarp he'd used to drag her down the hill. After clambering easily back up to the path, he shook out the tarp, rolled it the way they'd taught him, and placed it in the bed of the truck. Zedekiah would hose off the blood tomorrow, the way he did with the blood of deer and moose, porcupine and skunk. If anyone walked by and saw him, they'd be right in thinking the blood had come from one of God's creatures. And no one would pause in surprise if they saw Zedekiah lower his head in prayer over the tarp. They all knew this about him.

Kennedy Jackson
August 2010

They named the tour months ago. The T-shirts and logos and hats have been printed and sit in neat piles, ready to be sold by dozens of vendors. At the time they named the tour, *Shape of the Sky* was just a concept. Something he enjoyed thinking about and playing with, from his comfortable chair in his comfortable house, far from the actual Vermont sky. Now, lying in the grass behind the Zucker house in Resolute, Vermont, Kennedy Jackson looks up and tries to get his mind around the true shape of the sky. It's not a circle, even though some people might say that, since it's certainly hovering over a mostly round earth. But from his perspective at this moment, stretched out as he is in the field, there are enough obstacles blocking his vision that he can't call it a circle. There's the house, for one thing, which is a large old farmhouse with a lot of extra humps and bumps and cubes added on, and a ludicrous balcony off the back—the balcony from which Russell killed a girl two nights ago. It's an ugly house, after all the construction, but it's big enough for the band and it was offered in good faith by a man who does not know their music but needs the money.

Then there are the trees out back, a long, graceful line of them, in front of which Russell's poorly aimed arrow pierced the girl's torso.

Kennedy knew about this pretty quickly. Or he thought he knew. He was told Russell had shot the arrow, but everyone thought he'd missed. They all thanked God and their lucky stars that he was too drunk to hit anything— the apple or the girl's head on which it rested or the tree behind her. After Jeannie rushed in to tell them what Russell had done, Benji and Kennedy searched the woods near the house. They thought the girl had taken off, and in a way, they were right. She was the one they'd picked up in the bus a couple hours south of Resolute that first day they'd driven in. Lexie. Not finding her was a relief. Not finding a body, an enormous relief. They didn't find the arrow either, though, and this bothered Kennedy. Now he knows why. She was hit straight through the stomach. And she picked up the arrow for some reason, after it passed through her and embedded itself in the ground. She carried it off into the woods, and died down some ravine.

So far, Kennedy is successfully managing not to think of Lexie, the person. He didn't know her, but it had been his idea to stop the bus and pick her up on that dirt road last week. If he hadn't made the driver pull over, perhaps she'd be alive. His guilt is predictable and dull, and he keeps it from getting at all sharp or clear by not thinking of Lexie, the person. He is thinking of her as Lexie, the fan. Lexie, the hitchhiker. Lexie, Russell's final conquest before prison. If Kennedy repeats her name enough, it will become so much nonsense. Like lyrics shouted out over and over, night after night, inaudible half the time to the thousands of screaming fans.

Russell had been becoming a problem for months, but Kennedy hadn't been able to do what needed to be done: fire an old friend to save the band. So now a girl is dead, a very public arrest has been made, with sirens and streams of cars leading excited journalists down the Zucker driveway, so that even their well-paid security detail was powerless to keep them out. Since which, the security has gone haywire: keeping out their manager late last night when she came from her inn for an emergency meeting of the band, then letting in a few complete strangers this morning, none of whom, luckily, had darker intentions than a picture and an autograph. He makes a mental note—his third that morning—to ask Benji to have a conversation with security.

The maddest part of all is that the show will go on. Russell confessed. As flawed a person as he is, he took blame for the entire incident. There won't be a larger inquiry. The band is not being investigated. So the show will go on.

He will miss playing music with Russell. So far, that's as far toward sympathy as he's willing to go for his old friend. During their last concert, which he didn't know would be their actual last concert, Kennedy looked at Russell while he beat out a drum solo: sweat flying, hair tossing, studied gaze of concentration and unfathomable contentment. He envied Russell the instrument that could be heard over the screams of the fans. Of course, Russell never really minded the screams. He was in it for the screams, for Christ's sake, and had only ever pretended to understand that Kennedy didn't like them.

"They scream because they love you," he said once. "What's wrong with that?"

"Because they can't even fucking hear me over themselves, and that makes me feel powerless and stupid!" Sometimes, Kennedy would practically cry with frustration at how misunderstood he felt. You're supposed to like the screams.

And now another memory, this time from high school. Russell stands at the top of a flight of stairs, waving a book. Below him, a girl cries, "My algebra book!" But she smiles as she cries, and it's clear she's not upset, but only pretending to be. And Russell smiles as if he'll give the book back, but he won't. The whole thing is this pointless act that they're putting on for each other and the gathered audience of introverts, incapable of this game, and less attractive for it.

Kennedy was never good at acting. He used to try. He used to emulate Russell, but he failed. So he became quiet and serious. As a result, he is known to be difficult. Driven. Angry, even.

Russell has always known that Kennedy isn't an angry person, but a shy one. He might not understand about the screams, but he gets who Kennedy is: driven and difficult, maybe, but mostly shy. And Kennedy will miss playing music with Russell. He won't let him back in the band, ever, but he'll miss having Russell there beside him because they have known each other so long, and because Russell understands him better than anyone.

"Kennedy. Hey, man, you awake?" It's Benji. He wants to talk about the replacement drummer who's flying in from Germany. Something to do with picking her up at the airport without leaking the news that she's in Vermont. Benji's been after Kennedy all morning to have this conversation. But Kennedy squints at him and shakes his head. He does not want to be involved.

"You work it out, Benjamin. You're good at all that shit."

Even after all he's seen in this business, it shocks Kennedy to see that the death of this girl—call it murder or a really fucked-up accident—will be good for business. There's all kinds of buzz on the Internet about "how the rest of the band is holding up" and "who will step in to replace the irreplaceable Russell Maxwell?" Russell might have been irreplaceable once, but like so many people in this business, he fell victim to his own good press. He believed the idolatry—all the crap—and it affected his talent. First, it rendered him unable to hear criticism. And then, it eroded his passion for the music. By the time the Vermont state troopers folded him into their car yesterday, he hadn't been irreplaceable for a very long time.

From somewhere off his left side, a conversation is taking place in hushed female tones. He was vaguely aware of other people coming outside after he did, bringing blankets to sit on, and beach chairs. Kennedy closes his eyes against a headache, dehydration and his own inadequacy—squeezes them until he sees colors—wishing he could be alone, and not surrounded on all sides by people. For the hundredth time in two days, he considers going for a walk. But someone would follow him. Someone always follows him. Especially now, after Lexie. The press is everywhere. Reporters who wouldn't have covered the concert have shown up to cover this. Bow hunting magazines, bloggers who write about famous murderers, and the same old evangelists, seeming almost quaint in comparison, still looking to bring down the evils of rock 'n' roll, God bless them.

Benji is being quiet, tiptoeing around, picking up bottles and cans to recycle, picking up trash to throw out. His intentions are good, but his stealth is a distraction because he is everywhere and nowhere all at once, never making enough noise for Kennedy to follow his progress from point A to point B.

Kennedy opens his eyes. A pair of bare legs—female legs in very short black shorts—stand near him. They float hopefully at the periphery of his vision. He looks back at the sky and waits. People might leave him alone without being asked. If he's quiet enough, they sometimes do.

So there's the house and the trees and then there's a hill to the north, or not a hill actually, but something smaller than that. A hillock—one of his grandfather's words. The hillock also has trees, and that part of the sky is a gentle, feathered curve of treetops raised like an offering out of the earth. To the south, which he can't see as well because it's behind his scalp as he lies in the grass, there's some sort of green utility box which would also obstruct the hypothetical circle, if he could even see it behind him. But the shape of the sky is hindered as well by Kennedy's limitations: the extent to which he can see past his own face, his cheekbones, which are small hillocks in their own right.

The problem he's lately become aware of—a problem that has nothing to do with Russell and everything to do with Kennedy—is just outside of his line of vision as well. It flits around him like a moth, batting against other, well-formed thoughts and ideas, then darts away again before he can grab it and pull it in, or lash out at it, fling it away. It stays just outside his reach, but he knows it is there. He will have to confront it soon.

"Hey baby." He feels a hand on his wrist, which is resting on his chest. He sighs and looks over. He sees a pair of bent knees by his face and black stiletto heels sunk into the spongy turf. She is the owner of the short-shorts, not yet giving up on him. He doesn't look into her face, whoever she is. Maybe she is the girl from Monday night. They never finished what they'd started, because Jeannie knocked on the door to tell him about Russell and the arrow. So maybe this is that girl, come back for what he promised but never delivered. He does not even wonder what her name is. She is Monday night's girl. Today, he does not want a girl. He closes his eyes and her hand slips off his wrist. He hears a sound of mild effort as she stands up again, then another as she extricates her heels from the lawn and makes her disappointed way back to the house.

Kennedy Jackson is not exactly sure what has brought him to this point. If it's the endless stream of nights and days trying to sleep comfortably on the stiff, leather seats of the bus. Or the waves of people singing and screaming, arms raised in love or joy or pleasure at his songs. Or the girls, some of them half his age, who seek him out, bribing security or roadies or friends for a glance, a conversation, a touch of his hand, a brush of his lips, his strong, famous arms around them in the dark. Everything he once wanted and has doubtless achieved, that very list of goals, now smothers him from within.

His path used to be about the music. Not so very long ago, the music propelled him forward, and the people, the things, the money, these were side benefits. Now he has a bus, a driver. Other people tell him where he's going, and where he's going is always the next town in which he's scheduled to appear. If he'd been paying attention, maybe he'd have noticed when his path deviated from the music. But he wasn't paying attention. Russell's arrest, though, has neatly clarified just how much everything has changed. He wants the old path back.

People like to tell him that the music is just as good, just as strong as it once was. He doesn't know. He feels like, somewhere between Indianapolis and Kansas City, between the Melanies and Valeries and Marthas, he lost his ear for beauty. (And Lexies, he thinks. Don't forget the Lexies.) Not all beauty, not entirely. He can still hear the harmony of birds, the throaty calls of frogs in a summer pond, and know enormous pleasure. But his own music is something of a mystery to him. None of it fills him with joy, or even satisfaction. He sits with his guitar and pushes out sound, presses notes to syllables. Writing music feels like work to him, drudgery even. None of the chord changes sound sweet or even interesting, and the lyrics are all shit. This, of course, is the problem. For an instant, it shimmers directly in front of his closed eyes, opening and shutting its wings slowly, taunting him. Kennedy reaches for it, and it is gone.

They don't practice as much on the road, because they're playing all the fucking time. But they do have small practices where they discuss the things that went wrong the night before, and recap the surprises that went right. At three, they're supposed to meet in the large, odd room at the back of the house—clearly one of the later additions, because it has no right being where it is, poking out from between the kitchen and the dining room. They'd meet without amps, and if Russell were still with them, he wouldn't even have brought drums, just two chopsticks and a can. But Russell is not there. And his absence would, of course, be the main subject of any meeting. It's all they've talked about since he was taken. If they met at three, it wouldn't be a practice at all, it would be a bitch session. Anyway, the new drummer is the one who really needs to practice with them, and she won't be getting to the farm for a few more hours. So Kennedy finds Benji, who's making a pot of green tea in the kitchen. He accepts a cup, and they stand in silence drinking tea, staring out the kitchen window, both full of unhappy thoughts. After he finishes, he washes out his cup, leaves it draining, and asks Benji to deal with canceling the meeting.

Kennedy thinks of going to his room for a nap, because he hasn't slept well and, as of tomorrow, the whole fucking world will be watching to see if the band can survive Russell's abrupt departure. But he won't be able to sleep if he tries. He knows that. And he very much wants to find something else to do. He just doesn't know what.

A party is starting up. Even with Russell sitting in some Vermont jail cell. There's always a party, and he knows he doesn't want to do that.

He wanders down to the woods. It takes about six minutes before a girl follows him out there. Not a girl who's looking for him, though. It's Carrie, with the baby—Francis. He doesn't know why he let Evan bring his wife and son on this tour. The baby is mostly good, but he gets to crying in the early evenings and the sound makes Kennedy grind his teeth. She's walking around and jiggling the baby, just trying to calm him before his anxiety works up into something tense and difficult. And Kennedy doesn't want to be near them. He turns around, hears the party, turns back around. He feels like there's nowhere to go, and considers the woods vaguely. But then he hears an engine out front and jogs around the house, away from Carrie, as if he needs to be somewhere.

A pickup truck is pulling in, driven by a man who seems old at first, but isn't. His face is lined and red and when he takes off his cap to run a hand over his head, Kennedy can see that his brown hair is thinning. When the man puts the truck in park and gets out, it's with the slow movements of someone who's done hard labor all his life. A mason or a miner or, more likely in this area, a farmer. In his fifties, maybe. He has a dark look to his eyes, like he's angry, but when he sees Kennedy, he smiles and the look goes away. Kennedy thinks the expression is just what his face does when he's not thinking anything at all. And because he's used to seeing life in terms of lyrics, Kennedy makes a mental note to try to work this idea into a song.

"Afternoon," the man says. He's walking forward, hand outstretched.

"Help you?" Kennedy asks. He shakes the hand, relieved to see that the man doesn't appear to know him, but is just a friendly guy. Again, he tells himself Benji will need to talk to security about who they're letting through.

"I'm looking for Darren, owns the house. He been around?"

"I'm afraid he's not supposed to come around," Kennedy says, and he shakes his head. "It's in the contract, but I don't know why. If I could meet him, I'd have questions for him about this place."

"Right." The man puts his hands in his pockets and frowns. "Well, I'll probably find him in town. Just wanted to avoid going for the ride, what with all these people clogging the roads."

"Sorry about that," Kennedy says. "We've made a mess of your town."

The man looks sorry to have brought up the traffic, so Kennedy laughs and introduces himself.

"Bill Farnham," the man says in reply. They shake once more. Bill Farnham's face still shows absolutely no recognition, and in his anonymity, Kennedy feels a jolt of pure happiness.

"Well, I'm gonna be on my way, then," Bill says.

Kennedy has a thought as the man turns to walk to his truck. "Can I trouble you for a ride?"

"No trouble," the man says. He changes course and opens the passenger door, then sweeps a load of papers and books and cups onto the floor of the cab.

"Hop in," he says. "Don't mind those things."

With a last glance at the house, Kennedy gets into the truck. Various people will be incredibly pissed at him later, for taking off on his own, but he decides not to worry about it.

The truck smells of his childhood. Manure and tobacco. Not that he grew up on a farm, but many of his friends did, and he spent time at his uncle's farm in Rutland. When he was thirteen, Kennedy broke his collarbone and got a concussion falling off a horse named Whippit. He was lucky to come away with only a shoulder that clicks to this day and some memory issues. He never rode again.

"You hoping to go into town?" Bill asks.

"Actually, if you're passing it, I want to check out those new houses they're building out the back way between here and town."

Bill looks unfazed and nods. "Less traffic that way, in any case."

They sit in companionable silence, bumping out the long drive, passing security; neither guard seems to notice their main charge in the cab of the truck. He's thinking how incompetent they are when Bill says, "You in that band?"

"I am," Kennedy says.

"Must have been hard for you, what happened the other night."

"Yes."

"I hear they don't know who she is, to contact her family."

"No, not yet." Kennedy braces himself for criticism: how the band brought bad karma to this poor little town, or how rock 'n' roll incites violence, or even, perhaps, the evils of irresponsible bow hunting. But the man surprises him and says nothing about all that. He just drives quietly.

Finally, maybe a minute later, he says, "Your band: any good?"

After a confused moment, Kennedy realizes they're talking about music. "Are we any good?" he asks, to be sure.

The man nods.

"Used to be," Kennedy says without thinking. "Not so sure anymore." If a journalist heard him say this, it would result in an interview and a cover photo on *Rolling Stone*. But Bill Farnham just glances at him, then looks back at the road.

"I bought the new CD. What's it called?"

"*Brilliant Deep*," Kennedy says.

"Right." Bill nods. "I put it on in the barn a couple weeks ago, listened while I was milking."

"What'd you think?"

"Not my thing, actually."

This makes Kennedy laugh out loud. He likes Bill, with his simple, frank manner.

"No offense," Bill says.

"None taken."

Then the farmer holds up a finger. "There was one song I liked a lot. Reminded me of my father's music."

"Oh yeah?"

Bill nods. "You had an accordion on there."

"Sure," Kennedy says. "That one's called, 'When Meg Comes 'Round.'"

"Yes it was," Bill says. He looks impressed, like Kennedy just solved a math problem. "You play the accordion on that?" he asks.

"Yes sir, I did. Sang it, too." Kennedy's glad to be able to take credit for the only song this man liked. He finds himself wanting to impress him. And then realizes that this is how it all started: trying to impress people, then impressing them so much, he lost his way.

They pull off the road into a rutted, dried-out dirt area in front of a circle of four new houses, in various stages of completion. One other car is parked in the middle of the circle, a dirty green Honda with a mismatched white hood.

"Here you go," Bill says. He squints up at the houses for a minute, then looks sideways at Kennedy. "You buying a house?"

"Nah. Just wanted to see 'em."

"You meeting Carter, then?" Bill nods at the Honda.

So it is the kid's car. Kennedy nods. He climbs down out of the cab and salutes the farmer. "Much obliged," he says, suddenly aware that he's been trying to talk like simple folk, and feeling stupid for it.

"I'll see you around," Bill says. "I hear your concert's going to be out my back door. Good sound."

"Not your thing, though."

"Oh, hell. It's different when there's a concert," Bill says. "Like baseball. Much better up close."

Kennedy closes the door and Bill Farnham drives away, waving his hand.

He hears what he's come for almost immediately—doesn't have to spend time searching. The sound of a guitar, wired into some small amp, coming from the upstairs of the least-finished house. Loud enough that the kid didn't hear the truck leave, but not loud enough to bother anyone out here in the country. He smiles, because that's the house he'd have chosen, the one that's all bare joists and blue flapping tarps and sawdust. The boy is probably looking out the back, through the gaping attic, above which the peak called Mount Witness looms, the way the developers planned it. The house must have power already, or a generator, because the kid is playing his music.

Kennedy comes closer to the house so he won't be seen if the boy walks around and glances into the circular drive inside the ring of houses. He sits on the front step, and leans back against a jamb, eyes closed, taking in sounds. He came here without expectations, because he wanted something to do, but quickly realizes that the teacher was right.

Above his head, the boy is playing around, running up and down the strings as fast as he can, showing off for himself. But there's a mastery there, unconstrained dexterity. He spends hours a day practicing; that much is obvious. After a few minutes, the music stops. Kennedy hears him stand and walk across the room. Maybe he's glancing out to check on his car. More footsteps. He sits again. This is his routine, Kennedy thinks. He'll sit here for hours a day, playing his guitar, occasionally stopping to stretch his legs, wander around or down the stairs to another room, then play some more.

He and Russell grew up in Rochester, Vermont. Before they went to UVM and formed the band, Kennedy and Russell used to sneak into Saint Elizabeth's Church to write music, because it was quiet and haunting and a little scary. No amp, because they'd have been heard. But they'd bring a guitar and some paper and a stubby pencil, and let themselves in the back door, the way Mr. Leverton came and went some afternoons. A self-appointed, volunteer janitor who also cleaned at their school, Mr. Leverton had always let them be. He was a music man, too, Kennedy recalls now. A man with a sweet, high voice, always singing while he worked.

Russell will be all right. He admitted to the crime. He is cooperating with police. He'll serve some time, but he'll get a life back. This is what Kennedy focuses on when he is forced to think about Russell. And then, quick, before the girl named Lexie becomes a person, he thinks about something else.

The boy is playing again. He starts with a few simple chords, then touches on Kennedy's own 'Sleepy Sponge,' but only for a minute, thankfully. Kennedy is not in the mood to hear his own music played back to him. "The ego mirror," Russell used to call it. The sensation of hearing your music unexpectedly. Sometimes it was a rush, sometimes a disappointment. Always, ultimately, a bit weird. Russell had been working on a song about it: 'Ego Mirror,' of course. Maybe he'd finish it in prison.

Now the kid moves into something complex and well-worn. Something he's been working on for weeks or months. He teases at the emotional core of the thing, prods at ideas he hasn't yet figured out, then returns to the core.

But Kennedy can hear the promise of what Carter Akyn hasn't yet worked out. Within the song is both the pleasure and anger of being fifteen or sixteen or seventeen—the untapped potential of those years, and the yearning to be more than he is, to be in another place and time. Carter works the chords, then shifts into a labyrinth of finger-picking. Kennedy swallows and leans forward, elbows on his knees, intent. The song finishes abruptly, with a strong chord, like some kind of flamenco dance. It's not the way the song should end, but it sounds impressive.

Kennedy shifts on the hard floor, and the boards creak. He knows the boy has heard, because the floorboards upstairs creak in reply, as if Carter Akyn has taken a single step and stopped, nervous to come closer.

"Hello?"

"Hello there," Kennedy shouts. "Is that Carter up there?"

Footsteps, less hesitant now. "Ride?" he says, coming down the stairs.

"No," Kennedy answers. He stands and walks into the drafty house, stretching his back as he moves.

Carter appears on the stairs. He stops when he sees Kennedy there.

"What's Ride? Is that a person?"

"Yes." Carter looks around, like there might be people standing behind corners, ready to jump out and shout something. "Boo!" Or maybe, "Surprise!"

"Sorry if I startled you. I'm Kennedy."

"No shit," he says. He's rocking on his heels on the bottom step. "What are you doing here?"

"Well, I heard I might hear some good music if I came over, so I thought I'd check it out."

Carter smiles like this is a joke. He's a handsome kid, tall and gangly, with wavy, brown hair that's neither long nor short; probably he's growing it out. He has soft, insubstantial stubble on his chin and a wry smile that looks suspicious, like someone's pulling one over on him.

"Your teacher, Mr. uh … Guy somebody."

"Mr. Masters?"

"He thought I should hear you play."

"You came here because of Mr. Masters?"

In the kid's voice, Kennedy can hear how very little respect Guy Masters commands in his classes. It seems wrong, that the teacher should be helping this kid, and get nothing for his trouble.

"Fine man, Guy Masters," he says.

"Okay," says Carter.

"You don't think so?"

Carter shakes his head quickly. "No, I do. I mean, yes. Yes, I do. I think he's a good guy. A … fine man." He smiles unhappily.

Kennedy's seen this sort of thing before—the reticence to disagree with an adult, and a famous one at that. He wonders if Carter's shy, or just starstruck.

"Can you play another one?"

"Uh, sure." He picks up his guitar and it looks like a relief, like a pocket he can put his hand in. "What do you want to hear?"

"Something I didn't write, for damn sure."

Carter nods. "Well, here's …" His words trail off and he starts to play. It takes Kennedy a second to place the song, because the kid's got a few artistic riffs that throw him off, but it's Clapton, 'After Midnight.' Once he gets it, Kennedy likes the changes the kid has put in the song. Carter finishes and only then does a worried look appear on his face, as if he might have made a fool of himself.

"I like that," Kennedy says. "You did some interesting things there."

"I've been playing around with it."

"You a big Clapton fan?"

"Sure." Carter shrugs.

"Yeah, sure. Who isn't, right?"

The air in the house is dusty and full of late afternoon sunshine. Kennedy pulls his cellphone out of his pocket and glances at it. He has a load of missed calls, because the ringer's always off. It's almost seven o'clock. "That your car outside?" he asks.

Carter nods.

"Any chance you can give me a ride back to my house?"

"Yes." Carter says this very loudly. Too loudly, as if he's trying to wake himself up.

"And maybe we can talk about a spot for you in the show tomorrow night."

They look at one another. Carter's face goes through a funny series of expressions, from happiness to worry.

"You know I'm not in school, right?"

Kennedy nods. "Why is that, anyway?"

Carter sighs. "I forget."

"No, seriously."

"It felt like I was doing the right thing, when I dropped out," Carter says. He swallows and looks worried, like he thinks Kennedy might change his mind if he says the wrong thing. "I wasn't good at school. Maybe I was just lazy. Some people think that. But I really don't know anymore."

"Well, I'm breaking a rule, but that's nothing new."

Carter nods and smiles with relief, though it looks like he's trying not to. He's not good at acting. He's not good at the game.

For a second, Kennedy sees himself on stage with this kid. They're playing side by side, sharing a mic, singing a lyric. He's not sure which song—his own, or one that this kid has written. Then the imagined moment changes and it's Kennedy and Russell, and they're sixteen again. Not anywhere near as talented as this kid. Nowhere near ready for what's going to come their way.

Lexie Quinn was a real person. She was young and beautiful and lush. Her face had a sheen to it, very pale, and her kind, gray eyes showed her to be a person without guile. Few of the women he met seemed innocent in this way that Lexie Quinn had seemed innocent. She had a trusting nature; he'd seen it as soon as he'd let her on the bus. And now she's dead. Russell killed her for nothing.

Kennedy clears his throat. "You'd have to spend some time practicing with the other kids … pretty much all the hours left between now and then. That all right with you?"

"Yesss," Carter says, loud and long, smiling like someone just told a dirty joke. And just like that, Kennedy feels a jolt of joy again, that same feeling he had when Bill Farnham didn't know him. But it's not his fame that spreads warmth through his face and arms and chest, not how impressed this boy is, meeting a fucking rock star. It's got to do with the energy of youth, and the music that still seems to reverberate over their heads. It's about the mountain out back, and the way it whittles the sky into something sculpted but not quite tangible. It has to do with the bare boards under his feet, and the smell of sawdust, and the sound of plastic slapping wood in the hot wind. How real this moment feels to him. How alive and very real he himself feels.

Stella Blue Wheeler
August 2010

For a while, before actually approaching him, Stella watched the policeman who was supposedly her uncle. She'd never really thought about it before, but policemen all looked the same. They were rigid, strong, mean, and just a little shorter than they wanted to be. Race didn't matter much—the black ones looked the same as the white ones, and if there were any Asian ones, they probably looked the same, too. Her uncle didn't, though, and this was why she had the thought about policemen in the first place.

He was nice-looking, as in kind, and a little taller than he wanted to be: slouching, the way her mother always said not to. He had very dark hair—almost black—like Kenny Craig, a senior who Stella loved deeply and madly, who'd asked her to dance once. The supposed uncle didn't look like Kenny Craig; he just had his hair. His face was handsome, though. Eyes that squinted up a little when he laughed, and a serious expression when he wasn't laughing. Not serious-mean, but serious-caring. Like you could talk to him. Which was good, because that's what Stella was planning to do. Soon. But not yet.

She was trying not to think about her mother, who was a totally different person today than she'd been yesterday. Stella had woken up in the tent, excited about Day Two of the music, hoping they'd play 'Some Blonde,' because she realized all at once they'd never played it the night before and it was one of her favorites.

People outside their tent were laughing and shouting, as if they were still having a party, and she wondered if anyone had slept besides her. The tent flap was closed, but the skylight flap was open, and she was excited to see thin white clouds floating overhead through a pale blue sky. The sun was out—no more rain.

That's when she noticed the noise. Her mother was lying with her back to Stella, making this funny noise, and Stella had to ask, "Are you crying?" Because she was, it was obvious. And that's what started everything. That's when her mother told her.

Stella had always wondered who her father was. It wasn't a very original thing to wonder, and she tried not to be obsessive about it, because that was boring. But she was a girl without a father. And as much as she loved Martin and wished he was her father, she knew it wasn't true. Martin was gay. More importantly, Martin was black, and in real life if your father is black, you'll look at least a little black. Martin called her "All Set," because it was Stella with the letters mixed up. He always said she was the only one he'd answer the phone for, no matter what mood he was in, and she knew this was true, because she'd seen him ignore her mother's calls when he was painting.

Stella had asked Cricket who her father was a thousand times, and her mother had always avoided telling her a full story. His name, she'd say, was Bill. He was a friend. They'd lost touch. No, she didn't know how to find him. No, Wheeler wasn't his last name; Wheeler was her mother's last name. Every time Stella pressed the point, either asking for a picture, or a document, or even a name, her mother would stare at her, hospital quiet, looking wounded.

Stella's uncle must not have been a very good policeman, because he didn't seem to notice that she'd been following him all over the concert grounds. He'd talked to a group of kids, gotten them to show I.D., and confiscated a huge red thermos with a plaid pattern on the side, like a kilt. He'd sniffed the thermos, reared his head back at its smell, then emptied it by turning it upside down and letting it run out into the grass, while the kids stood around him in a small circle, looking forlorn. Then he'd patted their shoulders and sent the kids on their way. He'd walked another couple hundred feet and stepped in to break up a game that had something to do with a purple flaming Frisbee. Then he'd walked another hundred feet, bought a cup of coffee, and found a pole to lean on while he drank the coffee. All the while, Stella had been following. She wasn't trying to hide, because it would be easier to talk to him if he talked to her first. That was what she'd decided. But it wasn't working. If he knew she was there, he wasn't wondering why.

"I used to follow the Grateful Dead." That's how her mother had started.
"What?"

She was still crying, which had made it hard to argue with her, but of course Stella hadn't believed her at first. Her mother was the least cool of all the mothers. Which wasn't to say she didn't love her. In fact, she loved her more for it sometimes. Like when she didn't let any boys in the house after nine at night when Stella had friends over, a rule that made Stella's life easier, too. Because who really wanted to watch other people make out? That would be awkward. And the fact that her mother had never invited Stella and her friends to drink wine with her, the way Missy's mother had on Cape Cod in June. But she was just so, so hard on Stella, and that was unfair, especially if she was this impostor—this person she wasn't supposed to be.

Now that Stella knew the whole story, which had taken a couple hours, she thought the Grateful Dead had been a funny way to start. Because, really, it was the least important information. Her mother didn't even have the same name she'd grown up with and her whole life was a lie. It would have been hard to start there, though.

Stella was really proud of herself for not being mad at her mother about all the lies. She was in shock, maybe. So maybe she'd be mad later. For now, though, she felt kind of sorry for her mother, and kind of impressed. Cricket was like the hero in a book. She'd been a victim, powerless, out of control of her own life. And she'd turned it all around, leaving home, changing her name, getting away.

Her father used to rape her. At first Stella had tried not to think about this. She'd actually flinched—physically shuddered—when her mother told her. But now some time had gone by, and she was feeling angry. Nobody could hurt her mom. No fucking way! Maybe this was another reason she wasn't upset for herself or mad at Cricket. She was angry at this horrible old dead guy she'd never meet or get to kick in the balls the way he deserved. So she had all this disbelief and sympathy and anger and shock and nowhere to put it.

Maybe this was why she'd decided to talk to the supposed uncle.

The band was playing 'Dinner At Mitzy's,' which was a song she'd always thought was really dumb. Probably it was hard to come up with new material all the time, especially if you were going to play these long concerts that lasted two days. She supposed they'd had dinner at a friend's house and had written a song about it. But who really cared? It was like those people who would post anything at all on Facebook: *Bagel and lox for breakfast… Nothing good on TV… Dinner at Mitzy's.*

Who really cared? Musically, the song was okay. If you ignored the lyrics. This was hard, because it started out all about the words, with no instruments, just Kennedy, slapping a guitar and singing:

> *She got potatoes*
> *She got wine*
> *She got some pot and we're all feeling fine*
> *She got bread and she got lentil soup*
> *Dinner at Mitzy's and we're all getting looped*

The audience went wild at "we're all getting looped," just like they were supposed to. Then the guitars came in, and the drums, and the words got sillier and sillier, until he was saying *"we're all gettin' glooped,"* but you had to have seen the lyrics to know it, and the song picked up speed until it spiraled into chaos.

Maybe she would like the song now, having heard it here, at this moment, on this important day.

Her uncle, she was trying to think of him as Uncle Chris, finished his coffee, crumpled up the small cup, and tossed it into the trash. He turned away from the stage and walked a short distance to where he could watch people climbing the BFW. Set up for amateurs and experts alike, the BFW was a regular feature of Perilous Between concerts. It was a climbing wall—very big—as the name suggested.

Stella decided it was time. Enough wasting time. She wasn't nervous, really, except that her mother was taking a nap because she'd collapsed from exhaustion after their big talk, and she might wake up and not know where Stella was and be really upset. Stella had left a note, but she knew that might not make her mother less upset.

"Excuse me?" she said, approaching the policeman.

"I was wondering," he said, not looking at her.

"Wondering what?"

"When you were going to say something," he said. "You've been following me around here for over half an hour."

She grinned. "I didn't think you'd noticed."

"I noticed," he said, looking back toward the BFW. There were three guys on the wall. They all looked stuck, like they'd climbed higher than they were comfortable with, and weren't sure how to get back down.

"There's a safety net if they fall," she said.

He nodded. "Still looks dangerous, doesn't it?"

"I guess."

"I'll be glad when this whole show is over, between you and me," he said. "Puts a lot of pressure on this little town."

Close up, she thought maybe he had eyes that were a little bit like her eyes. The coloring was all wrong, but the shape …

"You weren't wearing a uniform yesterday," she said.

He looked down at the front of his shirt, as if he hadn't realized he was in uniform.

"You were with a woman yesterday, the one in the wheelchair," Stella said.

He nodded. "Becca."

"Is she your girlfriend?"

"Are you asking me out?"

Stella laughed and looked down. "No."

The cop turned and pointed at the BFW. "See the middle kid?"

She looked. The kid in the middle of the wall looked a little less frightened than his two friends. He was laughing wildly, throwing his head back and barely hanging on to his handholds. "He's the one who played yesterday," she said, realizing who he was. "The one who opened for the band. He was really good."

The cop nodded. "That's Carter. He's Becca's son."

"Really? He's an awesome guitar player." She wondered if she could meet Carter later, after the cop officially became her uncle. Then she felt ashamed for thinking something so selfish while her mom lay alone in their tent—

maybe still asleep, or maybe awake now, clutching a tissue, reading Stella's note with a racing heart.

"Yes, he is." The cop looked pleased that she'd said it first. Maybe he wanted to be able to agree without sounding all full of himself. "Anyway, yes, I'm in uniform because today I'm on duty. Yesterday I wasn't."

"You didn't arrest those kids who had the booze in the thermos."

He opened his eyes wide for a moment and regarded her.

"Aren't you supposed to arrest kids for underage drinking?"

"Well, your honor, just how do you know what was in the thermos?"

She thought about this. "Just a guess." He was treating her like a younger girl than she was, but she thought maybe that was all right. She felt raw with knowledge today, reborn and weak.

"Are you here to report a crime?" he asked. "Or turn me in for not reporting a crime?"

"No." Stella cleared her throat. "Your name is Chris Kozlowski, right?" she stumbled over the word *Kozlowski*.

He tapped the nameplate on his chest. "Like it says."

"From Philadelphia?"

He studied her for a moment, his smile fading. "Who are you?"

"I'm Stella Wheeler." The untruth of her name hit her. Wheeler, a made-up name. And Cricket, who yesterday had been just like any other mother in Cape Elizabeth, Maine, was suddenly a runaway rocker from Philadelphia.

"My mom is your sister," she said, to get it over with. And also, just to hear herself say it again.

Right then was when the first guy fell. He lost his grip about a third of the way down the BFW and whooshed down into the net laughing, as if that had been the point. The other two guys on the wall began making alternately amused and freaked-out sounds. If they wanted a cop's help, though, they weren't going to get it from Officer Kozlowski, who was staring at Stella with his mouth half open.

"It's true," she said.

"Andy has a daughter?"

"I guess." She shrugged. "I mean, yeah. Yes. Me."

"I thought I saw her last night. Was so sure it was her. But then I couldn't find her."

"She told me."

"I've thought I saw her before, though, too."

Stella nodded. Maybe he was about to cry. She couldn't tell. He looked away for a few seconds, and she could see his Adam's apple working even though he didn't make any sound.

"Is she still here?" he said then, looking back at her. He wasn't crying.

"In our tent. Probably wondering where I am." A breeze blew Stella's hair around her neck and into her face. She pulled it back with two fingers.

"She doesn't know you're talking to me?" He sounded disappointed.

"She was going to talk to you herself, but I decided to get things started, in case she chickened out again."

"Again?"

"I think she's tried to contact you before."

He looked away.

"And I think she would have talked to you last night, but she got scared."

"Why?" His voice was higher now than a second ago, and he looked a little lost. Like a kid, stranded at the fair.

"It's hard for her."

"It's hard for *her*?" he said, laughing. It was the first time he didn't sound nice.

"Because you look like your dad. Your father," she corrected, deciding dad was a safe-sounding word, a word for a nicer man. "You look like him."

She couldn't read his expression, and he looked away again when he saw her trying.

From behind Stella came a shout that made them both look around. "Hey, excuse me!" It was a man in his sixties, dressed like no one Stella had ever seen. He wore a short pink sarong wrapped around his waist, and beads on his bare chest, over an open shirt with embroidered flowers. His long gray hair was woven through with ribbons, and he had a pink turban on his head.

"Some kids are stealing my shit," the man said. "I've got a booth on the next row, and they're hassling my wife and putting my prisms in their pockets."

The policeman, her uncle, walked briskly by her, motioning for the man to lead him to the place. Then he paused and spun around. "What's your tent site?"

"What?"

"The number on your campsite," he said.

"333."

"Come on, man. It's happening now!" shouted the man in the sarong. "Shit!"

"I'll be there soon; keep her there for me," said her uncle. Uncle Chris.

He showed up an hour later. Her mom was sitting outside the tent, looking anxious and cried-out and eager. Cricket had sobbed and hugged her really hard and hadn't yelled at all when Stella came back to the tent. She never said why—whether she was mad or worried or scared about her brother or what. She just cried and cried until she ran out of whatever she needed to keep on crying, and she'd hugged Stella until it was awkward. Now she kept putting on her sandals, buckling them as if she was about to stand up or go somewhere, then undoing them again, slipping them off. Stella saw him coming and touched her mother's elbow.

"There," she said.

He was studying the campsite numbers, walking so fast he almost went right by. He came to an abrupt stop and stood, arms hanging uselessly. Staring. Cricket stood and walked toward him barefoot, despite all the preparation with the sandals. They didn't hug at all. They stood and looked at one another, and Cricket lifted her hand and touched his arm. She said, "I'm so sorry." And he nodded and dug in his pocket and handed her something. She laughed a weird choked-up laugh that might have been a sob, and they turned and walked away like Stella wasn't even there. As they walked, they started to talk. She could see her mother nodding, and her uncle's face turning to hear her better.

Stella found her cellphone in her sleeping bag. The battery was almost dead and she only had one bar. But she dialed anyway, because she needed to.

Martin answered on the fourth ring. He always answered on the fourth ring, because that's how long it took him to put on his glasses and see the caller ID, and if he didn't get to the phone in time, the machine would pick up on the fifth ring.

"All Set?" he said. She heard how he was happy to hear from her, and just a little worried, like a father would be.

"Hi," she said.

"What are you calling me for, baby? Is the music over? They're taking a break?"

"No."

He heard it, the way her throat was closing off words. How she was trying not to cry.

"What is it?"

"Did you know about Mom?"

"What about her?"

"That she's not who we thought. That she's someone else. Did you know?"

He was quiet. She imagined him walking the kitchen, fiddling with the plants.

"Martin?"

"Yes and no," he said.

"What does that mean?"

"There are gaps in her background. She is reluctant to talk about it."

"My name is really Stella Blue. Did you know that?"

"Yeah?" he said. "Stella Blue? Well that's even prettier, I think."

"It's from a song. It's on my birth certificate," she said. "Mom's going to show me, when we get home."

She saw her mother and her Uncle Chris again ten minutes later. Her phone had died, and she'd called Martin back on Cricket's phone to say goodbye. Then she sat out in front of the tent, listening to the band from a distance and trying to feel sorry for herself, but not really able to muster up the right emotions. Just then, 'Some Blonde' started up, and she saw them at a distance, walking slowly, her mother talking, her uncle's head bent low. They were eating Tootsie Pops, she saw. And she realized that's what he had brought her: a Tootsie Pop. Probably raspberry. Which made everything better somehow. Because in a single glossy moment, that turned her mother back into the person she'd always been.

230

Fisk Endicott
August 2010

Sitting on the flat rock, his eyes closed to avoid seeing the dead girl's body, his hands trembling more than usual, Fisk listened to the stream running at his feet. As water made its way around small branches and pebbles, it still sounded as it always had, like nature's bells. The water also coursed over the fingers of the girl's left hand, where her arm twisted awkwardly over her head. Fisk was not squeamish, but it bothered him that the music of the water would be the same with or without this girl's corpse lying in its path.

In other circumstances, this was a pretty place. It could be cool in the morning, even in July, but the chill made it bright and shiny and complete; it made the hovering blue sky even more startling. The mountain, rising up, promised an adventure if he wanted one. And he did still like the occasional small adventure. In winter, snow-covered trails had always drawn him. But at eighty-six, Fisk was finally too old for snowshoes anymore. He stuck to areas he could negotiate in boots, mostly paths in the valley beside streams, sparkling in long ice-edged rivulets. Summer was more his season now. He could still manage these hikes in summer.

A nearby scampering in the woods made him open his eyes, which he kept raised, for now. He scanned the steep bank, grateful for so many trees that would help him drag himself back up to the ridge when the time came. His house was only half a mile from this once-pretty place. After he climbed up, it would be mostly a flat half mile, although he'd have to watch for roots. His daughter did not know he was out here, and that would be a problem for him, later. No one knew that Fisk still took his walks.

"I don't want you falling out there in the woods, when no one knows you went out," she'd said at Christmas, when he found her in his house, waiting for him to return from the same walk. Almost the same. "What if you fell, Pop?"

"That would be the way to die," he'd said. "Fall down in those woods, I'd be gone quick and easy." She'd pressed her lips together and reared back a little, hoping to look wounded, but mainly coming across as priggish.

"That's how the Indians did it," he'd said. "An old Indian man like me would go off in the woods on his own when his time came. Make a quick exit."

"We're not Indians."

She was neither romantic nor pragmatic enough to see his point. And if he'd suspected for a minute that her objection was out of love or honest concern, he might have heeded her request. But it wasn't love that drove Rita. Oh, she cared about him. It would be unfair to suggest otherwise. More than that, though, she saw him as her duty. Since her mother had passed, Rita was in charge of Fisk, and she did not want him to die on her watch. Even in these sparkling, merciful woods. But Fisk had been hiking these trails for too long to stop now. He'd die wherever he happened to be when his time came. No one but God had power over that. Certainly not Rita.

The person who *was* dead had not met a merciful end. Then again, she had not died here. Drag marks on the ridge above had led Fisk to investigate in the first place. He did still love a small adventure, after all. Though he hadn't bargained on this one. As he'd made his way slowly down the bank, knobby hands reaching from tree trunk to tree trunk, slipping occasionally, then regaining his purchase, he'd noticed broken branches and skid marks—signs of something having been pushed down the bank to the river. He'd trekked these woods enough to know that he'd find something heavy at the bottom. Not heavy for a person; he hadn't expected a person. He'd thought some lazy fool had gotten rid of a piece of furniture, maybe. Or a box of paint cans they couldn't be bothered to dispose of properly. These things did show up in the woods from time to time. He'd expected to find a crate of trash metal or someone's broken dryer. Then he'd have called Chris Kozlowski, that very competent new policeman who'd been voted in as constable—the one everyone was gossiping about—and tell him Leander Hollins would need to drive out with his truck, gather whatever had been dumped into the stream. But Leander would not be the one to come, after all. Officer Kozlowski would have to drive out himself.

She'd been a pretty girl once, with pale gray eyes and a thin, angular face. Maybe she was twenty. Maybe sixteen. Who could tell, at this point? Her curly blonde hair was tangled, clotted with leaves and small twigs from the ground. She wore a denim jacket embroidered across the front and down the sleeves with flowers and bees and rainbows. She wore an orange top and leather sandals and a funny quilted skirt that looked homemade. Her features looked eastern European or maybe Irish. Fisk used to be good at guessing a person's heritage. But, like her age, it was hard to tell anymore with this girl. Her skin was unnaturally white, almost gray.

The look of her brought him back to other bodies he'd found. His wife, Rebecca, three years ago. She'd died in her sleep at the hospital, already sedated because of the cancer. It hadn't been a death without pain, but it hadn't been a terrible way to go, he supposed now. This girl's body reminded him more of finding Johnny. That had been in Germany, during the war. Woods again, but in winter. Fisk's friend, Johnny, only twenty-two years old, shot through the neck by an invisible enemy. Not the only body Fisk had seen during the war, but the one he'd carried with him daily since. Johnny's throat had been torn open by the bullet. Fisk could still remember, though it made him shudder, how the vertebrae in his neck had been plainly visible. Finding that body had made time fold over on itself, so that he couldn't believe it hadn't been yesterday— this morning, even that he'd found his friend. When something important is on your mind for many years—when, every day, you almost speak of it, but then don't—time loses meaning. The passage of sixty-six years becomes nonsensical, impossible.

This girl's corpse was wrong in this place. Without her, he had the charming music of the stream, the smacking blue sky, the small sounds of life in the woods and up on the ridge. Even this magnificent rock. In any other circumstance, Fisk would have been pleased to find this rock to rest on. A large, flat trapezoid, the rock slanted barely, so that his seat was higher than his knees as he faced the water and his miserable discovery.

Hers had not been the merciful death of these woods, but something much less compassionate. Had she been shot? Stabbed? He couldn't tell. Like Johnny's, this girl's pallor told Fisk she'd lost a lot of blood, and that had to be blood covering her jacket. But unlike his friend's, her eyes bore the fear of knowing what had been coming. No inappropriate part of her was visible to Fisk. No vertebrae, for example. No bones. Yet his hands were shaking. More than usual. He closed his eyes again, folded his hands, like in church (though also to still them), and tried to say a prayer. All he could come up with was, *Dear God. Dear God.*

Had he prayed for Johnny? He had every day since, but in the moment, had he prayed? He remembered kneeling, immobilized by the sight of all that shouldn't have been there. Other men had found them both—Johnny and Fisk—before he'd gotten off his knees. Other men had borne the responsibility of delivering Johnny out of Germany, out of the frozen mud. Home to his parents. Not Fisk. Dear God.

He'd been in shock then. Was he in shock now? He'd have to do something soon. Fisk opened his eyes. In Germany, he'd forgotten to worry about the invisible enemy, hiding, perhaps, watching him.

When a bird called from somewhere nearby, Fisk jumped. Animals would come for her soon. He needed to climb out. By the time he got home and called Constable Kozlowski, by the time he could lead the man to this spot, the sun would be low in the sky. The longer he waited, avoiding the shift of stones and branches beneath his feet as he hauled himself back up the ridge, the fewer clues they'd find.

Also, for once, it was important that Fisk not die out here in these woods today. He'd found her and he needed to deliver her out of here, back to her people. Because, as Rita had said, they were not Indians, after all.

Bill and Georgia Farnham
August 2010

Bill Farnham sat on his back porch and rocked in the chair that Georgia had bought at the Westmore Farmer's Market from one of the people in The Island Pond Community. *The Smiley Farm,* some people called them. Georgia always said that those people were God-loving, too, they just had different ideas about who God was, and how best to celebrate His word. She liked to support them because they were treated by many with such disrespect. Bill just liked the way that the rocker moved along the porch boards. Whoever had built the chair had done a good job. It was a dark, pretty cherry, and its smooth, full arc—front-to-back-to-front-to-back—seemed to follow the beat of the music.

Perilous Between, it turned out, was better in person than it had sounded on the stereo in the barn. Funneling toward him across the pasture, which was now dotted with tents and teenagers, the band's music had wonderful and intricate texture. Drums layered under keyboards layered under guitars. And alongside all of it, like a child running with a ball, that Kennedy Jackson sang. His voice—sometimes deep and resonant, sometimes twangy and sharp—was like no voice Bill had heard before in his life. It made him happy to have given the man a ride in his truck.

Jackson had pulled out his accordion and played it three times so far: twice today, once yesterday. He played 'When Meg Comes 'Round,' the one from the new album, as well as a couple of others that Bill took to be older releases. Even on the accordion, Kennedy Jackson had a unique sound: something both rolling and compressed, like excitement held in with a deep breath, then released in a shout. The push and wheeze of sound echoed Bill's rocking in the chair and brought him straight back to those concerts on the green from long ago, when his father would climb up on stage in the town gazebo and play music for Resolute with his old friends, men long-since dead, who shared names with Bill's own friends today: Grogan, Zucker, Piper, Lavring.

Through the open kitchen window behind him, Georgia hummed along to music she didn't know. She'd get about five notes right out of every ten, then would stop and listen for a lick before trying again.

They'd talked about the poor girl who had died. Of course they had. Georgia had said it was a terrible accident, and Bill hadn't said much more. From having met Kennedy Jackson, and having noticed the circles under the man's eyes and the guilty way he'd answered Bill's questions, Bill thought it was probably something darker than an accident, something avoidable. But he saw no reason to share that with Georgia, who had voted for the concert to come to town. Rita Frederick was making a regular project out of telling anyone who'd listen that she'd warned them all. Bill figured that was making everyone feel bad enough without his own observations added into the mix at home.

Georgia had enjoyed having the campers. People came to their door, asking for Band-aids, water, phone numbers, advice. *Is this plant poisonous, do you know? My son stepped in a patch. Where can we get some dog food for Buddy? Do you know where we might wash out a few things to wear tomorrow?* One woman had convinced Georgia to lead her five children on a tour of the farm. In the barn, Georgia had gently lifted up each boy and girl to touch the cows' velvety noses with small fingers. She liked people, Georgia. It made a lot more sense to Bill—their decision to offer camp space in their field—when he thought about how much she liked people.

It was a rare moment when he didn't feel the pressure to work, either because a thing needed building or a thing needed tearing down. That was farm work in a nutshell: plant it, till it under. Feed it, slop it out. Build it, tear it down. But today, he felt no such need. He would sit here on his porch. He would rock in his chair, and look out over his field, and take in the smiles and waves of people—strangers to him—enjoying his farm. In a little while, Georgia would bring out a tray with a pitcher of lemonade and glasses with ice and mint leaves, and she would sit next to him in her own chair and listen.

And rock.

Washing over him, the music left Bill spent and happy. It flowed up the sides of the house and into the air above and around the pasture. It rubbed down the itchy backs of the cows, making them sigh and snort. It echoed back over campers—some dancing, some eating ice cream or nachos or fries, a few packing up early to begin the long trek home before they got trapped in the exodus. The music twisted upward, filling the world above the stage, over Bruno Marza, who was hammering a single chord on the keyboard again and again, leaning into the mic to emphasize just the word heaven whenever the others sang it. Over Kennedy Jackson, playing guitar and singing, "When you're with me, the shape of the sky *adds up to heaven.*" Over Eddie Cullen on guitar and Walker Jensen on bass and Serena Costa, the woman who'd come to play drums after that other fellow got put in jail. All of these musicians were singing the end of the line together: adds up to heaven. Their synchronicity and mastery was a thing to hear, and Bill found himself closing his eyes and smiling at nothing in particular, head back on the chair, arms and feet pressing into the movement of the rocker. Like a boy on a swing, flying.

On the day of the clean-up, Georgia rose at four. She'd offered to take the milking. Bill was happy enough for a break from it. The truth was, she wanted to watch the new baby for a while. The morning before, there'd been a new heifer calf: all white except for smudges of black on her neck and behind one ear. The first few days in a calf's life struck Georgia as the most miraculous. She could lose herself watching as the slow, unsteady movements of slightly-too-long legs turn frisky and confident.

Outside, the moon struggled to light the way through dense morning fog. Where the world had smelled of so many competing odors just days ago, from savory to smoke to sweet to rotten, today it smelled the way it had before, of grass and manure and mud. Georgia picked her steps carefully; she could scarcely see a yard in front of her, and had no idea where the cows were. She listened, then followed the sounds of their wet, wheezy breaths. It didn't take long to move them into the barn, for which she was grateful; too many mornings lately had been spent playing an exasperating game of catch before the work could begin. Maybe, with the concert over and the campers gone, the cows would settle back into a calmer routine.

After the milking, Georgia made her way to the stall where they'd put Sugar and her calf. The baby was nursing, butting her head up hard into Sugar's udder every once in awhile to get more milk.

"Ouch," Georgia muttered. "We're gonna call her Crash, I think." She gave Sugar a smile, and enjoyed thinking the cow's eye-roll was intentional, like a private joke.

The sun was up and the fog had started to burn off. She was aware of the fields stretching out behind her, behind the barn: fields full of the small leavings of a party for 62,000 people. She turned and looked, but in the low orange light, could see only hints of it: random sparkles and flashes of color. As if it weren't trash at all, but a field scattered with jewels. She had to hurry. The morning was whisking out from under her, and she had things to bake.

People began to arrive three hours later. First to drive in was Stan Piper, of course. She saw him climbing out of that shiny blue Chevrolet he was so proud of, then noticed other cars and trucks just turning into the drive. The clock in the living room chimed 8:30. Right on time.

"Bill," she called. "Go head 'em off! I'll be out in a minute. I've got two more pans of muffins to finish."

She heard the door open and shut, then saw Bill standing in the front yard, hands spread wide in welcome, saying something to Stan that made them both laugh—something fresh, no doubt. They were joined a minute later by Nowell Heath, then Guy Masters, and then a minute after that by Gil and Baby Fassette. Probably Becca would be running things at the diner today, since it would be hard to do much clean-up from the wheelchair.

"Need any help?"

She turned to find Mel Zucker putting on one of the aprons hanging by the pantry.

"Well, sure!" Georgia gave Mel a hug, then put her in charge of pouring cider and lemonade into pitchers to bring outside.

She pulled the last pan of muffins out of the oven and turned off the heat.

"Have a look at that!" Mel said, nose to the window.

Georgia looked. Out of nowhere, it seemed as if their property was swarming with people. As if, instead of leaving, the 62,000 fans had taken down their tents and wandered over here, into the Farnhams' front yard.

"Quite a turnout," Georgia said. "Isn't that nice?"

"Nice, nice," Mel said, flapping a hand at her. "You're not paying attention. Look." She pointed. Then Georgia saw. Becca was here after all, and Chris Kozlowski was pushing her chair. A little ways behind them, Carter Akyn was walking with the Spragues' pretty daughter, Suzanne, and holding her hand.

Mel raised her eyebrows. "Looks like the Akyns aren't achin'," she said.

"That's awful!" Georgia spluttered, and the two of them set to giggling.

After all the food and drinks had been set up on folding tables under the shade of the white ash tree south of the house, Georgia assigned jobs for the clean-up. It wasn't that nothing had been done by the concert organizers. They'd hauled away a lot of trash, and had made sure a few stragglers cleared out. No one ominous, just a handful of kids sleeping late, talking in small vehement clusters, dancing to music only they could hear with their eyes closed and their mouths open.

"Don't they know everyone else left?" Georgia had asked, only half joking.

"Revelers," Bill had responded mysteriously, with a smirk that might have contained a hint of envy. She thought about quoting Proverbs: *Let your heart not envy the sinners,* but in the end, decided not to comment.

Despite the work of the organizers, there was plenty left to clean up, which was why the town had solicited volunteers to come help. Of course, in Resolute, that meant everyone.

Georgia gave people jobs. She gave them trash bags and recycle bins, sand to put out any smoldering ashes, rakes and shovels and rubber gloves. From there, they spread out over the property in small groups: dozens of them, all here of their own accord—except maybe the music students. The sounds of their work echoed across the trampled grass: plastic bags riffling in a light wind, the clunks and tintinnabulations of bottles and cans being tossed into bins, lively shouts and requests. "Anyone got a shovel?" "I just found my third busted skateboard!" "Are Frisbees recyclable?" "Toss it here!" "Don't try it, Stan, you'll hurt yourself." "Any more of that cider around?"

She set herself the task of replenishing the food and drink table, and being available to answer questions. So when Guy Masters asked where to throw the trash bags his students were carrying, all in a line behind him, she told him about how a dumpster should be arriving later in the day.

"Just line your bags up along the edge of the driveway," she said, pointing. "Down there, I think Bill said."

His students staggered off with their bags, Carter Akyn among them, and Guy watched them go, smiling.

"I see Carter escaped the weekend without drowning in his ego," Georgia said, looking at the kids' retreating backs.

"Oh, I wouldn't say that, necessarily," Guy said. "But he's a good kid. He'll do fine."

"Pretty exciting concert for him, wasn't it?" Georgia asked. "You must be feeling pretty proud."

Guy maybe stood up another inch at that. "This isn't public knowledge yet," he said, dropping his voice. So many sentences in Resolute began that way, Georgia thought with a tiny secret smile.

"But that Kennedy Jackson talked to Becca about maybe inviting Carter on tour with him next year."

"That so? Oh my!" Georgia put her hands to her face in excitement.

"Now, Georgia," he chided gently. "No one's to know."

A few people were watching them. Rita Frederick's curiosity was obvious, from where she stood pretending to work, really just rearranging the napkins on the food tables.

Georgia dropped her hands and tried to relax her expression. "Okay, right," she whispered. "That's so exciting, though, Guy!"

"Well, it's in the works," Guy said. "He's got to salvage his band first, figure out where it goes from here. But I think he's pegged Carter for an opening act maybe, or something like that."

Before walking away, he put a finger to his lips and she nodded, pantomiming a zipper across her mouth.

To avoid Rita's prying gaze, she turned and looked out across the fields. She said a small prayer of thanks for this town and these people—all of them her family, all of them.

She shaded her eyes with a hand and looked at the mountain. Maybe it was a trick of the light, but in the distance, Mount Witness seemed larger today. Just as, on some nights in the deep of winter, the moon seemed magically enhanced, bobbing up from the dark, eastern horizon like a full balloon. She'd been thinking a lot about what that band had referred to as the *Shape of the Sky*. It had seemed silly the first time she'd heard it. But since then, she'd remembered an art show that the high school had put on when Ray was a teenager. The kids had worked in collage: torn construction paper and tiny fabric cuttings and flower petals and bits of foil. As their teacher led a group of parents through the art room that day, she'd talked a lot about *negative space* and *symmetry* and *unifying colors*. Ray's piece was a self-portrait. It hadn't looked like him, because it looked like the green and brown tissue and newspapers he'd cut up to make it. But in another way, it had looked like him, because that was the exact shape of his nose, which had been his grandfather's nose as well, and how funny to see it made out of a grocery receipt like that. Georgia hadn't been sure she'd understood it, but she'd liked looking at it, because it had made her see her son in a slightly different way.

Now she tried to see what the shape of the sky might be, resting atop Mount Witness like so much torn blue paper, glued in place with paste. For a second, for just a blink, she could see it that way. Just like, when she'd happened to glance at the cedars lit from behind at sunset the other night, she'd noticed them as if for the first time: dark feathery tops redefining the world that lay beyond. She remembered spotting the cows that morning, after searching for them in the fog: amorphous dark shapes resolving suddenly into animals she knew, with unique personalities and names and habits.

She had no idea what all of these thoughts might mean, what they would bring into her life, but she felt buoyed by the hope that comes along with new insight. Maybe it didn't matter. Maybe none of these thoughts mattered. But she decided to keep her eyes open, see what else she might see.

CPSIA information can be obtained
at www.ICGtesting.com
Printed in the USA
FFOW01n0452171214
9622FF

Shape of the Sky tells the story of Resolute, Vermont—popu[...] trying to raise much-needed money by hosting a rock festival. D[...] is due to begin, a fan is found dead in the woods. State troope[...] world turns upside down as the case returns him to dark mem[...] disappeared when he was a boy. An account of one communi[...] fifteen minutes of fame, *Shape of the Sky* weaves tales of friends[...] loss through the viewpoints of townspeople, a police officer, fa[...]

*****

Shape of the Sky is that rarity, a work of literary fiction that is also a page-turner. Do your heart, mind, and soul a favor and read this wonderful book.
— David Jauss, author of *Black Maps, Crimes of Passion,* and *Glossolalia*

Much of Shelagh Shapiro's stirring novel transpires in the shadow of Mt. Witness. How appropriate the name! This narrative is "local," then, "regional"– but only in the sense that Robert Frost's poetry was. Firmly rooted in Vermont, the book witnesses a whole array of worlds, from the musical to the sexual (ribald or mordant, or tellingly both at once). Yet above all, it dramatizes and testifies to the always complex and always intriguing intricacies of how we deal with one another as human beings.
— Sydney Lea, Poet Laureate of Vermont, author of *I Was Thinking of Beauty*

Shelagh Shapiro spins characters that are brilliant, colorful strands, then deftly weaves these into a moving story of family. The family in question, however, is a small Vermont town. *Shape of the Sky* follows its residents and visitors as they plunge into one particularly eventful summer.
— Carol Anshaw, author of *Carry the One, Lucky in the Corner,* and *Aquamarine*

ABOUT [...]
Shelagh [...] appeared in *North Dakota [...]w, Short Story, Gulf Stream* and others. She has an MFA in Writing from the Vermont College of Fine Arts and is a contributing editor for the Vermont journal *Hunger Mountain.* Her radio show, *Write The Book* is heard weekly on 105.9 FM "The Radiator;" archived podcasts can be found on iTunes. Shelagh lives in South Burlington, Vermont with her husband, Jerry.

PQH381587

Published by

WIND RIDGE BOOKS
of vermont

Shelburne, Vermont 05482
$15.95

Wind Ridge Books donates 10 percent of the net profit from the sale of this book to Big Heavy World Foundation.

$15.95
ISBN 978-1-935922-55-1

51595>

9 781935 922551